"We can do things with crochet
that you knitters only dream about . . ."

Detective Heather appeared a little stunned by Adele's barrage, but quickly shrugged it off . . .

"As long as I'm here, I'd like to ask you all something. Was it common for Ellen to forget her hooks?"

"Not at all," CeeCee began. "I was surprised when Molly told me. It was completely unlike Ellen. She was highly organized and into detail . . ."

"Really," Detective Heather said, taking out her notebook and pen. "So, then you saw the bag of hooks after she left?"

CeeCee shook her head. "Not me."

The detective looked toward Adele, Meredith and Sheila. "You must have seen the bag of hooks?"

They all shook their heads.

"Hmm, so, Mrs. Pink, you were the only one who actually saw the bag?"

This wasn't sounding good. I didn't like the way Detective Heather was staring at me. I thought about what I'd said to Dinah about has it wasn't my job to find out who killed Ellen. I'd just changed my mind.

HooKeD oN MuRDeR

BETTY HECHTMAN

BERKLEY PRIME CRIME. NEW YORK

THE BERKLEY PUBLISHING GROUP
Published by the Penguin Group
Penguin Group (USA) Inc.
375 Hudson Street, New York, New York 10014, USA
Penguin Group (Canada), 90 Eglinton Avenue East, Suite 700, Toronto, Ontario M4P 2Y3, Canada
(a division of Pearson Penguin Canada Inc.)
Penguin Books Ltd., 80 Strand, London WC2R 0RL, England
Penguin Group Ireland, 25 St. Stephen's Green, Dublin 2, Ireland (a division of Penguin Books Ltd.)
Penguin Group (Australia), 250 Camberwell Road, Camberwell, Victoria 3124, Australia
(a division of Pearson Australia Group Pty. Ltd.)
Penguin Books India Pvt. Ltd., 11 Community Centre, Panchsheel Park, New Delhi—110 017, India
Penguin Group (NZ), 67 Apollo Drive, Rosedale, North Shore 0632, New Zealand
(a division of Pearson New Zealand Ltd.)
Penguin Books (South Africa) (Pty.) Ltd., 24 Sturdee Avenue, Rosebank, Johannesburg 2196,
South Africa

Penguin Books Ltd., Registered Offices: 80 Strand, London WC2R 0RL, England

This is a work of fiction. Names, characters, places, and incidents either are the product of the author's imagination or are used fictitiously, and any resemblance to actual persons, living or dead, business establishments, events, or locales is entirely coincidental. The publisher does not have any control over and does not assume any responsibility for author or third-party websites or their content.

PUBLISHER'S NOTE: The recipes contained in this book are to be followed exactly as written. The publisher is not responsible for your specific health or allergy needs that may require material supervision. The publisher is not responsible for any adverse reactions to the recipes contained in this book.

HOOKED ON MURDER

A Berkley Prime Crime Book / published by arrangement with the author

PRINTING HISTORY
Berkley Prime Crime mass-market edition / May 2008

Copyright © 2008 by Betty Hechtman.
Cover art by Cathy Gendron.
Cover design by Rita Frangie.
Cover logo by axb group.
Interior text design by Kristin del Rosario.

ISBN: 978-0-425-22125-9

BERKLEY® PRIME CRIME
Berkley Prime Crime Books are published by The Berkley Publishing Group,
a division of Penguin Group (USA) Inc.,
375 Hudson Street, New York, New York 10014.
The name BERKLEY PRIME CRIME and the BERKLEY PRIME CRIME design
are trademarks belonging to Penguin Group (USA) Inc.

PRINTED IN THE UNITED STATES OF AMERICA

10 9 8 7 6 5 4 3 2

For Burl and Max.
You guys are the best!

Acknowledgments

I want to thank Sandy Harding for her enthusiasm and excellent editing, and for being fun to work with.

This book wouldn't have happened without my wonderful agent, Jessica Faust.

Los Angeles police officer Kathy Bennett's online class Cops from A to Z was fascinating and gave me a lot of valuable inside information.

Thanks to Cathy Gendron, Rita Frangie, Kristin del Rosario and the axb group for making the book look so great.

Not only did homicide detective Michel Carroll of the Fort Worth Police Department put on a heartrending presentation for the Kiss of Death Chapter of Romance Writers of America, but he also generously answered my questions and gave me insight into what it's like to be a homicide detective.

I can't forget my cheerleaders, Roberta Martia and Judy Libby, who have been joined by Betty Mehling and Diana Lang.

Although, like Molly, I did teach myself how to crochet with a kids' kit, Alice Kan and the Tuesday group helped me get past the basics. Paula Tesla broadened my crochet horizons and became my go-to person. She also taught me about the generous spirit of crocheters, who really do make things to raise money for charity or to give to those in need.

Crocheters rule!

Joan Jones, Linda Bruhns, Jan Gonder and Jack Warford met Molly first and gave her a thumbs-up.

And thank you to my cake tasters, Burl and Max, even if you couldn't wait until it was cool enough for the icing.

CHAPTER 1

WHEN I STOPPED BY ELLEN SHERIDAN'S HOUSE to drop off the crochet hooks she'd left at the bookstore, I expected to be in and out with maybe a thank-you and a few brownie points. I certainly didn't expect to end up in handcuffs.

Finding her front door open, I assumed she was bringing in groceries. I did a courtesy knock and said a few hellos and went on in. I called out her name as I continued down the hall to the living room. It looked out on the backyard, and I was so intent on seeing how the landscaping had changed since I'd been there last, I didn't look down— not at first, anyway. Not until I screamed at the shock of stepping on something other than floor. I screamed again, even louder, when I realized I had stepped on Ellen's leg and she might not be alive. She was sprawled across the champagne-colored carpet with a fireplace poker next to her head.

My feet suddenly seemed unable to move and my mind unable to focus. The only thought that kept going through my mind was to check her pulse on the chance that her condition wasn't as final as it looked.

With my heart pounding, dry mouthed and light-headed, I kneeled next to her. Just as my fingers landed on her neck, I heard a rustle.

"Freeze." The voice was male and full of authority. I followed his command, turning my head ever so slightly to look over my shoulder and see who the voice belonged to. An LAPD officer with a crew cut and a grim expression had both his hands on his gun, and it was pointed at me.

"Hands on your head," he ordered. Without hesitation, I complied, though as I did, the tote bag on my wrist slid down my arm.

Only later did I find out how this moment of supreme bad timing happened. All afternoon, the Neighborhood Watch captain had been concerned about the open door. He thought it looked suspicious when I went in, and called to report it. The cop had been down the street, staking out a stop sign that was notorious for being ignored. He'd answered the call and been approaching the famous open door as I started to scream.

Not taking his eyes off me, the officer stepped toward Ellen, crouched down and, releasing one hand from the gun, put two fingers on her neck. He was close enough for me to see that the name on his badge was Steven James.

"That's what I was going to do." I hoped that would make it clear that I was trying to help Ellen. After a moment he stood up and shook his head with an even grimmer expression.

"This isn't the way it looks, Officer James. I just got here. I was dropping this off." I moved my elbow to show off the red tote bag. I had taken his command to freeze seriously and was still on my knees.

"Drop it," he commanded, then realized the impossibility of the order with my hands on my head, and told me I could move my arm to let the bag go.

As soon as the tote bag hit the floor, Officer James pulled it away with his foot and I put my hand back on my head. He stepped behind me, and the next thing I knew, he'd used his free hand to slap a pair of cuffs on me.

"What are you doing?" I squealed.

"Ma'am, I need to secure the scene, and I can't do it if I have to worry about what you're doing."

I promised I'd stay put if he took off the cuffs, but he didn't budge.

With me restrained, he holstered his gun and got busy on his radio. The truth of what had happened really hit me when I heard him say "homicide." Someone had killed Ellen. My knees felt weak, and I was glad I wasn't standing. Otherwise I might have collapsed. My stomach began to do flip-flops, and I pulled against the handcuffs.

When Officer James finished on the radio, he slid on a pair of rubber gloves, opened the red tote and dumped out the contents. A pile of red, green and blue metal rods hit the carpet with a jingly noise. He eyed them suspiciously. "Ma'am, you want to tell me what these are?"

"Crochet hooks," I said. "They're for making scarves, and blankets and those cute little cloche hats. Not that I know how to crochet. I work in a bookstore, so the only yarns I deal with are tall tales." The kneeling had become uncomfortable, and I asked if I could stand up. He agreed and even helped me up. I was glad to see my legs had recovered.

"Hmm, so then that's what that is." He gestured toward Ellen's hand. A wooden crochet hook lay across her palm, with a small ball of beige yarn next to it.

I nodded. "I think that's one of the fancy kind. Her name is Ellen Sheridan. She leads"—I faltered—"make that *led* the crochet group that meets at Shedd & Royal Books and More. That's the bookstore where I work. I'm the event-coordinator-slash-community-relations person. I handle author events and book signings, and usually arrange for groups to meet at the bookstore. But Mrs. Shedd is the one who invited the crochet group." I took a breath. "I know I'm rambling. It's what I do when I get nervous, and I'm really nervous for obvious reasons. And I'm afraid if I stop talking, I might throw up." Officer James's serious expression shifted momentarily, and now he looked nervous. He fluttered his hand quickly to encourage me to keep going with the chatter. "I've never been in the middle of anything like this before, and . . ."

"I have to check out the rest of the house," he said, apparently realizing that the only way he was going to get a word in was by talking over me. He took my arm. "And it looks like you're coming with me."

"Check the rest of the house? For what? Why do I have to go?" It came out like one continuous sentence. I couldn't see much of his face, since he was standing to the side and just a little behind me, but I heard him let out an impatient snort.

"First order of business is making sure it's safe. I have to make sure there isn't somebody with a shotgun hiding somewhere. Second order of business is to make sure there aren't any more bodies. And it's safer for you if you're with me."

After hearing the shotgun part, I was glad to go along.

As he took my arm to steer me away from the living room, it registered for the first time that it had been trashed. Cushions were strewn around with their stuffing coming out, and the coffee table had been upturned. Papers were scattered over everything. Officer James seemed to notice it, but not react. I shuddered.

He didn't seem bothered by going through the house, either. But, then, dealing with crime scenes was his business. It certainly wasn't mine, and I felt uncomfortable and intrusive going into the private areas. The worst was Ellen's bedroom. Did I really want to know that she had left her bra hanging on the door to the bathroom? Or that she had a pile of *Hollywood Reporter*s next to the bed that she was never going to get to read? The hardest were the photos of her children on the dresser. Her son and daughter had played soccer with my boys. Somewhere they were going through their day just like it was any other, only it wasn't.

I was relieved that we didn't find anyone hiding in any of the closets or under any of the beds. There were no more bodies, either. The rest of the house appeared untouched until we got to what looked like an office. The floor was a chaotic mix of papers, office supplies and furniture.

"What do you think that means?" I said, continuing with my rambling. "She must have interrupted the burglar before they had a chance to go through the whole place, huh?"

He didn't answer, and I'm not even sure he heard me as he pulled open the door to look into the powder room. Apparently, letting me blather on didn't include listening. I'd probably lost him at "crochet hooks." Though he did give me a couple of nervous looks when there'd been a lull in my one-sided conversation.

Maybe his not listening wasn't such a bad thing. In my nervousness I had veered off the topic of Ellen and started giving way too much personal information about my husband, Charlie, dying a little over a year ago and how hard it was to start a whole new chapter of my life. I imagine a shrink would have a heyday with where my rambling had taken me.

We made a brief tour of the kitchen. No one hiding in there, though coffee mugs, cereal bowls and even cereal were still out on the counter. Who would have thought the Sheridans ate wild-berry marshmallow puffs? I'd have figured they were more the shredded-wheat types. I also changed my opinion about Ellen's being a neat freak.

As Officer James continued to lead me back to the front hall, a flurry of activity interrupted the eerie silence of the house. Two paramedics were walking in, along with a cop carrying a roll of yellow tape. Suddenly a petite ball of energy with spiky salt-and-pepper hair roared through the door.

"Molly?" Dinah said, stopping short. Her eyes grew wide when she saw my handcuffs. "What's going on?" She glanced back toward the living room and noticed Ellen's body. She had the same response I'd had, and screamed.

Officer James let go of my arm and stepped in front of her, trying to block her further entry. "You can't come in here."

"Too late, I'm already in," she said, holding her ground.

He gave her a dirty look. "Okay, fine. But now you can't leave until the detectives talk to you."

"What are you doing here?" I whispered to Dinah. She explained that she had been driving by and had seen my car out front. It's a real standout, a vintage—i.e., old—Mercedes in teal green. The color of the 1993 190E was so rare that when I saw another one, the driver and I shared a wave of solidarity.

"When I saw the police cars, I had to find out what was going on," she said, glancing down the hall again. "Is that Ellen Sheridan?" she stammered.

I nodded, and she gulped. I think Dinah is somewhere in her fifties, though she won't tell anyone, including me, her best friend, exactly where, insisting that people peg you when they know your age. She's an instructor at the local community college, and she claims that teaching freshman English to kids who still act like they're in high school has prepared her for anything, but apparently not this. She suddenly appeared a little green around the edges as she pulled at the burnt orange scarf wound around her neck. Dinah goes for the arty look, lots of layers and scarves and dangling earrings.

Just when I thought Dinah was going to lose it, Officer James escorted us into the front yard and then began draping the yellow tape across the entrance. Ellen's house was a one-story white wood frame house that took up most of the width of the lot. A tall pepper tree shaded the front yard with its lacy leaves. The grass grew on either side of the half-circle driveway, and the white picket fence that marked the front of the yard was lined with coral roses. It didn't look like a murder house. It looked like the kind of place that gave out big candy bars on Halloween and had nice parties with rental tents in the backyard and A-list caterers. It just showed you couldn't go by appearances.

Beyond the low fence, it was beginning to look like a street fair. More cop cars and news crews were parked on both sides of the street. A police helicopter was circling, and there was the loud *thwack* of news helicopters in a hover pattern. And since all this activity was not a common sight in the upscale area, the neighbors had come out to see what was going on. I saw more than one familiar person look at Dinah and me and shake her head in dismay.

I thought things were turning around when I saw a black Crown Victoria pull up and Barry Greenberg get out. That's Detective Barry Greenberg, who just happens to be my sort-of boyfriend. Though the sort-of part was in my head. He saw us as a sure thing.

Barry would get this all straightened out and have me uncuffed. Then Dinah and I'd be out of there.

I didn't like the way his expression darkened when Officer James walked up to him and pointed at us. There was a lot of talking and head-shaking, none of which looked like the easy fix I was hoping for. Finally Barry walked over to us, holding up his hands apologetically.

"Sorry, but I have to step down."

"What?" I wailed, expecting him to tell the uniforms that he knew us and he'd take over.

Barry is your basic tall, dark and sexy in a mature sort of way. He was dressed in his detective outfit of a suit, white shirt and subdued gray-tone tie. He made a call on his cell with his back to us. When he clicked off, he turned toward Dinah and me.

"I can't handle this case. You just can't be the lead detective when your girlfriend was found hanging over a dead body."

"It works for me," I protested.

"Well, any defense attorney would make mincemeat of the prosecution if he knew that's what went down. I could lose my job."

"All right," I grumbled. It wasn't as if I had a choice in the matter anyway, so I might as well agree. There'd be another set of detectives in no time, he promised, and no, he couldn't take off my handcuffs. The new detectives would.

When I saw who the new detectives were, I almost choked. Detective Heather Gilmore and her partner took over. It wasn't her partner, Rick Allen, I was concerned about. It was Detective Heather.

Though Barry insisted it wasn't true, I knew she had the hots for him and a death wish for me. We had run into her at a beachfront restaurant, and it had been totally obvious to me how she felt about him, though Barry seemed mystified when I brought it up. All her hair-twirling and leaning in close to share some little cop story was just Heather being friendly, as far as he was concerned. All the hot looks she gave him didn't register, nor did the North Pole stare she gave me.

Detective Heather was darling. She was slender and young, and had white-blond curls that framed her face. Even in her dark suit, it was obvious that she had curves. I was a little soft around the edges, with nice brown hair but no flowery word to describe the color. Still, Barry preferred me.

I thought it might have something to do with my cooking. You knew Detective Heather was a microwave-heater of store-made stuff, at best. I was all about cooking from scratch, slow-cooked roasts with scalloped potatoes, cakes with buttercream icing. Not that any of this was going to help me now.

"Don't worry. She'll just ask you what happened and let you go," Barry said as he headed over to speak to her. Even at a distance I could see how her face lit up when he got close. It got worse as they were talking. Barry's back was to me, so I couldn't see his reaction, but she leaned in close and touched his arm. It was even worse than the hair twirling from before. Barry said something to her, and they both looked my way. He kept talking and she kept staring at me with a hard expression, as though she wasn't that happy with what he was saying.

I was getting more and more uncomfortable.

Finally she seemed to agree to something and turned back to face him. I couldn't believe what she did next. She flicked her hair back from her face in what had to be the most obvious flirt move in the book. As he turned to go, she touched his shoulder, and I groaned.

He glanced back at me and gave me a smile and a thumbs-up as he headed for his car.

Detective Heather took charge immediately. She sent Dinah off with her partner and then focused on me. I hoped she'd suggest we talk on one of the nice benches along the fence in the front yard, but she had other ideas. She led me to the backseat of one of the black-and-whites and gestured for me to get in.

"It's more private," she said.

And a lot more embarrassing.

She waited until I was about to slide into the car to remove the handcuffs. "The officer was within his rights, you know. His first duty was for his own safety and then to secure the scene. He can do whatever he has to, to anyone he sees as a threat."

I had a hard time with the last part. On what planet did I look like a threat? And I didn't buy her privacy comment. If that was really what she was after, there was always her black Crown Victoria. Even though it never showed in her even expression, I knew she was enjoying my discomfort. She stood next to the open back door and took out a nice-looking black ballpoint pen and a black reporter's notebook.

Not only was it claustrophobic with that cage separating the front from the back, but the seat itself was some kind of indestructible plastic that gave me the willies. It seemed way too easy for her to merely shut the door and signal a cop to take me away.

She started by asking the correct spelling of my name, as if there were many ways to spell Molly Pink.

"Aren't you supposed to read me my rights?" I asked warily.

She stopped writing and looked at me. "Only if I was going to arrest you." She paused for a beat, and then leaned toward me. "Unless you think I should arrest you." Her perfectly shaped eyebrows rose into a question. "Is there something you want to tell me?"

I rolled my eyes. "Don't be ridiculous. It was just a matter of bad timing."

I explained my Good Samaritan act.

I pointed to the red tote bag some investigator was bringing out. "Those are the hooks. You do know what crochet hooks are?" I asked.

She nodded and gave me a withering look. "Of course I recognize crochet hooks."

She held up her handbag. It had wooden handles, but the body was made out of a variety of stitches of blue yarn. I had seen something like it in a fancy store at the mall, with a fancy price tag to match. "Looks just like that Balboa bag, doesn't it? I made it," she said proudly.

"Oh, then you crochet," I said, thinking our conversation had turned friendly. But her eyes flared.

"No, I knit." She pointed out the intricate cable stitches that gave the purse its sculpted shape.

"Knit, crochet, it's all the same, isn't it? Yarn, metal things." I tried to sound light. She shook her head with a boy-are-you-stupid expression.

"No, they're not," she said in a clipped tone.

Who knew she was so serious about her yarn work?

She scribbled some notes in her notebook and then asked if I had noticed anyone outside when I'd gone in.

"Oh, you mean like the burglar?"

"What makes you think there was a burglar?" She moved just a little closer to me as if she wanted to hear my every word.

"I've seen enough cop shows to recognize a burglary scene. There was stuff all over the place. Obviously Ellen Sheridan walked in on them and they clobbered her. The fireplace tool was right next to her head."

Heather's blue eyes locked on me. "Or that's what somebody wanted us to think." Something about her look made the hair on the back of my neck stand at attention. Did she think that somebody was me?

After a moment she straightened and asked for my personal information. Though she explained that it was just for identification purposes, I thought there was a certain curiosity factor, too.

She began with age. I knew I wasn't under oath or anything, but I gave her the truth, forty-eight, which compared to her perky mid-thirtysomething probably seemed ancient. If she asked for my weight, I was going to knock off a few pounds, which I doubted even counted as lying. But she skipped right to my marital status, and when she heard "widowed," I half expected her to ask if I planned to marry again. Instead she just muttered an automatic "sorry." It was in the same tone someone says "you're welcome" after you say "thank you."

Finally she asked for some samples from me, so they could separate my fingerprints and hair from the others at the crime scene. One of the investigators showed up and took my fingerprints and a few strands of hair. Then, to my great relief, Detective Heather let me go.

I was thrilled to get in the greenmobile and head for home.

The phone was ringing when I walked in. I grabbed the cordless and started walking around the house turning on lights.

"Mother." The word stretched into a sentence of disapproval. "Why didn't you answer your cell phone? Are you watching the news?" It was my older son, Peter's, shorthand for "turn on the TV." I checked my cell in my pocket as I headed to the den. It had once again set itself to silent. I flipped on the flat-screen and swallowed hard when I caught the image of myself in the police car. Detective Heather certainly photographed well. I couldn't say the same for me. I looked like I'd felt, rumpled and upset.

"How could you?" he said, and I could just picture him looking heavenward.

How could I what? Did he really think it was part of my afternoon plan to trip over Ellen Sheridan's body and end up on TV so I could embarrass him? Peter's a William Morris TV agent and very concerned about his image. He's been the uptight Brooks Brothers type since he was a kid. He's a little short in the sense of humor department, though you'd think someone with a name like Peter Pink would have one.

He wasn't happy until I apologized—for what, I'm not sure. Then, when he'd heard the whole story, he asked me if I needed a lawyer.

"I hope not," I said with a shudder.

Call waiting beeped, and I hit the button. It was a frantic Dinah. The detective had let her go almost immediately, and she wanted to make sure I was okay since, when she'd left, I'd been sitting in the cruiser. I assured her I'd made it home unarrested.

Before I could click off, another call came in. It was my younger son, Samuel.

"Ma, are you all right?" There was concern rather than disapproval in his voice.

I was surprised he had even heard about my recent escapade, since he rarely watched television. It turned out Peter had called him.

"I could come over," he offered. Samuel was totally different from Peter, softer, less judgmental. But, then, he was a musician. Though he was head barista at a coffee place to pay his rent.

"Peter said you were in trouble."

" 'Trouble' is kind of a strong word. I had kind of a bad day, but it's over now." Samuel had taken his father's death hard, and I knew he was worried something might happen to me. I had to reassure him that I was fine. Well, I was, almost.

After hanging up with Samuel, I took a shower and changed my clothes, but I couldn't seem to wash away the image of Ellen sprawled on the carpet.

Blondie, the terrier mix I'd recently adopted, was sitting by the back door, staring at her leash. Her world was a lot less complicated than mine, and obviously she didn't think my finding a dead body was an excuse for skipping her walk. I thought it might do me some good, anyway. But I was still tense when we returned. Blondie had a catlike personality and went off to the bedroom to sit in her chair.

I tried watching TV, but it didn't help and I only made myself more nervous by constantly flipping through channels. I needed to do something. I wandered around the living room, feeling at loose ends. Normally I loved my house, even if Peter was trying to get me to sell it and move to a condo. He couldn't understand why I needed all this space now that I was alone.

But tonight nothing felt right. I didn't even enjoy the way the whole back of the house looked out on the yard. The flower bed and the orange trees barely registered. If Charlie had been here, he'd have known what to do to get me out of this funk. But, then, if Charlie had been here, none of this would have happened. I wouldn't have gotten the job at the bookstore, and I wouldn't have known anything about Ellen and her damn crochet hooks.

There was only one antidote to my nerves that always worked—cooking. I went into the kitchen, considered my options and chose caramel corn. I'd make it and watch an old movie and try to forget about everything.

None of that paper-bag microwave stuff for me. I poured oil and popcorn into the bottom of a saucepan, stuck on a lid and turned on the fire. The room filled with the smell of it popping, reminding me of movie theaters and events with the kids. I emptied the finished product into a bowl and got ready to make the caramel part. The candy thermometer was already stuck onto the side of the pan holding the butter and sugar, ready to go. The butter portion looked a little scant. I opened the refrigerator, and my gaze stopped on the six-pack of Hefeweizen. I had noticed it on sale and without thinking bought it for Charlie. He loved the wheat beer very chilled with a slice of lemon.

I felt my eyes tear up. "I'm past this," I said out loud, and then doubled the amount of extra butter.

Once the caramel mixture reached the hard ball stage, I poured it over the popcorn. While it cooled, I looked through my DVD collection and found a frothy Audrey Hepburn movie.

Popcorn in hand, I hunkered down in the den and started the movie. By the time it was half over, I'd stopped thinking about Ellen's body, and made a serious dent in the candy-covered popcorn. Was it my imagination, or were my khaki slacks already a little tighter through the hips? I really needed to find an outlet for my nerves with fewer calories.

Just as Audrey sat down at her typewriter and William Holden began to dictate a love scene, I heard my kitchen door open and shut, and Barry called a greeting. A moment later he came in the den. He was still dressed in his suit, and was pulling off his tie.

"You bought Hefeweizen?" he said, holding up a bottle before taking a sip. "I didn't know you drank beer."

There was an odd moment. I almost wanted to say, "That's for Charlie." Then logic kicked in. Charlie wasn't going to drink that beer, and neither was I.

"I bought it by mistake," I said, finally.

Barry's dark eyes clouded, and without my saying any more, he understood. He set the bottle down and didn't pick it up again. He eyed the bowl of caramel corn.

"Have some."

"There's no connection to Charlie with that, is there?"

I shook my head, and he grabbed a handful. As soon as the flavor kicked in, he got a look of ecstasy.

"Better than beer, anyway." He dropped his tie, took off his jacket and sank down next to me on the couch. "I wanted to make sure you were okay. Last time I saw you, you didn't look so good."

"I think stepping on the leg of your dead neighbor will kind of do that."

"Yeah, they always say your first body is the toughest."

"First body!" I squealed. "How about first, last and everything-in-between body? I don't want a repeat performance."

"And why exactly is it you were standing over said body?" he asked.

Here we go again. I repeated the story about being a nice guy and returning Ellen's hooks. "Next time I think I'll just call," I said when I finished.

"You understand why I couldn't take the case."

I nodded halfheartedly. "Well, Detective Heather ought to take herself off it, too. She's personally involved. She'd like to buy me a ticket to the moon so she could have you all to herself."

"You flatter me," he said, putting his arm around me and pulling me close.

"No, you're just blind." I reminded him of the scene in the Sheridan front yard. He didn't seem to have any memory of the hair flicking or arm touching.

"She's a good detective, fair and impartial. Besides, you didn't do it, did you?" he said, his mouth sliding into a grin.

I rolled my eyes. "Does the phrase 'all's fair in love and war' mean anything to you?"

Blondie ambled in and looked at Barry.

"Some watchdog," he said, shaking his head. "Doesn't she know how to bark?"

"When the mood suits her," I said, reaching out to pat her head.

"You shouldn't leave your back door open. You never know who might drop in," he said, leaning in to kiss me. "Got to go."

He didn't have to explain. I knew it was something to do with his son. Barry was divorced. His ex lived back east and had had sole custody of him. Jeffrey was thirteen and had recently come to stay with Barry, who was very serious about the father thing. It cut into his social life and mine. But he as always reminded me that if I was willing to kick up our relationship a notch, by moving in with him, getting engaged or, even better, getting married, then things would be different.

I got up and packed the rest of the caramel corn to go. We'd been over this before and again I told him I would rather have a chopped-up social life than a relationship I wasn't ready for.

"Sorry, babe," Barry said. "But for me the few months we've been seeing each other are enough to know I want to move on to something more. I understand you still need more time."

It wasn't just because of getting over Charlie. It seemed like all my life I'd been setting aside what I wanted, for somebody else. My older brother was conveniently always gone, leaving me to deal was my mother, the original diva. Her profession was backup singer, but she was all star at home. My father, the skin doctor, was either at work or quietly letting her be the center of attention. I felt more like her road manager than her daughter.

Charlie and I had married young. Peter and Samuel came along soon after. Whatever I had thought of for myself somehow went out the window after that. I loved doing all the PTA stuff, going on school field trips and attending every game either boy played in. I was glad to keep things together for Charlie at home and help him out at work. But then when he died, something had happened. Once I was semifunctional and realized I had to rebuild my life, I saw it was just that: my life. For the first time there was no one to defer to, and even with the occasional loneliness, I discovered I liked the freedom. I could do laundry at midnight, fall asleep on the couch reading or have ice cream for dinner, and not have to answer to anyone.

All those years I'd been the wind beneath everybody's wings. Now, for the first time, I was the one doing the flying, It was scary and exciting.

I walked Barry to the door and handed him the bag.

By now the fluffy feeling of the movie had worn off, and I had a stomachache from the caramel corn and was back to thinking full-time about Ellen's body and Detective Heather. There was something I'd forgotten to mention, or maybe I hadn't wanted to mention it. Either way, I'd said nothing about it. Ellen and I had more of a connection than crochet hooks.

CHAPTER 2

SHEDD & ROYAL BOOKS AND MORE FACED Ventura Boulevard, which was the main drag along the south end of the San Fernando Valley. Some city planner types had gotten the idea of trying to make Ventura Boulevard look different as it passed through the different Valley communities. Thanks to the Tarzan connection, the strip going through Tarzana had been designated "Safari Walk." They'd hung metal silhouettes of giraffes, lions and other animals from some of the streetlights and stuck some topiary elephants, giraffes, etc., along the sidewalks. The final touch was an occasional brick sidewalk square with a boulder stuck on it.

The bookstore had a topiary giraffe out front. The only time anyone seemed to notice it was when a red Ford Focus had jumped the curb and run into it. That ivy-covered animal was pretty tough. The picture in the newspaper had shown it on its side, unscathed except for the loss of a few leaves. The car, however, had been a mess.

The actual status of Tarzana was a little confusing.

Along with Encino, Studio City, Sherman Oaks and the multitude of other Valley communities, it was technically part of the urban sprawl of the city of Los Angeles. But in most people's minds, there was the City and the Valley. The City side of the Santa Monica Mountains was more temperate, thanks to the ocean breeze, and made up of odd-angled main streets that had started out as cow paths to the ocean. It had Hollywood, Westwood, Brentwood and the supertrendy shopping streets frequented by celebs. Some people considered it hipper.

The Valley had plenty of houses with rural-style mailboxes, and you could still find a lot big enough to have a horse. The streets were wider and mostly on a grid pattern. It was hotter in the summer and colder in the winter, but we had more trees, more parking, more sushi restaurants and the lure of mountain walks just minutes away.

I had been working at the bookstore for about six months as community relations/event coordinator. It was my job to bring new customers into the bookstore, and to that end I had placed the event area in the window overlooking Ventura. The plan was that passersby could look in and see something going on, and they'd come in and check it out. Though this morning it didn't look as though there was much to advertise.

Even from across the bookstore it was obvious that not much was going on with the crochet group. Actually, "group" was a bit of a stretch. There were only three women sitting around the end of the long table. And one of them, Adele Abrams, worked for the bookstore. But, then, it was only their first meeting since Ellen's demise. As I looked at them, I realized I didn't know much about the group. I heard they'd been together for a couple of months, although they'd only started meeting at the bookstore a few weeks earlier. Before that, they'd been meeting Monday, Wednesday and Friday mornings at the yarn store down the street until it went out of business.

My thoughts turned to Ellen, and I realized that several days had gone by with no further word from Detective Heather. As far as I was concerned, no news was definitely good news. She had just been trying to make me sweat that afternoon and must have moved on to look for the burglar type who had done it. I was glad I hadn't brought up my history with Ellen.

What would have been the point of telling Detective Heather that Ellen and Charlie had been partners in their public-relations firm, Pink Sheridan? Or what a mess there had been when he died?

I had made the mistake of thinking I could take over his position. It wasn't as if I had no experience. I had worked with Charlie when he started out on his own, and even after he had gone into partnership with Ellen, I had done a number of things, including setting up events and even some hand-holding.

But Ellen was against it from the start. She claimed Charlie's clients were calling her and had no confidence in me. I always wondered whether it was the other way around—like, maybe she had called them and talked me down.

After less than a month, Ellen had dropped a check on my desk and said I could take it and get on with my life, or we could bring in lawyers. She insisted that buying me out was doing me a big favor. Charlie's death was still too raw for me to have the energy to fight her, so, I took the check. Before I had even cleaned out my desk, Natalie Shaw arrived. She wasn't going to be a partner, just an associate, which really meant doing all the work while Ellen got the glory. The firm was still called Pink Sheridan, but all the Pinks had left the building.

I glanced at the crochet three again and debated what to do. True, it had been Mrs. Shedd who had invited them to move their meetings here, and they'd hardly needed me for the few weeks they'd been coming. But now that they were Ellenless, everything had changed, and I felt they were my responsibility. They were just sitting there with their balls of yarn and metal hooks lying idly on the table.

"Ladies, how are you doing?" I said, walking up to the group.

"Pink, I've got it covered," Adele said, giving me a look of dismissal. I tried not to clench my teeth at her calling me by my last name. She knew I hated it, which was why she did it. But why show her that it worked?

Adele and I'd had a problem from day one. She had been hoping to get promoted to my job, but when Mrs. Shedd hired me instead, Adele hadn't taken it well. Mrs. Shedd had given her the children's department and story time as conciliation, but it had just annoyed her. Adele wasn't a kid person to begin with, and the idea of having to read stories and be friendly was a real stretch for her.

I ignored her comment and glanced at the other two women. I recognized both of them. Sheila Altman worked as a receptionist at the gym down the street, and it was hard to miss CeeCee Collins's hair. It was that reddish-blondish, slightly acrylic-looking color that never occurred naturally.

"It's just horrible about Ellen. She must have interrupted the burglar," I said, shaking my head for emphasis. Adele gave me a dirty look when she realized I wasn't leaving.

Sheila Altman glanced up, the line between her eyebrows squeezed in tension. "They've already discounted the burglary thing. It was just a setup to make it look like that's what it was." She was drumming her fingers at an amazingly fast cadence on the table. No surprise, really. Sheila had a definite problem with her nerves. She came to every signing we had that featured a book with anything to do with de-stressing, dealing with anxiety, or learning relaxation techniques. None of them seemed to help. But, then, she had a lot on her plate.

We'd first met at the *Dr. Wheel's Guide to Total Calm*

signing. I'd been giving out samples of chamomile tea, and when Sheila came back for seconds, she opened up and told me her story. Apparently the grandmother who brought her up had recently died and now Sheila felt adrift. She had a boyfriend, and seemed to be hoping for some kind of happily-ever-after with him, though it didn't sound as though it was going to happen anytime soon. In the meantime, she was juggling her job at the gym with classes in wardrobe design. Her dream was a career at one of the film studios as a costume designer. All she could afford was a rented room in a house in Reseda. It came with kitchen privileges, but as part of the rent she had to babysit the owner's kids on weekends.

Sheila seemed to worry about everything, though, I gathered, mostly about not being good enough at things. And even when I told her that we all worried about that, it didn't help. Something about her seemed like a rubber band that had been pulled too tight and any second could snap.

"How do you know they've discounted the idea of a burglar?" I asked, talking in time to her finger drumming. It was making me nervous.

"One of the gym members' sister's husband's sister works in the West Valley Division of the police department. Everybody was interested in what happened. It kind of busts their image of living in a safe area when burglars go around offing people who get in the way of their business. The women were all relieved to hear it was a setup." Sheila paused a beat. Thank heavens, she didn't seem to be able to drum and talk at the same time and had finally let her fingers go still. "Supposedly Ellen was strangled some kind of weird way." She looked at me. "I can't believe you don't know, since you were at the scene of the crime and all."

"You know, dear, you looked pretty washed-out on television," CeeCee Collins said, giving me a disparaging glance. Her real name was Connie Collins, but everybody knew her as CeeCee. Easily recognized, she had been on television for years. She had starred in two sitcoms, then become part of ensemble casts on several long-running dramas.

Lately she seemed to be doing only guest shots where she played somebody's eccentric great-aunt or something, and commercial-spokesperson things. She claimed the spokesperson jobs were just for fun.

"Of course the lighting in the police car had way too much shadow," CeeCee continued. "I always wear this special makeup when I think I might end up on TV. You know, when you go to an award show or a premiere. It really does the trick. It doesn't have that thick orange look in person like so much of the stage stuff does, but it keeps you from looking pasty. I'll give you the name of it, if you'd like."

I thanked CeeCee but told her I didn't intend to make showing up on the news a regular occurrence. Did she honestly think I cared whether I looked pasty? To my thinking, if I hadn't looked bad, something definitely would have been wrong.

"What exactly were you doing there?" CeeCee asked. She motioned to the other two. "We really should begin. Ellen would want us to." She turned back to me and waited for my answer. I rolled my eyes and repeated the Good Samaritan story for the millionth time as they picked up their tools.

"Pink, we don't need you here." Adele glared, but I didn't move.

A thought crossed my mind as CeeCee began working her hook. She was a client of Pink Sheridan.

"This is a double whammy for you. You lost a group leader and a publicist," I said, touching her arm.

CeeCee's bright expression dampened, and she put her head down. "Yes, Ellen's been handling my publicity for years. I don't know what I'm going to do without her."

Her hook stopped in midstitch for a moment, as she appeared to blink back a tear. Then she swallowed and resumed by taking some black yarn and joining it to her work. Her dexterity was amazing. In the blink of an eye she had made a border of black stitches around a square with a blue and green pattern. It seemed almost automatic. She did the last stitch and put the square on a pile of similar ones. All had black borders and the same pattern of stitches and open spaces.

Adele was working on some kind of a square, too. But hers was twice as large and also had a black border. The inside was purple, and she was attaching a loopy pink flower. Funny how whoever you are shows up in everything you do. Adele's square was like her. She was wearing a flouncy full skirt with a pink, yellow and lavender design. On top, she had a hot pink camp shirt. Her voice had a look-at-me quality, too. It carried across the store even if there were all kinds of conversations going on. Of course, her voice was good for story time. Everybody could always hear her.

Sheila had a strip of royal blue stitches in one hand and a crochet hook in the other. She seemed to be struggling, and her knuckles were white. Whatever she was making, it didn't seem to be going well. Her face was squeezed in frustration as she tried to force the hook into the yarn.

"Dear, your stitches are too tight again," CeeCee said in her musical, sugary voice. She shook her head and reached out to touch Sheila's work.

Sheila pulled it in close. "I can do it myself."

"I was just trying to help." CeeCee looked from Sheila to me. "Ellen used to take her work and help her straighten it out."

"She didn't help me. She just did it for me. And I hated it," Sheila said, cradling her work protectively. "It made me even more nervous. She'd be hovering over me, saying I worked too slow, and then she'd just snatch it away." Sheila's breath seemed uneven as she tried harder to force the hook into the line of stitches.

"What are you making?" I said, hoping to lighten her

tension. I made sure to keep my distance so she wouldn't think I was going to make a grab for her work. The way she was holding that hook, even with its round ends, I had a feeling she might do some kind of damage if I did.

She looked up at me, her eyebrows squeezed together with worry, and held up a picture with a lot of directions under it. It showed a square with an intricate lacy pattern that to my noncrocheting eyes appeared impossible to make.

"Nice," I said in my best calm voice. Sheila's face lit up with my tidbit of praise. Adele handed her a smaller hook and suggested she try it.

"Take some deep breaths, dear," CeeCee said in an encouraging voice. "We can't afford to have you freak out now. We have a deadline." She watched as Sheila easily poked it into the line of royal blue stitches.

"Now, make nice loose stitches." CeeCee said it slowly and stretched the word *loose* out as Sheila looped the yarn to CeeCee's rhythm. Even I could appreciate the looseness of the first stitch she produced with CeeCee's prompting. Sheila beamed with pride and started to pick up speed again, but CeeCee stopped her. She repeated the whole *loose* thing again, and Sheila produced another loose stitch. CeeCee kept pacing Sheila until she had picked up the rhythm on her own.

"Pink, it's under control. Why are you still here?" Adele snapped.

"It's my job to make sure things go smoothly, and now with Ellen . . ."

"You can't lead the group. You don't even know how to crochet." There was definite triumph in Adele's voice.

"Actually, I should lead the group," CeeCee said. She gestured toward the pile of black-edged multicolored squares on the table next to her. "I do have a few more done than you." She glanced at the two large squares with loopy flowers in the middle. "And more experience. I learned how to crochet during all the waiting on my first show. You probably remember it—*The CeeCee Collins Show*." She did a few minutes on how they knew how to name a show in the old days. None of this *Friends* or *Entourage* business. They went right for the name of the person who pulled in the audience. CeeCee finished by making sure we all realized her show was still on the Classic Channel; then she got back to the point. "Adele, dear, I know you mean well, but I was really so much better at helping Sheila."

Adele got a huffy look. "I am the one who gave her the smaller hook so she could get out of the too-tight-stitch trap."

Were they honestly arguing over who was going to be the leader of the three of them? Talk about all chiefs and no Indians.

Meanwhile, immune to their fighting over who helped her the most, Sheila had settled into a steady rhythm of looping the yarn around the hook and pulling it through. Even yarn-challenged I could tell she was making loose, even stitches.

CeeCee and Adele seemed to have come to some kind of truce. I suspected that each of them thought they had convinced the other they were in charge, and they had gone back to crocheting. CeeCee took some red yarn and made a little tail of stitches, then joined the ends, forming a circle. From there, she began making stitches around the circle. It was fascinating to watch the birth of a new square. She was like a machine and barely seemed to look at what she was doing.

"What's with all the squares?" I asked. All three of them turned toward me, apparently surprised that I was still there.

Adele rushed to speak first. "I can't believe you don't know. Being that you're the event coordinator and community-relations person." The edge in her voice grated on me. "The whole point of the group is that we make things for charity."

"Yes, dear," CeeCee interrupted. "Ellen came up with the idea of us making an afghan with all different squares. The only common thread is that they are all edged in black. She donated it in advance to a charity she has"—CeeCee stopped and swallowed—"had as a pro bono client. You've probably heard about it: Hearts and Barks."

Of course I had, and I'd seen the signs for their upcoming fair being held on the back lot of Western Studios, over in the eastern part of the Valley.

Sheila took out a brochure that described the services Hearts and Barks offered.

"I had no idea," I said after reading how Ruth Klinger had been faced with choosing between her meds and keeping her dog, Fluffy, until Hearts and Barks had come to her rescue. "How wonderful that they not only helped with Fluffy's vet bills, but her day-to-day food as well." There was a picture of Ruth hugging Fluffy. She looked so happy and relieved, I couldn't help but tear up.

"Even though it's called Hearts and Barks, they help cats, too," CeeCee offered. "They do a lot of wonderful things, like sponsoring spaying and neutering clinics."

"They're going to sell our afghan at the silent auction," Sheila added.

"Isn't that four weeks from Saturday?" I asked, looking at the paltry supply of finished pieces.

"It's actually three weeks," Adele said.

CeeCee pulled out a sheet torn from a magazine that showed a large throw made out of what she called granny squares. She explained that theirs was going to be different. Instead of all the squares having the same pattern of stitches, they were making all different kinds of squares, and the result would look more like a crazy quilt. Since Adele's were clearly larger, I asked how they were going to fit in.

"They may be larger, but they're proportionate. My squares are going to make up the center." Adele picked up her finished square, laid it in the center of the table and demonstrated how hers were going to be arranged with all the other smaller squares around them.

"Are you sure the three of you can manage all those squares in that amount of time?"

"Ellen made a lot . . . and there's four of us," CeeCee said, gesturing toward a woman approaching the table. "This is Meredith."

I'd seen her across the store but never met her. I introduced myself. She appeared to be in her late twenties and was the youngest in the group. Her long, light brown hair was pulled back into a ponytail, and she wore loose white cotton pants, a long top and an amethyst necklace.

Sheila set down her work for a moment and stretched. She acknowledged Meredith with a somber nod.

"It seems so strange without Ellen," Meredith said, taking out some yarn and hooks. "I just can't believe she's gone." After Meredith finished laying out her work, she looked toward the café. "I'm going to get an herb tea. Anybody else want something?" The other women shook their heads, and she left to get her drink.

"Meredith used to be a masseuse at the gym," Sheila said, moving back to the bigger hook.

"Until Ellen found her," CeeCee offered. "Meredith was already doing this special massage she developed. Ellen showed her how to market herself and introduced her to a lot of people and . . ."

"She got all these big-deal show-business types for clients." Sheila sounded impressed. "I've had her massages, and they're really great."

I knew Sheila had tried everything to relax, so her endorsement meant something. CeeCee explained Meredith's unique hook: She took her massage chair and special aromatic oil to the exec's office. Her clients had to remove very little clothing and barely even had to stop working. "She calls her massages 'Refresh, Relax, Renew.' And that's how her clients feel when she's finished," CeeCee said.

It sounded good to me.

"Has anyone talked to poor Lawrence?" CeeCee asked. Everyone at the table shook their heads.

Hmm, poor Lawrence indeed. He was Ellen's husband of a million years. When Charlie was alive, we'd been on the regular circuit of award shows and assorted events and run into him often. He was always Lawrence, never Larry. He and Ellen were a real power couple. She had the PR business and he was a talent manager who'd recently added TV producer to his title.

For years, Lawrence had managed a stable of musicians and comedians, all recognizable but not superstars. Then Jed Frank, a singer-songwriter client of his, ended up with a TV show, and Lawrence became a producer. The show was a monster hit, and it had fueled Jed's music career as well. Suddenly Lawrence was at the top of the heap. Too bad he didn't have as much charm as he had power.

Meredith returned with her tea and settled in to crocheting.

"You're doing Ellen's favorite," Adele said, looking at Meredith's square. It was certainly beautiful. The center resembled a scarlet flower, and around it were airy white stitches. Meredith was just adding the black border.

They all fell silent as their hooks moved through the strands of yarn.

Suddenly I felt like an outsider. Adele picked up on it and glanced up at me.

"Told you it was under control."

I hated to admit it, but she was right. There was nothing for me to do. I looked back as I walked away from the table. Sheila had gotten into a rhythm of crocheting. She was mouthing the word *loose*, stretching it out with each stitch as CeeCee had done. Her whole demeanor said *calm*, something I'd never seen in her before. Suddenly I had an idea. If crocheting could relax a jumble of nerves like Sheila, maybe it could help me with my caramel corn problem. Instinctively I pulled at the waistband of my black slacks, willing them to be looser.

There was just one major problem. I didn't know how to crochet. I could ask Adele. A possible lesson played over in my mind. Adele, with a superior smile, would seize the opportunity to lord her hook prowess over me. She'd hover over me, correcting my every wrong move, which I would undoubtedly make lots of, and do her best to make me feel as though I had two left hands.

No way.

A figure in a dark suit, with white-blond hair, slipped into my peripheral vision. My tension level kicked up a notch, and I was suddenly hungry for caramel corn.

"Mrs. Pink, may I speak to you?"

As if I had a choice.

"Detective Hea—Gilmore," I said, catching myself in time. Calling her *Detective Heather* sounded too much like calling her *Detective Barbie Doll*, and would endear me to her even less. I lied and said it was nice to see her. Glancing back at the table of yarn ladies, I noticed that all four sets of eyes were locked on me.

"Why don't we go into the café," I suggested, moving toward the entrance without waiting for her answer. What bookstore worth its weight in paper didn't have a café these days? No more not letting people in with food and drinks. Now bookstores made their customers feel as if they were missing something if they didn't take a latte-schmaatte, decaf foam-only cappuccino or some other whipped-up party drink right in with them while they browsed. We weren't any better. In all honesty, Shedd & Royal needed the added income.

Before we walked in, the smell greeted me. Our angle

was that we baked fresh cookies, and the smell worked like a magnet to pull people in. Detective Heather wasn't immune. She got that fluttery-eyed look as the sweet fragrance of melting chocolate and buttery dough hit her nose. Maybe I could soften her up with sweets.

A batch of freshly baked chocolate chip cookies was cooling on a tray. "How about some cookies and a drink?" I offered as we approached the counter.

"Thanks, but no thanks on the cookies," she said, eyeing the treats with resolve. "I don't usually discuss cases over coffee." She hesitated as if she was thinking it over. "But I suppose it's all right—as long as I buy my own." She nodded at Bob, our main barista and cookie baker. "How about a large decaf nonfat latte with a shot of no-sugar vanilla syrup, ice blended." She smiled at me. "We don't all do donuts, you know."

It was one of the longest drink orders I'd ever heard and probably was a prizewinner in the hyphen department. I tugged at my waistband with regret. I bet Detective Heather never had caramel corn evenings, or if she did, it was with no-sugar, no-fat, no-taste caramel corn. I got a plain coffee, and we headed to a table.

She made small talk at first, commenting on how good the drink was, weather was nice for September, etc. It only upped the tension level for me. I wanted the conversation to be like a Band-Aid removal: Rip it off fast and get it over with.

Finally she got to the point.

"It's come to my attention that you knew Ellen Sheridan more than in passing. I was curious why you didn't say anything when we talked before."

Talked? Is that what she called that thing in the back of the police car? I had been so freaked out by stepping on Ellen's leg and being questioned, that at the time I had barely remembered my name, let alone my history with Ellen. "You mean about Ellen being my late husband's partner?"

Detective Heather nodded and added, "And there was something about you trying to work with her and it didn't work out."

My shoulders sagged, and I swallowed hard. "Okay, I admit that when I tried to step into my husband's position, there were some problems. Ellen forced—I mean, I let her buy me out. But I have tried to put all that behind me, and I don't really think much about it. Things have turned out really well for me. I have this great job." I made an expansive gesture toward the bookstore. "And I'm even dat—" Oops, caught myself just in time. There was no reason to bring up my social life, particularly since I had the social life Detective Heather wanted.

For just a moment, I wondered about Barry's eyesight. Being this close to her, I could see that Detective Heather had no crinkly lines around her eyes, was obviously smart and a professional, and as much as I hated to admit it, was in better shape than I was. Yet Barry claimed to notice her only as a colleague. Unless—a dark thought passed through my mind—it was all an act just to throw me off.

Detective Heather wrote a bunch of notes in her black reporter's notebook. It seemed as though she wrote more than I said, which didn't make me feel good. Somehow when I'd thought about what happened when I attempted to step into Charlie's business shoes, it hadn't sounded so bad. But saying it out loud to Detective Heather—well, it sounded like a motive.

"There's just one more thing," she said, keeping her incredibly sparkly blue-eyed gaze on me. She let the comment hang in the air, making my heartbeat kick up. The woman sure knew how to throw me off balance.

"I spoke with Ms. Sheridan's associate, Natalie Shaw. Do you know her?"

Should I answer quickly, or think about it? Which way made me look worse? Too fast and I sounded nervous; too slow and it would seem as though I was trying to hide something. The good part was, she was asking about somebody else.

"Natalie started working for Ellen when I left. I don't really know her." I let out my breath, relieved that the spotlight was off me, but it didn't last for long.

"Well, she mentioned your recent disagreement with Ms. Sheridan."

"*Disagreement* is such a strong word," I began, keeping my tone light. "I suggested something and she turned it down. That's all." I hoped that would satisfy Detective Heather, but of course it didn't.

"Do you want to give me the details?" With her pen poised, Detective Heather looked at me.

I hesitated. No, I didn't want to give her details. I didn't want to talk to her at all.

"You don't have to give me the details if you don't want to," she said finally. "I heard Natalie's version, and I can go with that. I'm just curious how you saw it."

Barry was right. The detective was good at her job. No way was I not going to answer her now. I didn't know what Natalie had told her, but I was sure it made me look bad. I took a sip of my coffee and cleared my throat. "Part of my job is to arrange book signings. Ellen had a client, an actor turned author, who was coming out with a memoir, *Walk a Mile in My Shoes*. Maybe you've heard of him—Will Hunter?"

As if anybody hadn't, including Detective Heather, She unsuccessfully tried to hide her reaction. The guy was hot in a laid-back slacker sort of way, and apparently made an impression even on the perfect detective. I noticed her pupils dilate just a touch at my mention of his name. She nodded and gestured for me to get on with it.

"Celebrities bring in foot traffic. Foot traffic leads to sales, and . . ."

"I got it, I got it," she said impatiently. "Stick to the part about Ms. Sheridan."

I started talking faster. Her impatience had made me nervous, and I just wanted to get it over with as quickly as possible. I explained how I'd approached Ellen about hosting his signing and how she had turned me down, preferring to stick to the hip, trendy bookstores the other celebs had been using. I didn't see any reason to mention that I had still hoped to get her to change her mind.

"So, then, you weren't about to lose your job over not landing the book signing?"

I shook my head vehemently. "Of course not. Mrs. Shedd and Mr. Royal are completely happy with me. Besides, one signing isn't going to make or break the bookstore." I finished my coffee and started to get up, thinking we were done. Detective Heather flipped her notebook shut, and then as an afterthought flipped it back open.

"There's just one more thing. . . ."

I pushed back against the chair. Who did she think she was, Columbo, with her *just-one-more-things*? Then I got a sinking feeling. Columbo always said that to the person he thought did it.

This *one more thing* was a question about Ellen's husband. "Several people have said they thought Lawrence was having an affair." Detective Heather moved a little closer and looked me dead in the eye. "I thought you might know something about it, being that you're a widow and a neighbor." How unsubtle could you get? Did she think I was two-timing Barry? Or maybe it was just wishful thinking.

Okay, I wanted to laugh, but I restrained myself. Lawrence, never Larry, was totally not my type. The only way he'd have been my type was if we were the only two people left in the world and I honestly thought it was my duty to start repopulating the planet. And even then I'd have to pretend he was somebody else.

The trouble was, I protested too much and Detective Heather kept nodding and writing things down.

I figured I'd better cancel my plan to take a casserole over to him as a condolence gesture.

By the time Detective Heather packed up her notebook and annoying questions, my nerves were on high alert. When I went back into the bookstore, the crocheters were working away on their squares. Sheila looked positively calm. She was still mouthing the *keep it loose* directions, as if it was some kind of mantra.

Maybe crochet was something for me. It was certainly a better occupation for my hands than acting as conveyers of caramel corn. I guess I was staring. Adele picked up on my gaze and looked at me. If expressions could talk, hers would have said, *This is my domain and don't even think about coming back here*. As I said before, I wasn't about to ask her to teach me. I didn't do well with diva types. I had been through way too much of that with my mother.

Ah, but there might be another way.

CHAPTER 3

MAYBE I HADN'T BEEN 100 PERCENT TRUTHFUL with Detective Heather. Mrs. Shedd wasn't totally happy with my job performance, and I'd never met Mr. Royal. Mrs. Shedd did a lot of her work from home and usually came in before anyone was there or after closing, which was why I had been surprised to find her waiting in the office the week before.

She was somewhere in her late sixties but, thanks to a fabulous hairdresser, had blond hair that looked totally natural. Nobody ever called her anything but Mrs. Shedd. I didn't even know what her first name was. Mr. Royal was even more elusive. He always seemed to be traveling around the world on some book-finding mission. I had begun to wonder whether he was just an imaginary partner.

"Molly, it's too bad about Will Hunter," Mrs. Shedd had said when she'd closed the door. "Particularly after you sold me on what a celebrity signing could do for the bookstore. I would love to give those oh-so-hip-and-in-love-with-their-coolness independents in the city a run for their big-name signings. I thought you were so sure you could get it."

I had made it sound that way, hadn't I? It was just that Mrs. Shedd had sounded so excited when I proposed the celebrity idea. And she'd gotten even more excited when I'd said who I was thinking of. I foolishly thought Ellen would like doing something fresh and different with her client. I guess I was just naive.

Mrs. Shedd didn't say anything threatening, like she was thinking of letting me go over it. It was worse than that, really. She said she was disappointed in me, and I felt terrible. She'd given me a chance, and I had let her down.

Wrenching my thoughts back to the present, I glanced toward the event area and watched Sheila struggle with her hook. I thought of her worries over not being good enough, and could instantly relate. But maybe all wasn't lost yet. Maybe whoever took over Will Hunter's publicity would be more open-minded than Ellen.

In the meantime, I had something else to take care of.

I made sure Adele was busy with her square and not looking anywhere close to my direction; then I slipped over to the children's department. It was a sweet area with soft carpet featuring cows jumping over moons. There were little people–size tables and chairs, and books with pretty covers.

There was also a big selection of craft kits in the corner. There were kits for everything, from making your own clock to designing your own doll clothes. Tucked at the end was just what I was looking for. I picked up the small, suitcase-shaped basket that said *Crochet for Kids*. I opened it and looked inside. There were little balls of yarn, a plastic hook, a plastic needle and what I was looking for— instructions.

If the instructions could teach a kid how to crochet, they would probably work for me. I closed it and held it out of view as I slipped up to the cashier.

"You buying this for your grandkids?" Rayaad asked. She was our main register person.

"Who?" I said quickly. I had never mentioned grandchildren. Did she think I looked old enough to be a grandmother? I instantly touched my hair, wondering whether there was some gray I hadn't noticed. "It's a present for some kids. Kids I know who like to make things." I was explaining much more than necessary. "I'd appreciate it if you didn't mention it to Adele—that I'm the one who bought the kit. I mean, tell her somebody bought it so she can keep up with inventory, just not that it was me."

Rayaad shrugged and agreed. I stowed the package with my stuff, making sure it was well hidden.

When the crochet women left, I took down the long table and set up a smaller one at the front of the area, along with rows of chairs, for our next event. Daniel Cheeseboro was putting on a program to promote his book *Clean Up With Soap Making*. Actually, it covered more than just soap. The subject of the book was how to make a home business out of personal-care products mixed up in your bathtub. Of course, he was going to do a demonstration.

"Did somebody buy the *Crochet for Kids* set?" Adele called to the cashier. Rayaad looked toward me with a question. I hoped she understood the stern shake of my head meant not to tell Adele it was me.

It turned out to be more of a rhetorical question, because Adele dropped it before Rayaad could speak. I just hoped I could get through the rest of the day without Adele noticing the odd-size store bag with my things and putting two and two together. It would lead to too many questions and lots of awkwardness.

I had thought I would get a chance to go home before the evening program, but there was too much to do at the bookstore. Before I knew it, people had started coming in and sitting down. While the author set up, I made a last-minute check of the book display, and mentally rehearsed what to say.

"Hi, folks," I said into the microphone set up on the table. I went through my spiel introducing Daniel Cheeseboro. He was next to me, basking in the attention as I described his expertise in the personal-products area.

"Tonight I'm going to demonstrate making shower gel." He held up a square plastic tub. "You mix up a batch in here for a few bucks, which gives you enough to fill a ton of these babies." He gestured toward the row of small bottles. "Then drop in a little glitter, stick on a bow and a big price tag, and there you go. All the details are in the book."

He began pouring clear, slimy stuff into the tub. He talked too fast for anyone to get exactly what the mixture was, but he assured everybody that when they bought his book, they would find a full list of the ingredients. I always appreciated an author who was also a good salesperson.

"Fragrance is a key element. It is what will make your product memorable," he said, showing off a set of small brown bottles. "I make my own mixture of essential oils. Remember, a little bit goes a long way." He explained that for the sake of time, he'd already blended the scents. That recipe, too, was included in the book. Daniel held up a glass bottle with an eyedropper in it. He squeezed the bulb until it filled halfway; then he started to carefully measure out a few drops. It was a waste of time, because as he turned toward the tub, he lost hold of the bottle and it hit the side, flipped and went facedown into the slime. A moment later, a cloud of lavender mixed with eucalyptus along with something else spread around the bookstore. I glanced at the people in the chairs and saw that they were starting to gag.

Before Daniel could finish apologizing, the place had emptied out. He seemed flummoxed and kept going in circles, talking to himself. I grabbed the tub and, breathing though my mouth, took it outside. On the way out, I got sloshed with some of the slime. The mouth-breathing didn't help much. While I avoided smelling it, I could still taste it. The only good thing was, there was no chance I'd be making more caramel corn. The taste was going to take a while to get out of my system.

"YOU SMELL FUNNY," MY FRIEND DINAH SAID later that evening, wrinkling her nose. She leaned closer, took a bigger whiff and then stepped back. "What is it? I recognize lavender, eucalyptus and something else."

"Rose geranium," I said. Daniel had filled me in on the last addition just before he carted the tub into the bushes and dumped it. I had done my best to air out the bookstore, then gone home when we closed. I had already showered and changed clothes, but the smell seemed to have dissolved into my skin.

Dinah had reluctantly left her computer to come over and help me with the crochet kit. It was a real sacrifice, because she had been busy chatting online with a new potential Mr. Right. Dinah was divorced and anxious for a new companion. After striking out with all the in-person ways of meeting someone, she'd gone Internet with a vengeance. I explained Daniel's goof, and she opened a window and then turned on the fan. I pulled out the basket shaped like a suitcase and showed it to Dinah.

"Isn't that cute," she said, opening it. She took out the plastic hook and yarn and finally the instructions.

"Did you hear anything more about Ellen?" she asked, and I mentioned Detective Heather's visit.

"You don't really think she believes you did it?" Dinah asked as she flattened out the rolled-up pamphlet.

"It seems too ridiculous. Me, a murderer?" I pointed to myself and shook my head. I told her about the Lawrence affair questions, and we both laughed. Dinah didn't find him any more appealing than I did.

"I bet she'd just love to tell Barry you were cheating on him," Dinah said, and then her expression grew serious. "But somebody did kill Ellen. Aren't you curious who it was?"

"Well, yeah, but I'm glad it's not my job to find out who. I don't want to think about it anymore. Let's crochet."

Dinah nodded in agreement and began to read over the instructions. I figured anybody who could teach English to freshmen could help me figure out these directions. The first step was to make a slipknot. She read the instructions out loud, and I tried making one. I wanted to rename it a slippery knot because the yarn kept falling out of my grasp. Being nervous will do that to you. I finally got it and triumphantly waved the hook and knot above my head.

Then she read the directions for making chain stitches. It sounded simple. I slid the hook under the yarn, made a loop and pulled it though the slipknot, and presto, I had made a chain stitch. I did it again and now there were two chain stitches. I kept going, and suddenly there was a trail of little circles of lime green yarn hanging off my hook.

When I had completed a bunch of chain stitches, Dinah told me to put the hook under both strands of the second-closest stitch to the hook, put the yarn over the hook and pull it through. Now there were two loops on the hook.

"What do I do?" I said nervously.

"Put the yarn over the hook again and pull it though both of the loops."

"I did it," I squealed.

"Congrats. You just made your first single crochet."

I repeated the whole process and kept going until there was a single crochet in each chain. I was glad to see I had kept everything very loose. I had learned that much from watching Sheila. I made a chain and turned my work. Once again I began stabbing the hook under two strands of each of the stitches in the previous row. I looped the yarn over the hook and pulled it through, got two loops on the hook, yarned over and pulled the hook through both loops. It was starting to look like something.

"Hey, hey, time-out," Dinah said, making a T with her hands. "What about my turn?"

I reluctantly pulled out the stitches and gave up the blue plastic hook and the yarn. Dinah had been watching me and barely needed the directions. Pretty soon she had formed a little snake of circles and then made rows of single crochet just like I had.

"Okay, it looks like we both got the snake thing and single crochet down. Let's make something."

After the basic directions on how to crochet, there were directions for making a little pouch. It was really just a long piece of crochet you folded over, sewed together and then put a button on the front of. We took turns doing the rows of stitches and managed to finish the whole thing.

"Wow," I said, proudly holding up the tiny bag. "We're as good as any ten-year-old." Dinah glanced at her watch. I knew she wanted to get back to her online chat. She assured me this guy had real promise—unless he wasn't telling the truth. When she left, I looked at our little creation with amazement. I couldn't wait to join the crochet group.

"ARE YOU SURE YOU KNOW WHAT YOU'RE DOING?" Dinah asked. We were standing in the bookstore, looking toward the event area. The crochet group was gathered around the end of the table. There were still only four of them.

"They need us. There is no way they are going to make enough squares for that blanket without some help. They'll welcome us with open arms."

"We only know how to single crochet, and we barely know that." She still seemed troubled by the idea of our joining the group.

"We made the little pouch that came with the set. Before we folded it and stitched it together, it was almost a square. We'll just make single-crochet squares. They won't be as fancy as the other ones, but they can still fill in a lot of blank spots. It's the least we can do for Ellen."

Dinah shook her head. "But you didn't even like her."

"Shush." I glanced around to see if anyone had heard. There was only a man buying a magazine within earshot, and he didn't even seem to notice us. "Okay, I didn't exactly like her, but I respected her abilities."

"Which abilities? Her ability to be rude to you? Her ability to push you out of Charlie's business?"

"She bought me out."

Dinah snorted. "I stand by pushed because you couldn't have said no."

"Whatever. I have a personal interest in making sure they finish their project. Having groups meet in the bookstore is supposed to help build our image. How good would it look if the charity crochet group didn't finish their project?"

Dinah obviously wasn't going to make the first move, so I did. Mumbling something about she wasn't sure it was the image she was after now that she was considering dating younger men, she followed me anyway.

"Hi, ladies," I said with a bright smile. They were crocheting silently, and all glanced up from their work. Adele was the only one who didn't seem happy to see us.

"What's up, Pink?" Her eyes drifted to my tote bag.

"We want to join you. We want to make squares for your charity blanket."

Adele laughed. "Since when do you crochet?"

"Ah, I learned a while ago. I just never thought to bring it up . . . until now." I pulled out the pouch Dinah and I had made together. I had thought it looked pretty good, but now, compared to what they were doing, it suddenly didn't look so hot. The lime green color seemed harsh in the bookstore lights, and maybe the stitches weren't exactly even, and when we'd sewn it together, we'd left a piece of yarn hanging.

"What's it for?" Adele asked, reaching for it. She turned it over in her hand. "This looks kind of familiar. Have I seen this before?"

I didn't want her to put it together with the kids' kit in her department. It would kind of blow my story. I snatched it back and put it in my bag. "I don't know why you're being so fussy. You guys need us."

"It's very nice of you to offer, dear," CeeCee said. "And as the leader of the group, I say welcome."

"Excuse me, but I'm the leader," Adele said, her face clouding up.

They immediately went back to a contest of who had helped Sheila more with her tight stitches.

Sheila looked up at the mention of her name. The calm in her face disappeared, and her eyebrows shot up in worry. "Please don't argue about me. You both helped." She sniffed the air. "How come it smells like massage oil in here?"

Even with all the airing out, some of the shower gel fragrance still lingered. But it was now light enough to be pleasant.

Meredith took a drag of air. "It's a little different from massage oil. I smell lavender and eucalyptus, but there's something else in it."

"Rose geranium," I said, and then told them about the shower gel incident.

Meredith chuckled as she listened, her hands busy putting the black border around a square of the same pattern she'd been making before, only this one had the colors reversed.

"I'll agree to let Pink and her friend in, as long as there is no chance Pink ends up the leader." Adele nodded to the group.

"I don't want to be the leader," I said.

With that agreed, they let us sit down with them. Dinah and I chose seats near CeeCee and as far away as possible from Adele. The last thing I wanted was her staring at me while I crocheted. She was bound to be critical. CeeCee on the other hand seemed likely to offer help, which we needed immediately. We'd had the directions in front of us the whole time we were working at my house. Now, without them, I didn't know where to start.

"You'll want to make a slipknot," CeeCee said out of the corner of her mouth. Then she surreptitiously showed us how. I looked down at my selection of crochet hooks, and CeeCee suggested using a J to start with. Dinah and I each took out our Js and then tried the slipknot. We were both nervous and had some trouble, but then got it down. Adele was already back into her own square and didn't notice.

I remembered the part about making a bunch of chain stitches, but had no idea how many to make.

"Why don't you two make a practice swatch to begin with?" CeeCee suggested. Then she said she'd be able to calculate out how many stitches and rows we'd need to do to get the size square they needed.

I listened to what she said, but it didn't process. Dinah seemed as confused as I was. Finally CeeCee said just to crochet ten rows of ten stitches and she'd help us from there.

Sheila put her work down and stretched her arms. "Those aren't Ellen's hooks, are they?"

The question caught me off guard, and my hook slipped out of my hand and clanged on the table.

"Of course not." I retrieved my hook. In the meantime the few stitches I had done had come unraveled. I started again. I was clumsy with the hook, but still watched with amazement as the stitches started to accumulate. On one side there was a plain old ball of royal blue yarn, and on the other a row of sweet little single crochets. Not to make a pun, but I was hooked.

Dinah was already frustrated. She kept getting distracted by a nice-looking guy in a warm-up outfit in the reference section.

"It helps if you look at your work," CeeCee said to her, then, following Dinah's gaze, "unless there is someone like that to admire." The man picked up a book, unaware that he had an audience.

Dinah dropped her hook and ten chain stitches on the table. "I just remembered I need a crossword puzzle dictionary." She was off before I could stop her.

There was a twinge in my shoulders. I was trying too hard. "I thought this was supposed to be relaxing," I said, rolling my neck and stretching my shoulders.

Meredith smiled at me. "Not so much when you first start. It seems like you're so worried about how you're doing, it's just the opposite of relaxing." She got up and walked around the table. "Sorry I don't have my chair, but this ought to help."

She kneaded my neck and moved down to my shoulders. She had magic fingers. The tension seemed to just melt. "Wow," I said, hoping that if I encouraged her, she wouldn't stop. "I can see why you're so popular." She took my arms one at a time and worked out the kinks. She moved back to my back and put pressure on various spots on my shoulder blades. "I mix in a little acupressure," she said, finishing and going back to her seat. "I do legs and feet on my regular customers."

"Your regular and very lucky customers. Thank you."

"My pleasure. It is very satisfying to provide such a necessary service."

I rolled my shoulders a few times and picked up my work again.

Just when I was beginning to enjoy the relaxed feeling

the massage inspired, I caught sight of a woman in a suit with a familiar knit bag.

"Mrs. Pink," Detective Heather Gilmore said. "I was hoping to find you here."

Oh, no, not again. I put on a pleasant smile, but inside I was groaning.

"That's a magnificent bag," CeeCee said, touching the sculpted blue yarn stitches of Detective Heather's purse. "Did you make it?"

Detective Heather nodded with a pleased expression.

"Maybe you'd like to join our crochet group," CeeCee continued. She explained the squares and the charity sale, and the fact that we were a little behind.

"Sorry I don't crochet. I knit." There was just a touch of haughtiness to the word *knit*, as if it were somehow on another planet from *crochet*.

Adele's head shot up, and for once the storm-cloud expression wasn't directed at me.

"You know, I'm tired of people like you who think knitting is the be-all and end-all of everything. We crocheters are tired of being the poor stepsisters of knitting. We can do things with crochet that you knitters only dream about."

Detective Heather appeared a little stunned by Adele's barrage, but quickly shrugged it off.

"I came to return your pen," she said to me. "How would it look if word got out police detectives were filching pens from people?" She held out an attractive gold pen.

"It's not mine," I said, wondering whether it was just an excuse.

"Really," she said, taking it back. "Hmm, I wonder whose it is." She glanced around at the group. "As long as I'm here, I'd like to ask you all something. Was it common for Ellen to forget her hooks?"

"Not at all," CeeCee began. "I was so surprised when Molly told me. It was completely unlike Ellen. She was highly organized and into detail. She couldn't have run her business and managed to lead the crochet group if she hadn't been."

"Really," Detective Heather said, taking out her notebook and regular pen. "So, then you saw the bag of hooks after she left?"

CeeCee shook her head. "Not me. I left before her. I had a meeting about a project I'm working on. I'm going to be a spokesperson for a new face cream." She looked toward Adele, Meredith and Sheila. "You must have seen the bag of hooks?" They all shrugged and shook their heads.

"Hmm, so, Mrs. Pink, you were the only one who actually saw the bag?"

This wasn't sounding good. I didn't like the way Detective Heather was staring at me. I thought about what I'd said to Dinah about how it wasn't my job to find out who had killed Ellen. I'd just changed my mind.

CHAPTER 4

"I DON'T THINK YOU SHOULD GO TO ELLEN Sheridan's funeral," Barry said. I was just clearing off the dishes from supper. Since his son, Jeffrey, was at a friend's, Barry had time for once. I'd thrown together a casserole and some salad, and we'd eaten at the built-in booth in the kitchen. No detective suit today—Barry wore jeans and a pocket T-shirt. They weren't the high-fashion jeans that get abused to look broken-in. His were a soft blue from being worn. Barry looked good in everything, but I liked him best like this.

As soon as I took away the dishes, he spread out some tools and my toaster. The popper-upper had stopped working. Barry could fix everything, and whenever he came across anything that was broken or barely working, he did his magic. My house had never been so functional.

"Why? What aren't you telling me?" I stopped halfway to the sink.

"Nothing." His face as usual was inscrutable, probably

from too many years of working in law enforcement. "You've been mixed up in it enough. Let it go."

"Let what go?" Barry and I both turned as the back door opened and my son Peter walked in. His tone was confrontational, as though he'd immediately assumed whatever Barry was suggesting was wrong. Peter had called earlier to say he'd be stopping by to pick up his golf clubs. Though he had his own apartment, all his sports equipment was still here. He looked at Barry and the tools on the table, and his eyes narrowed. "I would have fixed your toaster."

Not in this lifetime. I loved my older son dearly, but I knew him for what he was. Peter could fix deals, not things. He would have just bought a new one. Not that it was really about the toaster, anyway. Peter had shown a certain degree of animosity toward Barry from day one. I gathered it was something about the idea of my dating and whatever else I might be doing with Barry that didn't sit well with him.

The first time they'd met was at a party I'd thrown for my son Samuel's birthday. Peter took one look at Barry and pulled me into the kitchen, wanting to know who he was and how I'd met him. He wasn't any happier when he heard the details.

"You picked up a stranger in the grocery store," Peter said, looking at me as though I'd lost my mind.

"He wasn't a stranger." I explained that I knew Barry from traffic school. "He was the last-minute stand-in teacher, taking over for the motor cop who came down with food poisoning. I was there for making a right turn on a red light without stopping, though I still say it was yellow."

Peter glared with disapproval as I continued.

"So, you see, when I saw him in front of me in line at the grocery store, I already knew him, more or less." Peter had seemed no more sympathetic when he heard about Barry's handheld basket containing a single box of frozen macaroni and cheese, along with a six-pack of beer. "His groceries looked lonely." I'd gestured toward the counter crowded with food ready to be served. "And I had a cartful of pot roast and potatoes and fixings for that." I pointed toward the German chocolate cake on the pedestal plate. "I invited him to join the party."

Despite Peter's giving Barry the evil eye for most of the party, Barry had enjoyed the company and the food, and had fixed my electric can opener. Since then he had fixed every broken and half-broken thing in the house and become part of my life, and Peter had never changed his opinion.

I recognized the same unhappy look now as Peter took out a glass and poured himself some orange juice.

"I was telling your mother she should skip Ellen Sheridan's funeral," Barry said, wrangling the toaster innards. I guess all his cop work had taught him to deal with disapproval and confrontation, because he never seemed bothered by Peter's manner.

"But she was a neighbor," I protested. "And Charlie's partner. She came to his funeral. It would be strange if I didn't go to hers."

Peter drank the contents of the small glass in a single swallow and set it down on the counter. "He's right. You shouldn't go."

"What?" I stammered.

"You should do what he says. Let it go."

I don't know who was the most surprised by Peter's comments. In all the times his path had crossed Barry's, Peter had never even come close to going along with anything Barry said.

I almost wanted to skip the funeral to cement their newfound agreement.

But only almost.

"How do you think I'd look as a blonde?" Dinah patted her spiky salt-and-pepper hair. "I'm thinking it would knock off a few years." Dinah had offered to come along with me to the funeral even though she'd known Ellen only in passing. She kept the mood light as I drove through the gates marked HILLSIDE MEMORIAL PARK.

"And that is off of how many years?" I smiled at her expectantly.

"Ha, ha. You didn't really think I'd fall for that?"

It was more of a tease than an effort to get at the truth. Dinah was determined to keep her age vague.

"People know your exact age, and they start to judge you. Of course," she continued, her expression growing serious as we passed a grassy hillside marked with headstones, "getting older is definitely better than the alternative."

Dinah had jazzed up her black jacket and pants with several intertwined long scarves in shades of green, earrings so long they almost hit her shoulders, and a lot of silver bracelets, which jangled as we walked toward the chapel. It was a gorgeous September day, with warm, dry air that felt like silk, and it seemed a shame to have to go inside. By the time we got there, all the seats were filled and we had to sit on folding chairs in the back. Ellen would have been pleased at the turnout and the fact that Lawrence Sheridan had gotten the A-list celebrant to handle the proceedings. She managed to soften all of Ellen's edges and build up all of her good points. Even with all the differences between Ellen and me, I couldn't help but tear up.

After the service, Dinah and I followed the snake of cars to the burial site, but we didn't join the proceedings. It reminded me too much of Charlie's funeral. It was a relief to head to the reception.

The street in front of the Sheridan house was usually empty, but by the time we drove by, every inch of curb space was taken. I drove home and parked in my own driveway, and Dinah and I walked the two blocks.

"I might have to duck out. I'm expecting a call," Dinah said as we got in sight of the white picket fence and coral roses that marked the front of the Sheridans' yard. "Mr. Online wants to go live-voice." Her face beamed with a hopeful smile before going back to funeral-somber. "I understand going to the funeral, but are you sure you want to go to the house?"

I repeated what I had told Barry and Peter—about Ellen's being a neighbor and Charlie's partner—but added what I hadn't told them. "To see if I can find out anything about who really . . ." I gestured with my hands, hoping Dinah would fill in the blank.

Dinah got it and started to say something, but her cell phone interrupted. "I'll catch up with you," she said, stopping as she pulled it out.

As I continued toward the house, I noticed a throng of people gathered at the entrance to the yard. I was straining to see what was going on, when CeeCee stepped next to me. She knew how to dress for a funeral. I had worn my all-occasion black pantsuit with flats, and left my shoulder-length hair moussed and loose. CeeCee wore a white silk shell under a perfectly tailored black suit with a pencil skirt, designer sling-backs and a matching purse. She completed the look with a wide-brimmed hat and sunglasses.

"I can't believe paparazzi showed up here," I said, seeing that the throng had cameras.

"Well, dear," CeeCee said, straightening the jacket of her suit, "they go wherever they can get some shots of celebs." She adjusted the tilt of her head to show off her best side. "I'm surprised you came, under the circumstances."

"What circumstances?" I asked.

She stepped closer and lowered her voice, even though there was no one to hear. "Oh, you know, dear, after being questioned by that detective, well, I thought you'd want to keep your distance." It was disconcerting that CeeCee stayed with the posed look instead of turning toward me as she spoke. "You know, some people think that murderers like to show up at the funeral." Her voice had such a sugary innocence, she made murderers sound as benign as caterers.

As we approached the photographers hanging by the gate, she assumed a more appropriately funereal expression. "You should have let me give you the brand of makeup." She gestured toward her face. "See, no orange, but enough color so I won't look pasty."

As if on cue, the jean-clad group with camera bags slung on their shoulders focused on us and began to shoot. The flashes blinded me, and I almost tripped on the curb.

"Hey, here comes Will Hunter," one of the photogs shouted. They all turned toward the man with the unruly hair getting out of a Prius. CeeCee looked a little pouty at the loss of attention.

He grabbed my attention, too. Something about his tousled dark brown hair and slightly baggy but probably very expensive jeans paired with the black Armani jacket made me want to look at him. I think that is what they call charisma. I swallowed a laugh when I noticed that he was wearing slippers, the sheepskin moccasin kind. How funny that the guy who wrote *Walk a Mile in My Shoes* didn't wear them. Not that I thought for a minute he'd really written his memoir. Ellen had probably hired a ghostwriter, who'd done the real work.

I couldn't take my eyes off Will as he made small talk with the photographers before passing us and going into the house. So what if I was old enough to be his very much older sister; I still found him adorably attractive.

A woman greeted him as he entered.

"Who's that?" I asked CeeCee.

"Natalie Shaw. She's . . . Sorry . . . She was Ellen's assistant."

"*That's* Natalie?" I said, taking a closer look. I had seen Natalie at the Pink Sheridan office, but something about her seemed different. It took a moment before I realized what it was. Before, she had appeared somehow bedraggled, with her head down. Today, she was standing tall, and her whole demeanor seemed confident and in charge. For the first time, I realized that she had amber eyes and big lips.

I knew what was going on. I'd been through enough events with Charlie to understand that while this was an after-funeral reception, it was also business. Will Hunter was a client and had to be coddled. He and Natalie exchanged a few words as she ushered him inside. I had seen Ellen Sheridan act similarly toward clients at Charlie's funeral.

When Charlie died, I wasn't up to having a mob of people come to the house. In fact, I'd barely been able to walk and talk, so we'd gotten a banquet room at a restaurant. To have put all this together, Lawrence Sheridan had to be much more functional than I'd been.

A woman greeted us in the foyer, introducing herself as someone from Pink Sheridan. I got a mere welcome, but CeeCee got the client treatment. As I walked away, the woman was still talking to CeeCee, touching her arm with a reassuring gesture.

The interior was barely recognizable as the same place where I'd walked in and found Ellen. Now it was full of life, but, then, that was the point of the reception—to say that life goes on.

How strange to be in the Sheridan house again. After not having been there for a long time, I'd been there twice in a few days. I supposed I ought to find Lawrence and give him my condolences, since I had missed him at the service. I headed back to the living room, avoiding the spot where I'd found Ellen. The carpet smelled newly cleaned, and the room was filled with flowers and people. A bar had been set up on the patio, and uniformed waiters were circulating through the crowd, serving platters of elegant baby quiches, shrimp with cocktail sauce and puff pastries with a mushroom filling. Lawrence Sheridan walked through the room, and I considered approaching him, but he was with another of Ellen's celebrity clients.

One minute I was fine, and then suddenly a wave of emotion poured over me. This scene brought back memories of Charlie, and I reexperienced that punched-in-the-gut feeling. Charlie had gone to Las Vegas to do some hand-holding and oversee the publicity for a soap-star client who was opening a boutique on one of the hotel's indoor shopping streets. Somewhere in the midst of it Charlie had collapsed. He died before the ambulance reached the hospital. Even now I teared up, remembering that waving to him as he'd pulled out of the driveway on the way to the airport had turned out to be our last good-bye.

It seemed totally unreal. Charlie had always seemed immune to middle age. He played racquetball several times a week and worked out at the gym regularly. He ate right most of the time and all his numbers were in the good range, but none of it had mattered in the end. His heart had simply given out.

Ellen had actually helped me get his body back home and make all the arrangements. Jewish tradition insisted that the funeral take place as soon as possible, so Charlie was buried within two days. It was over before I had processed what had happened. Throughout the next week, people had come by the house, though I had been in too much of a fog to even notice. I suppose the fog was a protection against being overwhelmed with all the emotion.

I wondered about Lawrence. As I'd watched him walk through the room, he had seemed too in control, too distant. I wondered whether he really was that cold, or whether he was a master of shutting off uncomfortable feelings.

Natalie came into the room with Will Hunter in tow. They stopped within earshot, and I couldn't help but eavesdrop.

"I just want you to understand that everything is moving along. I'm working out the details to have the publicity for the book and your new movie coincide," she said. "I know you always talked to Ellen, but since I've been the one actually handling your publicity for a while, the transition will be seamless. Lawrence will be involved, too."

"It's okay, Natalie," he said. "I'm fine with giving you a chance. And if Lawrence is in the background, all the better."

When they moved on, I glanced around for Dinah. Her call was taking a long time, which must mean it was going well. I nodded to a few neighbors and followed the smell of hot food into the dining room. More uniformed servers manned stations with a lavish array of poached salmon with hollandaise, baby lettuce salad with walnuts and pomegranate, whipped potatoes, and green beans with mushrooms and almonds. To finish it off, there was a dessert table with three tiered trays of miniature pastries.

I passed on the food, thinking back to my intent to gather information on who had killed Ellen. What did I know about being a detective? I certainly hadn't learned anything from Barry. He almost never talked about work, except when he'd had a satisfying end to a troubling case, and even then he didn't tell me how he'd solved it. Frankly, it seemed a little unnatural to me. Charlie had talked about work nonstop. But apparently Barry and his fellow cops talked only among themselves.

Even though I had been in this house twice in a few days, it seemed doubtful that I'd have this opportunity again. Should I have a look around? Nobody seemed to be paying attention to me, and they probably wouldn't notice if I slipped off. Thanks to my handcuffed tour with Officer James, I knew the exact layout of the place. Who says there isn't some kind of silver lining to every cloud?

But before I could make a move, I stopped myself. Was I actually thinking of snooping during a funeral reception? It seemed a little too much, even for me. I noticed the coffee bar set up along the wall. A young woman in the same white shirt and dark pants as the other servers was at the espresso machine. Perhaps a coffee drink would up my courage, or at least give me a buzz.

"A red-eye, please," I said to the young woman. I waited to see whether she would recognize the drink or whether I would have to explain that it was a cup of coffee with a shot of espresso. Her eyes definitely brightened, but I realized it had nothing to do with my drink order and everything to do with the fact that Will Hunter had stepped up behind me. She seemed to forget my order, and asked him what he wanted.

"Dude," he said in a disapproving tone, shaking his head at her. "The lady was here first."

I smiled at him. Wow, an actual gentleman. Who would have thought? She made my drink, then his, but kept her eyes on him even as she handed me my red-eye. As he sipped his soy-milk latte, he made no move to walk away. Should I bring up the book signing? It seemed inappropriate, but I'd already heard him discussing business with Natalie.

"Didn't you write a book?" I said, testing the waters.

His crooked smile widened, and his eyes grew more alert.

"Yes, I did. I really did. People keep thinking I used a ghostwriter, but I wrote it myself, even that poem at the end." His gaze narrowed. "How'd you know about it, since it isn't officially out yet?"

He made it easy for me to segue into what I did and why I was so interested.

"Book signing, huh, at a bookstore out in the boonies? Interesting thought." He considered it for a moment. "Ellen . . ." At the mention of her name, his expression grew serious, and he swallowed hard before continuing. "Ellen wanted me to stick to ones she'd used before. There was one in Hollywood and one in Santa Monica."

We had a clear shot of the living room from where we were standing. The crowd hadn't thinned; if anything, it seemed to have grown. Lawrence and Natalie were working the room separately. Even without hearing what was being said, it was obvious by body language that people were offering condolences, and Lawrence and Natalie were in turn consoling the guests.

Will nodded toward Natalie. "She'll be the one handling that sort of thing now. I have to hand it to her: She stepped right up to bat," he said before taking a sip of his drink. "No disrespect of the dead, but I have to worry about my career. Dude," he intoned, shaking his head as he looked over the crowd. "Do you think whoever killed Ellen is here? In a show I did, the murderer showed up at the funeral to gloat."

I was considering his comment when Dinah reappeared just as Natalie grabbed Will and whisked him away. Dinah's eyes were bright, and she looked happy enough to dance.

"You and Will Hunter?" she said with a giggle. "My lips are sealed. Barry will never know."

I rolled my eyes at the thought as Dinah chirped on about her potential Mr. Right. She went into a long description of his deep baritone voice, which sounded like a growl. She didn't realize it, but little by little I moved us to the edge of the room. The coffee and her presence had given me courage.

"What's going on?" she whispered as I took her arm and led her off toward the private part of the house. Dinah was quick on the uptake, and before I could answer, she'd figured it out.

"Snooping, huh? So what are we looking for?" She banged into me when I stopped short in front of the office door.

"I don't know," I said in a low voice. There was a slight problem. What did I know about investigating a murder? "This room is one of the ones that was ransacked."

"Let's have a look." Dinah turned the handle, and both of us gasped before we could step in.

The room was in better shape than when I'd seen it last. The floor was clear and the drawers of the filing cabinet were shut, but it still had the feeling of disarray. In the center, CeeCee was hunched over Ellen's desk, rummaging through a bunch of files. Her hat kept bobbing every time she moved. She didn't notice us at first, and flinched when she did.

I was all ready with our excuse. We were looking for the restroom. I couldn't wait to hear hers. But all she did was drop the file she'd been examining.

"So there you are," she said, as if she'd been waiting for us all along. "C'mon, the crochet group is in the den."

What? She didn't even make an attempt at an explanation. She just went out the door and took us with her.

You didn't have to know anything about investigating to figure out she had been looking for something. But why was she sneaking around to find it? If it was something in her file, why not just ask Lawrence or Natalie? Now that Ellen was gone, surely they'd give her anything she wanted. Unless . . . unless it was some sort of secret she didn't want them to know. Charlie had always known embarrassing information about his clients. That was part of his job—to know where the bodies were buried but keep the public's attention focused somewhere else. What if Ellen had known something about CeeCee and had some kind of proof?

I glanced over at CeeCee as she led us down the hall, and I wondered whether I should consider her a suspect.

When we got to the den, Adele and Sheila were gathered around a chestnut-colored leather coach. Sheila's eyes were darting around the room, and it was obvious her nerves were out of control. She said something about Meredith having gone off to get some food. Adele had toned down her look to merely a black-and-white polka-dot skirt and a black-and-white print blouse, and was talking to a twenty-something woman who looked remarkably like Ellen. I realized it was her daughter, Dakota Sheridan. She had been in Samuel's class in elementary school.

"So, you're the Tarzana Hookers?" Dakota said, letting her gaze take us in.

"My mother was making a messenger bag for me. I talked to her last week and she said she'd almost finished it. But I can't find it anywhere." There was a frantic touch to Dakota's voice. "I thought you might know." The *you* referred to all of us, but the only one who answered was CeeCee.

"I know just the bag you mean, dear. It had that special yarn in the middle. Let's have a look in the crochet room."

Crochet room? I thought back to my tour courtesy of Officer James, but couldn't recall seeing a crochet room. There had been a few rooms where he had just opened and closed the door without going inside. It must have been one of those. Then, I hadn't been interested in crochet. Now I couldn't wait to see the room.

"Oh, my," I said to Dinah when we walked in. Ellen had taken the front corner bedroom and turned it into a crafter's paradise. One wall had cubbies for yarn. The groups of skeins were arranged by color and gave the wall a rainbow look. A fabulous afghan was draped on the arm of an olive green love seat, which had a full-spectrum floor lamp next to it. Adele explained that the lamp was good for working at night.

We all checked out the other wall of shelves, which held crochet books and samples of Ellen's work. An involuntary "wow" escaped my lips when I compared the little square I was working on to the elaborate motif of the squares in a yellow and white baby blanket. There were more baby blankets in soft colors. The next shelf had a child's poncho and several shawls. Everything had a small white note attached to it.

"My mother gave away most of what she made." Dakota picked up the poncho and looked at the note, then explained that it gave the name of a women's shelter and detailed the kind of yarn the item was made out of, plus how to launder it. The rest of the displayed items all had notes with destinations and washing instructions, but the messenger bag wasn't among them.

"Let's check the closet," CeeCee said, opening the door, which revealed a pile of clear plastic containers with lids. They were filled with an overflow of yarn and more completed items.

"I'm sure she wouldn't have given it away," Dakota said, pulling the tops off. Her voice sounded as though she was on the verge of tears, and her movements were frantic as she took out the contents of the containers. All the emotions she had been holding in seemed about to boil over, but then, as if realizing she was coming unglued, Dakota pulled herself together and her composure returned. She accepted CeeCee's promise that the bag was bound to turn up, and started putting everything back into the boxes.

Adele went to help her, and Sheila was commenting on the peace of the room when it was suddenly interrupted as Lawrence Sheridan rushed in. The tall man had a purposeful air. At one time he had probably been handsome, but so many years of being bossy and difficult had left an imprint on his face. His mouth seemed naturally set in an expression that shouted, "I'm going to win." He seemed to be looking for something or someone, and made a hurried check of the room. Just then, a small ball of black fur rushed in, jumped on a chair and off again, circled the room barking, and headed back for the door. As the poodle was about to exit, Lawrence made a dive for it. He picked up the squirming dog, and his whole demeanor softened. "Poor ittle-bittle dog. All these people . . . Let's put you back in your room. I have some special chicken for you." Suddenly Lawrence seemed to realize he was among a bunch of people. He glanced around, nodding when he saw his daughter; then his gaze moved on to me, and his whole face exploded in anger. I half expected flames to start shooting from his eyes.

"You," he shouted. "What are you doing here? You should be in jail." He took a step closer, and I instinctively backed away. All eyes were on me now, including those of Detective Heather, who I noticed was standing behind him in the hall.

"I think it's time to split," I said, grabbing Dinah's arm.

CHAPTER 5

"YOU JOINED WHAT?" PETER SAID. "THE Tarzana Hookers?" Peter had come to drop off the golf clubs he'd picked up days earlier. I couldn't help noticing even his sports wear was designer. Peter had been an agent even before he knew what an agent was. In first grade he'd convinced Mrs. Quinn to give the lead in the year-end play to Amanda Sanders. Years later when he was still a trainee at William Morris, he'd used the same bravado to get a fledgling actress one of the leads in the pilot of *Everyone Loves Lulu*. The show had been picked up, the actress was tabbed as the breakout star and Peter became an agent at 24. I just wished he could use some of his expertise to get some work for his brother. But he always said the same thing when I brought it up.

"If he wanted to play a musician, I could, but since he wants to be one, it's not my area."

I couldn't help but laugh at my elder son's expression. "As in crochet hookers." I held up a size-J hook and the fuzzy red yarn scarf I'd started. The directions promised easy, easy, easy. All you had to do was make a foundation of eight chain stitches and then start the next row with a single crochet in the second chain from the hook. From then on, it was just row after row of single crochet. I had quickly discovered that the fuzzy yarn looked great, but kind of knocked out a couple of the easys. The stitches seemed to disappear in all the fuzz, and I kept missing or adding an extra stitch on a row, which led to lots of unraveling. The only way to keep at seven stitches a row was to count each one as I did it. The piece was only about three inches long so far, but I was very proud of it.

"I suppose you think the name's funny," Peter said, clearly implying that he didn't agree. He didn't seem that impressed with my scarf-in-progress, either. "I thought when you got the job at the bookstore, you'd sell the house, get a condo and . . ."

"Fade into the background," I said, finishing his thought. "I don't think so. I'm beginning a whole new chapter in my life. It wasn't my choosing, but I'm going to make the best of it."

He held up a copy of *What's Up?* magazine. There was a picture of CeeCee and me walking into Ellen's. Well, we were really in the background; the focus of the shot was Will Hunter. The caption read: *Will Hunter arriving at funeral of his publicist, Ellen Sheridan, of Pink Sheridan Public Relations. Veteran actor CeeCee Collins and friend trail.*

"That was quick. It was what, two days ago? We weren't going into the funeral. It was the after thing at the house." I looked at the photo again. CeeCee was right about the makeup. She looked great, and I looked pasty again. "You know, if I'd moved to a condo, you wouldn't be able to leave your golf clubs, bicycle, tennis rackets, skis and boxes of old toys and video games here."

Peter rolled his eyes. "Mother, that's not the point. . . ."

"Relax. I'm just listed as 'friend.' I don't see how any of

this reflects on you, anyway." I glanced at the picture one more time. CeeCee's pose had looked so weird in person, but it photographed perfectly. I was not only pasty but had a dorky expression. "You deal with actresses," I said. "Can you think of what CeeCee Collins could have been looking for in Ellen's home office?"

Peter's expression darkened. "Mother, how do you know she was going through Ellen's office?" He hit his forehead with the heel of his hand. "You didn't wander off during the funeral reception, did you?"

When I didn't answer, he shook his head. "I'm going to tell Barry on you."

"Oh, so you two are friends now?"

"Not exactly, but we do see eye to eye on this. Mother, stay out of the Ellen thing."

"Okay, but first, can you answer my question?"

Peter had rolled his eyes so many times by now, I thought he was going to get dizzy. He threw his hands into the air. Apparently I had graduated from difficult to impossible. "I don't know. Maybe Ellen had some embarrassing picture of her and she wanted it back. So now you'll drop it?"

When I didn't answer, Peter just gave up. It was probably just as well that he didn't know about Lawrence's little outburst.

It was already after the official ten a.m. start time for the crochet group when Dinah got to the bookstore. I grabbed my tote bag, and we headed to the event area. Mrs. Shedd had been thrilled when she'd heard I'd joined the crochet group. She said I could do it on work time. Of course, she expected me to keep an eye on things and make sure the charity blanket got finished.

The Tarzana Hookers were already at the table. It was obvious who they were: Adele had made a big sign in red calligraphy and stuck it on the table in full view of the window. Apparently the original shock of Ellen's demise had worn off. This time there was lots of activity. Everyone looked up as Dinah and I set down our tote bags and pulled out chairs.

I took out the square I had completed. Well, almost completed. I had done the main part in a medium blue yarn, all single crochet. Some of the stitches were a little wobbly, but I thought it looked pretty good. All it needed was a black border.

"And I remembered what you said"—I nodded toward CeeCee—"about working on my own project, too." I took out the fuzzy scarf gonna-be. I had added another inch or so, but it still had a long way to go.

CeeCee picked it up and examined my work. "Nice job." She pointed out how even the edges were.

"How could you tell if the stitches were too tight?" Sheila took it from CeeCee and ran her fingers over the top row. "It's so hard to see them in all the fuzz."

Adele checked it out and said nothing, which was as close to a compliment as I was going to get.

Dinah apologized for not having a square, but she had brought in things for her own project. She pulled out a crochet magazine and opened it to a page featuring a crocheted yellow bikini. "I thought I'd try that." Dinah put down a ball of yellow cotton yarn and a pink crochet hook next to it. CeeCee examined the instructions, pointing out that it said "intermediate level."

"You don't want to defeat yourself, dear, by trying something too hard, to start." She flipped through the magazine and found a section featuring washcloths. "Why not try one of these? It won't take too long, it features a couple of different stitches and the yellow cotton you have should work fine."

Dinah didn't look sold. It was a bit of a shift from a bikini to a washcloth.

"It's nice that you two want to make your own things, but first we should concentrate on our group project," Adele said.

CeeCee unfolded a piece of paper and laid it on the table. It showed the dimensions of the proposed blanket and a lot of squares. All the squares were the same size except in the middle section, where she'd marked four large ones. I tried figuring how many squares there were in total. Adele picked up on what I was doing.

"Pink, there are sixty-five small squares and four of mine, each of which is equal to four of everybody else's."

"And how many are done?" I asked.

CeeCee appeared uncomfortable. "I haven't had time to count. But when we have them all done, we'll connect them into strips and then put the strips together."

Adele rolled her eyes. "It's irrelevant to be talking about finishing when we've barely started." She turned to all of us and in a drill-sergeant voice told us we better get moving. She pointed her hook at my partial square and said she'd show me how to finish it.

I had been hoping CeeCee would be the one to help me.

Adele whizzed through a description of making a slip-knot on the hook with the new color and told me something about making a slip stitch to the edge of one side of the square. "Then you just keep going around all four sides until it matches the size of the rest of the squares."

When I didn't get it immediately, she took the blue square out of my hands and finished it so quickly, I couldn't tell what she was doing. It reminded me of how someone can demonstrate something on a computer, but the cursor moves so quickly and the screens change before you can tell what they did. Adele was about to hand back the completed square, but CeeCee shook her head.

"Adele, dear, perhaps you haven't heard the one about how if you give someone a fish, they have food for today, but if you teach them how to fish, or in this case crochet a border, they're set for life."

Adele viewed CeeCee with consternation as she unraveled the border and gave me directions about how to begin.

Meredith arrived just as Adele let out a loud groan at my ineptness when my slipknot slipped out of my fingers.

"I know that blond detective talked to Molly, but did she get in touch with the rest of you?" Meredith asked as she set out her things.

Adele, Sheila and CeeCee all nodded and gave me funny looks.

"Dear, that woman really doesn't like you," CeeCee said to me in her usual sweet tone. "Did you do something to offend her?"

So it wasn't my imagination. I couldn't wait to tell Barry.

Sheila cleared her throat to speak. "Detective Gilmore wanted to know what I knew about Ellen, and about the rest of you." Her eyes passed over the group but stayed on me too long. "I told her I knew Ellen from the crochet group and the gym. I just said she did weights and treadmill early Monday, Wednesday and Friday mornings, and that I didn't know anything about any feud between you two." Her gaze rested on me. "And I said the last time I'd seen her was when I left the group to go back to work."

"The detective asked me the same kind of stuff," Meredith said as she took out some ruby yarn and a hook. "I told her I'd gone to Ellen's right after the group and given her a massage, though it hadn't seemed to help her. She seemed as tense when I left as when I'd gotten there. I think Ellen was upset about something or someone. She mentioned a client coming for lunch."

"Really?" I said. "Did she say who? Maybe that's what she was upset about."

"Maybe. She didn't name any names," Meredith said. "You know Ellen worked out of her home office a lot. I think she didn't want anyone to overhear whatever they were going to discuss."

"Ellen was cooking lunch?" Sheila chirped.

Meredith stifled a laugh. "Ellen didn't cook. She called and got food delivered. We had lunch once, and she had a whole spa meal brought in."

"Really?" Dinah said. "What was it? Some kind of egg-white frittata?"

"Who cares about the menu, dear. The real question is, who was the guest the day she died," CeeCee said.

All eyes were on me.

"It wasn't me, if that's what you're thinking."

"Whatever, Pink," Adele began. "We're losing sight of our crochet problem. We've got a map for the squares and an idea for how to assemble them, but there is one major thing wrong: We don't have enough squares."

"We should have checked when we were in Ellen's crochet room for the ones she made. I'm sure she'd want us to use them," Meredith said.

"Why doesn't somebody call her husband and ask if we can have them?" Sheila suggested.

Why were they all still looking at me?

"Maybe you didn't notice, but Lawrence wasn't exactly friendly toward me," I said. "He basically accused me of killing Ellen. I think that excludes letting me come over and hunt through her crochet room." Then I had a much better idea. One that would open the door to getting the squares and help me get the Will Hunter book event. "I could call Natalie Shaw instead. She's taken over Ellen's business, and I'm sure she could help us get the squares." And who knew what else I might find out?

CHAPTER 6

AND I THOUGHT DATING WAS TOUGH THE FIRST time around. Aside from the occasional broken heart, all I'd had to contend with were my mother's problems with my dates. For example, according to her, Zak, my boyfriend in high school, looked like a windup toy and his moustache like it had been drawn with eyebrow pencil. I thought his moustache made him look worldly but, much as I hate to admit it, as I look back, she was probably right. Before that, there was the Greg disaster. At a family party, my mother was going to sing something from her girl-group days. Everyone knew what, since the She La Las had only one hit—"My Man Dan." By then, my mother was reduced to doing backup, but was still convinced she was just one shot away from the big time. Greg offered to accompany her on the piano. The trouble was, he played better than she sang, and she practically threw a fit. Seeing it through adult eyes, I kind of got her point. It must have been hard being upstaged by a fourteen-year-old.

All that seemed simple compared to this middle-age

dating. Now there was so much baggage. Ex-wives, late husbands, and sons of all ages. Jeffrey's arrival had definitely made things even harder. Barry had never gone into detail as to why his son was suddenly coming to live with him, but obviously something wasn't working out with his ex, as Jeffrey had been living with her all three years since the divorce.

Trying to be Super Dad, Barry had originally decided that unless we were in some kind of committed relationship, such as engaged or married, it wouldn't be good for Jeffrey to meet me. I understood his reservations, because my sons were much older and still were weird about my dating. We had a don't-ask-don't-tell arrangement regarding what time Barry left my house. Though the last part was no longer an issue once Jeffrey arrived. Barry was home with him every night unless he was working.

But once Barry finally acknowledged there wasn't going to be any status change in our relationship in the near future, he changed his mind and decided Jeffrey and I should meet after all. Technically we had already met. Barry had picked up Jeffrey once before dropping me off, and we'd exchanged hellos in the car, though Barry had never explained who I was. This time I was getting a title.

Barry decided we should meet over dinner, which was why the three of us were sitting outside a Northridge restaurant shaped like a log cabin. Barry was holding the pager, Jeffrey was busy with a handheld game thing and I was watching the two of them.

Jeffrey had barely reacted when they'd picked me up and Barry introduced me as his girlfriend.

Barry tried to make conversation and asked about my day. Somehow I morphed from talking about the crochet group to telling him that CeeCee said Detective Heather didn't like me.

"I told you she had it in for me."

Barry looked uncomfortable. "We all know you didn't do it. There's no evidence you did. I can't say anything to her—you know, obstruction of justice and all."

"Didn't do what?" Jeffrey asked, suddenly paying attention. "What's going on?"

Barry Super Dad gave me a little nod as a signal that he would handle Jeffrey's question.

"Molly got into the middle of a crime scene by mistake." He said it like it was an event on *Sesame Street*. Didn't he realize that Jeffrey was thirteen?

Jeffrey suddenly viewed me with new interest. "Wow. Was there, like, a body? A dead body?"

Barry cringed on *dead body* and appeared relieved when the pager went off and we were led to a table next to the salad bar. But as soon as we sat down, Jeffrey picked up the thread of the conversation.

"So, like, how did it happen? How did the person get killed and how did you end up there?"

Barry was clenching his jaw, looking very uncomfortable. This wasn't what he'd planned for our dinner conversation.

"Do you want to be a detective like your dad?" I asked, deflecting his questions. I'd noticed politicians did that a lot. They simply ignored an awkward one and talked about something else. Personally, I would have just told Jeffrey the whole story, but Barry looked like his blood pressure was going up, and I just wanted the evening to go well.

Jeffrey shook his head decidedly. "Naw, I'm going to be an actor."

The answer was not good for Barry's blood pressure. His eyes kind of bugged out, and his mouth fell open in surprise—clearly not happy surprise. Then Barry calmed himself and even chuckled. "You're still a kid. When I was a kid I wanted to be a race-car driver. You have lots of time to figure out what you really want to do."

Jeffrey shook his head again. "I don't need years. I know

I'm going to be an actor. And I'm not a kid anymore. I'm a man in the eyes of God." He mentioned his Bar Mitzvah.

"That's just a ceremonial thing," Barry said. "You can't vote or drive or buy a beer. Maybe in God's eyes you're a man, but in everybody else's you're still a kid."

Jeffrey shrugged off Barry's comments. "You might as well know. I joined the drama club at school."

"Drama club?" Barry said in a tone of disapproval. "I thought you were joining the Junior Forensics."

"And from now on I want to be known by my stage name, Columbia."

"What kind of name is Columbia Greenberg?" Barry said, giving the waitress the evil eye when she arrived to take our order.

"A very good name. An unusual name. The name of, like, a superstar," Jeffrey said defiantly. He was trying to sound so serious, but he still looked soft and round, kind of like an unfinished sculpture. In contrast, girls his age all looked like women, wearing eyeliner and push-up bras. Not that Jeffrey wasn't trying to look more manly. He'd gelled his hair into spiky clumps and worn a blazer over his T-shirt and jeans.

I realized it was time to turn the direction of the conversation again. I picked up my menu and pushed one toward each of them. Barry opened his in a huff. Jeffrey took a second, then picked his up.

"Do you think Detective Heather questioned Lawrence Sheridan?"

"The husband?" Barry said, looking at me from behind his menu. He seemed relieved the question had nothing to do with Jeffrey's future ambitions. "Of course."

"I bet he was having an affair."

Barry scowled from behind his menu and started gesturing toward Jeffrey.

"What's everybody going to have?" Barry said.

"My dad thinks I'm four," Jeffrey said in a world-weary

voice, looking at his father. "I know about affairs and I'm not going to freak out." Jeffrey's voice did kind of crack as he said it, and I gathered an affair must have had something to do with his parents' breakup.

It couldn't have been Barry. He was too play-by-the-rules Mr. Solid. No wonder Detective Heather was so hot on his trail. He was excellent husband material.

"Let's talk about something else," Barry said, putting down his menu. "Molly, why don't you tell Jeffrey about your crocheting?"

Jeffrey and I rolled our eyes in unison.

After dinner we went back to their place. Barry had a two-bedroom town house. He wasn't much of a home-maker, and while the place had the basic TV and couch in the living room, there weren't any homey touches like col-orful pillows or nap blankets draped over the end of the couch. Once I got finished with my inaugural scarf, I was definitely making an afghan to brighten up the place.

Jeffrey trailed off to his room, playing his video game as he walked. Barry started coffee and we sat in the living room. I took the couch and he sat in a chair.

"I don't think Jeffrey would faint if we sat next to each other," I said, patting the couch cushion. "I don't think Jeffrey would even notice."

Barry got the coffee and went back to the chair. "Kids want to believe their parents are going to get back together. Not that it's going to happen here." He looked down into his cup. "His mother has been through a few boyfriends, and all the coming and going has been hard on him. It got worse when her latest boyfriend moved in and my ex started buying his favorite cereal instead of Jeffrey's. Per-sonally, I don't understand why she couldn't have bought two kinds of cereal." He looked at me. "Of course, you don't have that sort of problem. Your boys are grown." He chuckled. "They don't feel displaced by me."

I stared at him, my arms folded over my chest. "Are you

blind? Haven't you noticed how Peter always disagrees with everything you say?"

"He didn't last time. He didn't think you should go to the funeral, either."

"Okay, so one time you agreed, but it was the only time. Every time he sees you fixing something for me, he says he can do it."

Barry laughed. "But he can't. I saw him looking at a screwdriver and wondering which end to use."

My eyes narrowed, and the mother-protector came out in me. I might have thought that Peter was only good at fixing deals, but nobody else could say it. "He's not that bad. He even knows there are two kinds of screwdrivers. But that's not the point. Haven't you noticed that whenever Samuel sees you, he gets that hangdog expression, like I'm not paying enough attention to him? I thought you detective types were supposed to be superobservant."

"I thought we were, too. Hmm, so then your boys see me as your boyfriend, lover . . . ?"

My eyes widened in shock as I shook my head. "Lover? I don't think they even want to get close to that."

"Okay, then, but they consider me a serious contender?"

I shrugged. "I suppose . . ."

"Well . . ." He left the rest blank. This was where I was suppose to throw myself into his arms and say, *Yes, yes, I accept you as The One. I'll marry you and be the new Mrs. Greenberg.* I just changed the subject.

I took a sip of my coffee. It was surprisingly good, a dark, smoky roast made strong, just the way I liked it. "So you think Lawrence Sheridan is a likely suspect?"

Barry shook his head in capitulation. "You're doing that again. You think I wouldn't notice the change of subject? Remember, we detectives are an observant bunch. Yes, if it was my case, I'd talk to the husband first and to everybody I could about him. He probably had an insurance policy on her. What about the assets of her business? Maybe he wanted to start over with a younger woman with no financial strings attached. It wouldn't be the first time . . ." Suddenly Barry stopped. I was listening too intently, and the fact that I was making a mental list of what he said was obvious. "But it's not my case or yours. Oh, no, Molly, you can't go asking Lawrence Sheridan a bunch of questions. . . ."

I chuckled. "You don't have to worry about that."

"And why is that?" Barry looked at me levelly. I hadn't told him about my abrupt departure from the funeral reception thanks to Lawrence Sheridan practically throwing me out since it kind of proved that Barry and Peter had been right in advising me not to go.

"I don't think he's really likely to talk to me."

"And why is that?" Suddenly Barry had turned into Mr. Interrogator. When asked a direct question, I can only tell the truth, so, trying to make it sound not so bad, I told him about Lawrence Sheridan's suggesting I ought to be in jail.

Barry closed his eyes and shook his head.

Poor Barry. He'd had the best of intentions for the evening. Jeffrey and I were supposed to get to know each other, but the one who got to know the most was Barry, and none of it was information he wanted.

CHAPTER 7

I NIXED THE IDEA OF DEALING WITH NATALIE Shaw about the crochet squares over the phone. It would be too easy for her to answer and hang up before I had a chance to talk about other things, like Will Hunter's book signing. Even though Ellen had given me a flat-out no, I hoped Natalie might be more open-minded.

The Pink Sheridan office was in Encino, which was a notch above Tarzana in status. Maybe more than one notch, at least as far as the Encino people thought.

I hadn't been there since Ellen pushed me out. The parking lot looked the same, with the ancient California oaks spaced along the front as striking as ever. These weren't the back-East sort of oaks with their dancerlike graceful shape and leaves like hands. California oaks had blackish green leaves that held on to moisture for dear life and looked like football players, with their broad, solid trunks and low-spread branches. Along the side were tall eucalyptus trees, with their pale, smooth bark and gray green leaves. When it rained, they filled the air with their faintly medicinal scent.

The ground level had small boutiques and restaurants. The upper three floors of the U-shaped building were all offices. The inside of the U faced a courtyard, and each floor had a balcony running its length, accessible by wooden stairs. Charlie had made sure they got an office that faced the balcony. He'd liked being able to look out on the pond and the graceful white-barked sycamore trees that surrounded it. Sometimes when he'd worked late, the boys and I would bring dinner and surprise him. We'd open the sliding-glass door and have an impromptu picnic on the balcony, even if I was always a little worried about the boys falling through the railing.

I went in the front entrance and barely looked through to the courtyard. It made me think of Charlie too much. As the elevator took me to the third floor, a not-so-idyllic memory washed over me.

I had come in to finish setting up a press reception for one of Charlie's clients. I should have figured then how things were going to go with Ellen. What was it she had said to Charlie?

"Molly means well, I'm sure, but this isn't a PTA bake sale. You need to keep it professional-looking."

It had hurt when she said it, and it hurt now thinking about it. I wasn't one to call people names, but Ellen definitely deserved the B title. You shouldn't think ill of the dead, I told myself as I headed down the familiar hall.

A workman was doing something on the outer door to the offices. When I got closer, I realized he was taking off the metal letters that read PINK SHERIDAN PUBLIC RELATIONS. Now that there was neither a Pink nor a Sheridan, maybe things had changed, and the business was closing up shop.

I wondered what that would mean for Will Hunter's

publicity. Then I felt a pang of guilt for being so concerned with my own interests.

Inside there was a small reception area with a lot of boxes and a few chairs. A man in his early twenties sat at a desk, talking on the phone and looking at a computer screen. He looked up when I walked in.

His expression seemed slightly hostile, probably figuring I was either selling something or collecting for a charity. Pink Sheridan wasn't a drop-in sort of business. I explained that I wanted to see Natalie and didn't have an appointment. Of course, being a good gatekeeper, he wanted to know why. The crochet business seemed to sit well with him, and he went in to announce me.

"She's on the phone, but said for you to wait." He pointed to a folding chair.

I sat down, and when I leaned back, I realized I could see into Ellen's old office. Natalie was in there, standing over the desk, talking on the phone. The office looked pulled apart, but Natalie seemed in full work mode. It wasn't that I meant to eavesdrop, exactly, but it was impossible not to hear her end of the conversation.

"No, CeeCee, I haven't gotten all the papers from Ellen's home office yet. I'd be happy to send your file to you if I had it." It was obvious CeeCee had interrupted Natalie. "No, I'm sorry. There is no such thing as client privilege when it comes to publicists. That's only for lawyers and doctors. So if the police want to look at your file or at anybody's, there isn't anything I can do. But the good news is, as far as I know, nobody has asked." Natalie chuckled and seemed to turn on the charm. "I really think you should reconsider leaving us. Someone of your stature shouldn't be without a publicist." She stopped while CeeCee said something. "I'd really like to talk to you in person. I'm sure we can come up with something that will work for both of us."

I leaned closer, trying to hear better, but there was nothing more to hear. Natalie hung up and looked down at an open file on the desk. I was too far away to see even the label, let alone what it said, but I'd bet money that it was the file she had just told CeeCee she didn't have. And that it was what CeeCee had been searching for at the Sheridan house.

The obvious questions were: Why was Natalie lying to CeeCee, and what was in the file?

I sensed Natalie looking up, and I sat back in my seat to make sure I was out of view. A moment later she walked out of the office and greeted me.

"Then you know who I am?" I thought she would recognize the name but not remember my face. We'd only met a few times, once when she was just starting with Ellen, and a few times when I'd come to pick things up.

Natalie nodded in a friendly manner. "I remember meeting you, and of course Ellen spoke of you." I waited for her to take me into her office. Then, with a few nonchalant glances, I'd get a glimpse of the file and maybe see what CeeCee was so concerned about. But Natalie didn't, and we carried on our conversation in the reception area.

Ah, Natalie was definitely in public relations. She knew how to put a positive spin on something like Ellen's talking about me. By saying it in a positive tone and not giving any details of what Ellen had actually said, it appeared to be something positive. Of course, I knew differently.

"Leo said you were here about the crochet group?" She waited for my answer, but I glanced around at the chaos. There were boxes everywhere, and furniture was pushed against the wall.

"What's going on? Are you shutting down?"

Natalie followed my gaze. "I suppose it does look that way, but it's quite the opposite. L.S. and I worked out an arrangement." When I looked perplexed, she explained that L.S. referred to Lawrence Sheridan. "We're adding Shaw to the name, and I'll run the firm, but he's going to be very involved. With all his experience as a manager and producer, he brings a lot of clout to the table. There's so much over-lapping of responsibilities in the entertainment industry, it'll work out fine."

I don't know what surprised me more—that she had made some kind of deal with Lawrence, or that she referred to him as L.S. Lawrence Sheridan was always Lawrence, never Larry or anything resembling a nickname, and now he was known by initials?

"We're updating everything. Ellen was a little too old-school." Ellen's desk, it turned out, was just waiting for some charity's pickup. It was big, with curved legs and a parquet top—too fussy for me, and apparently for Natalie, too. She showed me catalog photos of the furniture to come. Her desk had a glass top and a large black blotter. They were getting wireless headsets and all the chairs were going to be er-gonomic. It all sounded spare and a little cold for my taste, and I was glad, for once, that I didn't have to work there.

Leo stuck his head into the office. "I got you the mas-sage appointment for this afternoon, Natalie."

She scowled at him. "Leo, what are you supposed to call me?"

"Sorry, Nat." He said the shortened version of her name as if it were all in caps, before he slipped back out.

"Everything is about being short these days," she ex-plained. "You know, Burger King is now BK. Who ever calls CPK 'California Pizza Kitchen' anymore? Any day now Dunkin' Donuts is going to wise up and become DDs. Have you looked at your e-mails lately? No one writes out *you* anymore. Everything is *4 u*, *c u*, *lol* or *imho*. The 'now' thing is to go for short, short, short. So I'm encouraging Lawrence to go by L.S. and I'm going by Nat instead of Natalie. It sounds more contemporary."

I guess Leo didn't have to worry about getting his name shortened. If I was going to make a move to secure the book signing, I had to find a way to bring it into the conversation now. With all of Natalie's short talk, she was bound to try to keep our conversation that way, too. "So, then you'll be keeping all of Ellen's clients?"

Natalie nodded. "Trying to, anyway. As shocked as they are about Ellen's death, most of the clients are more concerned with their own business." Natalie seemed to be glad to have someone to talk to, and she relaxed a little. "They don't know that it was all smoke and mirrors. Ellen had the relationships with her clients, but I was doing most of the actual work. Lawrence has been helping me, and almost all of them are going to stay. Except for CeeCee Collins. She wants to terminate."

"But you do still have Will Hunter—or should I say W.H.?"

Natalie chuckled. "No, no. Clients go by full names. I'm efficient, not stupid. Will's been a doll. He was Ellen's star client, and he says he's staying."

"So, then you'll be handling his book release publicity?" I tried not to sound too eager, but I had my fingers crossed.

"Ellen had started making plans, but I'll be making some changes. His book is going to be big. He's amazing, you know. Not only is he a class-A film star, but a damn good writer, too," she said. Spoken like a true publicist.

Personally, I was still having trouble believing he'd really written the book, but I wasn't going to rock the boat by casting any aspersions, and just nodded appreciatively. I brought up the subject of book signings and pitched her on doing his local one at Shedd & Royal.

"He's an outside-the-box kind of guy. Why not do an outside-the-box kind of book signing?" I said hopefully.

"Interesting," Natalie said when I'd finished. "Very interesting idea." I wanted to high-five myself. She was going for it. I was already making a mental note about needing extra chairs and all the end caps I planned to set up. And we'd need extra cookies and two baristas. Then my plans ground to a halt.

"I have a lot riding on the success of the publicity for Will's book. It sounds like a great idea, and one that I could squeeze a lot of press out of, but before I commit, I'd like to see one of your author events firsthand."

"No problem," I said, grateful that we'd already done the soap guy's event. The stink bomb disaster wouldn't have helped me with Natalie. "Our next signing is in honor of the crochet group. We're holding an event for a diet book called *Hook Down the Pounds: The Magic Way to Lose Weight with Crochet.*" I gave her the date, and vowed to myself I would make sure this one went right. Natalie walked over to her computer and typed the information into her calendar. It reminded me of the other thing on my agenda.

"I heard Ellen was supposed to have someone over for lunch the day she was, uh . . ." I had a hard time saying *murdered.* "Do you know who it was?"

Natalie stopped typing. "That's sure the hot question. Detective Gilmore asked me the same thing. Well, actually, she asked if you were scheduled for lunch with Ellen that day. She had some idea that you were trying to make some kind of business arrangement with Ellen, and it went sour."

I felt my anger level rise. "That's ridiculous. I have a job, and Ellen and I settled a long time ago."

"That's exactly what I told her—that you and Ellen worked everything out just when I was starting. I also told her I couldn't help her in the who department. Ellen's computer calendar got wiped out." Natalie went on to explain that Ellen wasn't exactly a computer whiz and could have done the damage herself. "Like I said, she was very old-school. She wasn't very good with computers, nor did she trust them." Natalie looked skyward. "I had to set up her home-office computer, and she still barely used it."

"Maybe she used a written appointment book," I offered.

"I never thought of that," Natalie said, "but you're probably right. Ellen would never admit it, though. It would have made her seem too old-fashioned."

"Since you didn't know if she had one, I don't suppose you know where she would have kept it?" I asked hopefully.

Natalie thought a minute. "She'd probably have kept it with her all the time, but other than that, I don't know." Natalie suddenly appeared impatient. "We've gotten way off the reason you're here. What is it you need for the crochet group?"

She seemed relieved when I said we needed to get Ellen's squares. "I'm glad you aren't abandoning the project. I'm taking over Ellen's charity work, too. The chairman of the silent auction committee called me yesterday and said she hoped the promised blanket would still be donated. She thought that in light of Ellen's death, it would be sort of a memorial and probably would bring in more money."

Natalie was only too happy to arrange a time for the group to come to Ellen's house. She knew about Lawrence's outburst toward me and said he was just expressing his grief and frustration that the police hadn't caught Ellen's killer yet. Then she added that she'd make sure he wasn't there when the group came.

By now Natalie was moving me toward the outer door. I noticed that the workman had finished with the sign. It read PSS PR.

"I thought using the initials looked more contemporary than 'Pink Sheridan Shaw Public Relations.'"

When I suggested that she could have shortened it by taking off the P, Natalie gave me a disparaging look. "SS PR sounds like some Nazi thing, so I decided to keep the P."

"So then it's pronounced like the initials PSS, rather than the sound?" When she didn't get what I meant, I demonstrated that the letters said as a word sounded like air escaping a balloon. I thought she would laugh; instead she nodded.

"Hmm. Catchy. I might just use it."

I rolled my eyes.

CHAPTER 8

"L.S. AND NAT SOUND PRETTY COZY," DINAH said. We'd met for coffee before the crochet group's start time, and I had just finished telling her about my trip to Pink Sheridan. I couldn't bring myself to call it PSS PR yet. I was glad for the break. Even though Mrs. Shedd had said my time with the crochet group counted as work time, I wasn't about to shirk my duties. So I'd already updated the event calendar, put up the signs for the upcoming *Hook Down the Pounds* program and placed copies of the store newsletter in strategic places around the bookstore.

Writing the newsletter was my job, too. The latest edition had spotlights on the mystery lovers' and romance readers' monthly gatherings; a notice that we might be starting a writers' group (if I could get Dinah to run it); and of course, a big article about the Tarzana Hookers, including a note about Ellen's passing; along with the usual list of staff-recommended books and a calendar of events.

Just before I'd joined Dinah, I'd set up an end cap displaying *Hook Down the Pounds* along with other books on crochet. Even though the event wasn't happening for almost a week, I wanted to start generating interest for it. For obvious reasons, I wanted it to be a stupendous success.

"If she's got Lawrence, never Larry, going by his initials, something is going on for sure," I said. "Though, frankly, I don't get his appeal."

"That's because you're a romantic. Believe me, to a lot of women, money and power trump charm, hair and six-pack abs."

I knew what she said was true, but personally, Lawrence was still in the life's-too-short category. "Detective Heather was off the planet when she implied I might be having an affair with him. I wonder if she picked up on the Natalie–Lawrence connection when she talked to her. I guess there isn't any way to help her along in that direction."

Dinah gave me her best are-you-kidding look. "The best thing you can do with her is keep your distance." I had to agree. It was a relief that several days had gone by and I hadn't seen or heard from the blond detective.

"Barry said that if he was investigating, the first person he'd check out would be Lawrence."

"Barry talked about work?" Dinah said, incredulous. "I thought you said he never did, that he was almost weird about it."

"I think he was so nervous about me and Jeffrey meeting, he wasn't thinking straight and it just slipped out." I took a long drink of my red-eye and paused. Something Barry had been doing lately was bothering me, and I thought I'd run it past Dinah. "Ever since Jeffrey arrived, Barry has started just showing up—like without calling or anything."

"What's wrong with that?" Dinah asked, breaking off a piece of her peanut butter cookie.

"I don't know exactly. It feels like he's acting as if . . ."

"As if what?" Dinah seemed perplexed.

"As if I'd committed to something more than *seeing* him. I know he wants something more concrete, and preferably with a name like at least 'engaged.' But I am not ready for that. I want my space and the freedom to walk around with some kind of green facial mask on without being worried about being seen. And as long as I'm still buying beer for Charlie, it's too soon, anyway."

"If the worst he does is show up without permission, I wouldn't get upset. You don't know what it's like out there." Dinah stirred her coffee and broke off more cookie. "Mr. Online wants to meet in person. I'm just hoping he doesn't turn out to be another weirdo. Barry is probably trying to stake his claim and thinks by acting as if it's so, he'll make it so."

With all of Dinah's relationship woes, it was hard for her to understand that I didn't want to be claimed. I guess the old "grass is always greener" saying applied here. I drained my cup, hoping that the doubly caffeinated drink would go straight to my brain. Not only had I come in early to do everything before the crochet group met, but I'd been short on sleep. Too much on my mind had kept me rolling around and refluffing my pillow for what had felt like forever.

Thank heavens I'd gotten up and found my red fuzzy scarf-in-progress. I'd sat on the couch and begun working on it. The repetitive motion was soothing, and counting the stitches to make sure I didn't add or lose one became like a mantra. Just a few rows in and my eyes were heavy and all the tension had disappeared. After that, I had fallen into a good sleep, but it hadn't been long enough.

"So, do you think Lawrence did it?" Dinah said, turning back to my investigative efforts.

"He is certainly acting very together for someone who just lost his wife, like maybe he isn't so brokenhearted," I said. "But if you want motive, Natalie had plenty. Suddenly she's in charge and running everything. And she did something strange." I told Dinah about overhearing Natalie's call with CeeCee and being sure Natalie was lying to her.

"I wonder what's in that file," Dinah said.

"You and me both," I said with a nod. I watched as Dinah took off another mini cookie piece. At this rate, it would last forever. "What's with the cookie?"

Dinah mumbled something about meeting Mr. Online and suddenly being weight-conscious.

"You've got to be kidding." Not only was she slender to begin with, but Dinah was such a ball of energy that she had to use up every calorie she ingested. "Here, let me help you out," I said, taking the last of the cookie and eating it whole as we tossed our coffee cups and headed to the event area as the others arrived.

"GOOD WORK," CEECEE SAID WHEN I TOLD HER Natalie had arranged for us to go through Ellen's crochet room.

"Since Natalie wanted to lock in a time, I suggested we have our next meeting at the Sheridans' house. I hope that's all right with everyone." I waited until CeeCee, Adele, Dinah, Meredith and Sheila nodded their assent, and then told them about the changes Natalie was making to Ellen's business. "Though there is no way I am ever going to call her Nat. I wonder if she really thought it through. Nat sounds like g-n-a-t, which is hardly positive." I turned toward CeeCee. "Is it true you're terminating?"

She stopped unpacking her tote bag. "With Ellen gone, there is no way I could stay."

Sheila gave CeeCee a puzzled look. "I thought I overheard you telling Ellen that you wanted to leave the PR firm a while ago."

CeeCee's demeanor changed, and she flashed an annoyed look at Sheila. "You must have misunderstood."

"I don't think so," Sheila said, gazing intently at the actress. "Because Ellen got that tone of hers. You know, kind of like, *don't cross me* or *uh-oh*. And she said something about some information she had . . ."

"Oh, that," CeeCee said, interrupting with her signature light giggle. "That, my dear, was just good acting. Ellen was helping me with a part I was going to audition for. It was a TV movie called *Laugh Till You Die*. The log line was 'veteran sitcom actress turns crime fighter'. Unfortunately Marion Ross got the part." CeeCee pointed at her work. "Now, let's get crocheting. We've got a lot of squares to do."

CeeCee was quick on her feet with that story, but I had a feeling it was just that—a story. So she'd wanted to leave Ellen. I wondered what kept her from going. Maybe the mysterious file had something to do with it.

Dinah and I sat together. It was still slow going for us. So far we'd finished only one square each that CeeCee found acceptable, and we were just beginning on our second ones. They were single crochet and not nearly as fancy as the ones the others were doing, but they would fill in some of the blank spots.

Sheila was ripping out her stitches. The royal blue square looked good to me, but CeeCee had pronounced the stitches too tight. CeeCee turned to Dinah and me.

"Remember, the correct gauge is essential, dears. That's the only way we can be sure the squares will all turn out the same size." She took out a gauge measurer and showed us how to check ours.

Oops. Dinah and I started unraveling our second squares. We had gone too small.

"Hey, Pink, try this larger hook," Adele said. I went to take the hook, but my eyes were drawn to the pink beanie she had just put on. She noticed me eyeing it.

"I made it. Isn't it great? And so easy and quick." Adele angled her head model-fashion to show it off.

I was speechless for a moment. The hat was great, just not

on Adele. Every time I looked at her, all I could think of was a soft-serve ice cream cone that had been dipped in that strawberry topping that hardened. It turned out Adele wasn't just modeling it, either. She kept it on and seemed to be making a lot of extra gestures with her head to show it off.

I glanced over at Meredith, who was intent on her work. With her longish wheat-colored hair and fine features, she would look great in the beanie. But, then, she was the kind who seemed to look great in just about anything.

She was making another of the squares CeeCee called "Ellen's flowers." The middle portion was scarlet and looked like a flower; it was surrounded by a pale cream yarn with a lot of open spaces. The black border was more solid, and the effect of the three colors and the change in stitches was stunning. I noticed that even Meredith occasionally had to consult the pattern's directions, which made me feel a little less backward about needing to keep a sheet with the basic stitches in view at all times.

As always, Meredith was between appointments and had worn what she called her work clothes. The flowing white pants and loose top appeared comfortable, like they'd be easy to move in. She had added a lavender scarf and turquoise necklace in a casually artful manner. It was just the opposite of Adele's calculated look.

Rayaad came up to the table, with two women in tow. "Here they are," she said, pointing at us.

"Hi, I'm Trish, and she's Nicole," the first woman said. "We're thinking of joining your group."

CeeCee, still trying to establish herself as leader, explained that we were making an afghan for charity, and then she invited the newcomers to sit down, as Rayaad left.

"Are you guys twins?" Sheila asked.

"Of course they're not." CeeCee appeared distressed by the comment and gave Sheila a cease-and-desist shake of her head.

The women did resemble each other a lot, but I didn't think it had anything to do with family. It had more to do with their matching chin-length, deep mahogany color-enhanced hair and their matching, perfectly pert noses that had probably been sixteenth-birthday presents. Both, though clearly in their late forties, were missing any trace of a fur-row between their brows, a giveaway that they'd been Botoxed. Ditto for the lack of crow's-feet. Trish and Nicole had pouty lips that shouted "collagen," and the way their mouths pulled a little too much to the side suggested face-lifts. Trish and Nicole were attractive and didn't have a wrinkle between them, but in the process they had lost their expressions and everything that made them look unique. Not that I was passing judgment. So far I'd done nothing to myself, but I'd learned long ago never to say never.

Trish said her husband was an orthodontist and Nicole's husband was some exec at Paramount, and both of them lived in Encino.

Unaffected by Sheila's comment, they sat down and set their designer tote bags on the table. Their megabuck bags must have felt like they were slumming when they ended up next to my red plastic one from Trader Joe's.

CeeCee began to introduce the group, but Trish's gush-ing interrupted her.

"Omigod, you look familiar," Trish said. "I know, I know. It was that weight-loss commercial, right? Wow, you looked great in that black dress at the end. That herb pow-der must really work."

CeeCee nodded, not altogether pleased, instinctively tugging at her garnet velour jacket so that it came down a little farther. "That was just a little something extra I did. I've done a lot of other work lately. You probably saw me as Aunt Tilda on *Melrose Housewives*."

"Really? You were on that show?" Trish said. "But it's the commercial I recognize you from."

CeeCee ended the discussion by moving on with the introductions. There was no big response to Sheila, Adele, Dinah or me, but when CeeCee got to Meredith, Nicole started to gush.

"Omigod, you're that masseuse everyone is talking about. I have to have your card. Your instant massages are supposed to be magic. I heard you use special oil and some kind of healing stones." She turned to Trish. "Can you believe the people in this group? Who would have thought? At a bookstore, no less." She turned back to the rest of us. "We've been going to a group at a yarn store, but this is way better."

"We'll just work on our regular projects this time, and start your charity thing next time," Trish announced, taking out her work as Nicole did the same. Adele gasped and her beanie started doing a mad bobbing dance when she saw what they took out. Trish showed off a piece with iridescent white stitches, explaining that it was going to be a throw for her couch. Nicole held up a fuzzy turquoise scarf-to-be. It wasn't what they were making, but how they were making it that had Adele's beanie bobbing. Their work was on needles. Unaware of Adele's explosive expression, they laid out a whole array of supplies—counters, needle protectors, gauge things and stitch holders.

"That's knitting," Adele sputtered.

"Yes, it is," Trish said, patting her blanket.

I caught the label on Trish's yarn. It was cashmere. I'd seen yarn like that online, and it cost a fortune. She obviously wasn't making things to save money.

"We're called the Tarzana Hookers because we use hooks, not needles. We crochet, not knit," Adele said, putting her hands on her generous hips, in full attitude mode. "Otherwise we'd be called the Needle Heads."

Trish rolled her eyes. "Nonsense. It's always knit and

crochet, with the spotlight on the knitting. Everybody knows that. Who ever heard of a group that just crochets?"

Trish's comments were like waving a red knitted blanket in front of a bull. Adele had gone total storm-cloud face now, and it looked as if her pink beanie was going to fly off.

"We may be the new kids on the block, since crochet isn't nearly as old as knitting, but we will not be treated like the poor stepsister anymore." Adele raised her fist in a sign of crochet power, and you could practically hear some kind of anthem start in the background.

Trish picked up my finished square. It was orange with a black border, and all single crochet. "This is what you're making such a fuss about? It's nothing compared to this." She held up her fancy yarn blanket, which had some kind of repeated pattern.

Adele snatched my square from her. "Lay off the square. She," Adele went on, pointing at me, "is just beginning. It's actually quite good for a novice."

I thought my mouth would fall open. Was Adele actually giving me a compliment?

Adele grabbed a hook and a ball of green yarn. She quickly made a small foundation chain, then joined it into a loop. Her hook was really flying, and it was hard to make out what she was doing, but the end result was evident. She had made the center and two rounds of a granny square before I could blink. The stitches were even, and the combination of spaces and double-crochet groups perfect. She held it up proudly. "Do that with your needles."

Trish picked up her blanket and began to knit at warp speed. She flew through a row, then held up her work and gave it a tug, showing off its stretchy quality.

"Try that with your crochet." She held up Dinah's half-done washcloth and pulled on it. It barely stretched. "Knitting is the *in* thing now. Everybody is doing it. It's hip, it's cool, it's now," Trish said defiantly.

Adele shook her head haughtily. "Crochet makes a better washcloth. It's sturdier, with more surfaces to scrub with."

"Yeah, but it takes more yarn," Nicole threw in, and then went off on the proud history of knitting. I held my breath, afraid she might know about crochet's past and bring it up. I'd looked into it to write a little piece for the newsletter, and it wouldn't exactly help Adele's cause. Though I could never find out exactly how or when crochet had begun, it was how imitation lace had been made in the 1800s in Europe. The real stuff was only available to the very wealthy, and apparently they weren't happy when regular folks started showing up with what looked like fancy lace. The rich people put down the crocheted lace as something only a common person would wear and further besmirched crochet itself by saying it wasn't on the same level as knitting and other needlework. It seemed as though Adele had it right about crochet's being the poor stepsister. But luckily Nicole didn't seem to know, and ended by holding up her turquoise scarf triumphantly.

The rest of us watched, aghast, as Adele continued. CeeCee even called out to her, "Dear, I think you're a little over the top." But it did no good.

"So what, when you can do this." Adele showed off one of the loopy crocheted flowers ready to go onto her square. And then she went for her grand finale, dangling a lacy crocheted snowflake she had pulled out of her bag. It was all dainty white string and pretty amazing looking.

"I'd like to see you knit this," Adele said. Her beanie was on the small side, and her head big. Little by little the beanie had been inching its way higher and higher, and now looked like a gumdrop had landed on her head.

Nicole was already packing up her designer tote, muttering something to herself about how maybe the other group was better for them after all, since they knew the truth about knitting. Trish followed suit and the two left in a huff.

Adele smiled victoriously. She had kept our crochet world pure.

I DIDN'T MEAN TO BE LATE FOR THE TARZANA Hookers' meeting at the Sheridans' house, but it was a lot different from joining them at the bookstore. There, I could just take a break from my work when they arrived, but leaving to go somewhere else was much more complicated. First, I had to cashier because Rayaad was late coming back from her break. Then there were a bunch of last-minute phone calls, and as I was walking out, one of our regular customers stopped me and tried to sell me on having weekly séances at the bookstore. When I finally pulled up to the Sheridans' house, Dinah was waiting out front.

Natalie answered the door and looked uncomfortable when she saw us.

"There's a little problem," she said in a whisper as she stepped outside. "Lawrence hasn't left yet. Now, I have no doubt that you had nothing to do with Ellen's death, but he seems to be fixated on it. He was very specific about not wanting you here." It wasn't the collective *you*, either.

There was only one *you* she was talking about, and it was me.

"I thought you said he wouldn't be home."

"I thought he wouldn't be," she said, appearing frustrated. "But he is. It *is* his house." She scanned the inside of the home quickly, apparently looking for him. "He has to leave soon. His dog has an appointment at the groomer's. I really need you to go now. If he finds you here, I'll get the blame." She glanced behind her again. "Too late, here he comes. Hide!"

"Hide? Where?" I looked hopelessly around the yard. Dinah pointed me toward a large bush that grew next to the house, and without taking a moment to consider the absurdity of late-fortysomething me having to hide from a neighbor, I went for it. I had barely squeezed behind the scratchy branches when Lawrence marched out the front door with his small black poodle in close pursuit. By peeking between the leaves, I managed to get a clear view.

Lawrence stopped between Dinah and Natalie. He looked like a graying giant next to my petite friend, and he wore his usual arrogant expression.

Dinah smiled and started to say hello, but he totally ignored her and turned to Natalie.

"Is she one of the crochet women?" he asked, and Dinah stiffened at being talked about when she was standing right there.

Natalie nodded and started to introduce them, but Lawrence cut her off by walking away. The man had turned rudeness into an art form. Only when he'd gotten halfway to the garage did he realize that the dog was still on the step. The poodle looked like a roly-poly little black sheep and was definitely in need of a trim.

"C'mon, Felix," Lawrence cajoled, holding up a leash. "Daddy's little boy is going to get a bathy-wathy and a haircut." The dog sat down. Lawrence tried a few more versions of doggie baby talk, but the poodle didn't move. Then Lawrence changed his tone to that of a dog trainer. "Felix, come," he commanded, but Felix merely looked the other way. As a powerful manager/TV producer, Lawrence could make people jump, but apparently not his dog. Finally he retraced his steps, slipped the leash onto Felix and gave it a little tug as he headed back toward the garage. Now the dog ran every which way, winding the leash around his master's legs, almost tripping him. Just as Lawrence got it all straightened out, Felix's eyes focused on the bush where I was hiding, and he started barking. Lawrence tried to keep going, but Felix wouldn't give up.

I cringed, sure that any second Lawrence was going to notice that the bush had some khaki slack branches. I searched my mind for some excuse, any excuse, to explain why I was back there. A lost contact, perhaps? Then I hit possible pay dirt. Maybe I could distract the dog.

Before work, I'd been trying to teach Blondie to give her paw. It's really a stupid trick, but cute. To help with the training, I had been giving her treats if she made any move with her foot. I still had a pocketful of liver pops.

I lobbed one toward the dog, hoping it wouldn't bop Lawrence. My sons never wanted to play catch with me, rightly saying I had no sense of aim. I missed Lawrence, but also missed the dog's scent range. Felix kept yapping, and Lawrence started peering into the bush. Frantically, I tossed another liver pop over the top. It sailed over Lawrence and landed at Felix's feet. He stopped the noise as he picked it up.

Lawrence noticed that the dog had gotten something off the ground, and he freaked, ordering Felix to drop it. The poodle looked up at him for a second, then must have realized that possession wins over a bossy owner's commands, and went back to chewing. Shaking his head with resignation and telling the dog he better not hear from the groomer that he got sickie-wickie, Lawrence finally continued on his way to the garage.

If I had to hear any more doggie baby talk, I was going to be "sickie-wickie" and was grateful when Lawrence's black Bentley pulled out of the garage and the door rumbled shut.

I brushed off some twigs and a stray spider as Natalie ushered Dinah and me inside. She left us, saying she had to get something from her car.

"Money and power be damned. You're right about him belonging to the life's-too-short department," Dinah said. "Even with the points he gets for being nice to his dog, he still rates below my rudest freshman students." She wasn't about to get any argument from me.

We both automatically looked back toward the living room, where Ellen's body had been, and had a communal shudder. I caught a whiff of a faint fragrance I couldn't define. It gave me an instant headache—or maybe it was from being back in the murder house.

Dinah and I had already come up with a plan to make the most of my visit. The day of the funeral, when I'd tried looking around the house, I hadn't known what I was looking for. This time I had a goal: Find Ellen's date book.

"So, the plan is, I cough twice if someone is coming," Dinah whispered.

"I thought it was cough once," I said, rubbing my temples, trying to lose the headache.

"No. Remember, we said one cough could just be a rogue cough by someone else in the room. To be on the safe side, I think we should go with cough three times," Dinah suggested.

The whole crew was in the crochet room. CeeCee and Adele were sorting through things in plastic bins. Sheila was going back and forth in a rocking chair. Meredith was checking out a shelf of crocheted teddy bears I had missed the first time. Whatever negative things I could say about Ellen, she had been a master craftsperson.

"Can you believe Trish and Nicole called me?" Meredith said, referring to the knitting women from Encino. "They were frantic about getting massages as soon as possible and grabbed the only bit of time I had available. I did them both at Trish's house. Before I'd even finished, they were trying to book me for a wedding shower one of them is giving." Meredith chuckled. "Ellen sure knew how to build an image. Those two women raved about the massages and were thrilled to pay me a fortune. When I think it used to take me days at the gym to earn what I did in a couple of hours with them . . ."

"That was certainly nice of Ellen," Dinah said with just a touch of surprise in her voice.

"She came out okay. She and Lawrence got unlimited massages at no charge," Meredith said.

"It wasn't just Ellen's publicity," Sheila said, getting up and taking one of Meredith's hands. "Your hands are magic."

Meredith seemed pleased with the compliment. "That's just what Trish said. You should see her house. It was bigger than this place, and in the hills with a view to die for. She sure knew how to marry well."

"You'll meet someone, dear," CeeCee said reassuringly. She looked around at the rest of us. "I didn't think of it until now, but Ellen was the only one of us who was married."

Without thinking, I started to protest and say I was married, too.

CeeCee touched my arm. "Dear, when your husband dies, you aren't married anymore." I swallowed hard, realizing that of course she was right.

CeeCee went back to her sorting. She opened another plastic bin, which was marked SAM, and pulled out a ball of tan yarn. It was a most unusual color, kind of like a latte made with whole milk.

Something about the color seemed familiar, but I couldn't place it.

"This is that special yarn Ellen used for her daughter's missing bag," CeeCee said.

"So that's the stuff," Adele said, examining it before putting it back into the bin.

Dinah and I kept checking the door for Natalie's return. I wasn't going to start snooping until I knew where everyone was.

As if in answer to my thoughts, Natalie came through the door, seeming preoccupied. "How long is this going to take?" The question wasn't directed at anyone in particular. CeeCee had gradually been assuming lead of the group, but apparently Adele wasn't giving up, and spoke first.

"It will take as long as it takes to find Ellen's completed squares," she said with her hand on her hip. No one could accuse Adele of easing up on the attitude. Natalie didn't seem happy with the answer, but her cell phone rang and she walked out the French doors onto the side patio to answer the call.

It was the perfect time to make my move. I nodded to Dinah, then took out my cell phone, acting as if it had vibrated. "Oh, I have to take this," I said to all of them. I was out the door and down the hall before anyone even reacted.

Once in the hall, I started to sprint. I had to be quick. My first stop was the home office. It looked the same as it had the day of the funeral, picked up but still in disorder. I checked the desktop, opened some drawers and thumbed through a pile of papers. There was nothing resembling a date book. Another possibility occurred to me. Ellen had already been out that morning, and if she kept her appointment book with her, maybe she'd never taken it out of her purse. After checking that the hall was empty, I moved on to the master bedroom. I knew from my own experience that Lawrence had probably left Ellen's stuff as it had been. Somewhere in an irrational part of your mind, you think the person might come back, and you want their things to be there.

The bed was made, but I noticed something that made me stop short. There were water glasses on both sides of the bed. When I felt them, both were cool to the touch, and there was condensation on the outsides, meaning the water was fresh. Had Lawrence had overnight company? It seemed really cold, with Ellen's clothes still in the closet and her gold necklace sitting on the dresser.

I turned on the light in Ellen's closet. It was like a cavernous room. On one side all the hanging clothes were neatly organized on bars at various heights, with the back portion left for evening wear. The other side featured shelves filled with purses, shoes and color-arranged sweaters. There was a built-in dresser toward the door. As I looked around, I realized there was a flaw in my plan. If Dinah coughed way across the house, I wasn't going to hear it in here. To compensate, I tried to move faster.

If the appointment book was in a purse, it had to be the one she had used that day. I tried to remember what Ellen had been wearing when I found her, since she was the kind who still matched her purse to her outfit. But the memory of the awful purple-blue of her face blotted out any memory of the color of her clothes. Then I noticed a black leather tote bag sitting on the dresser at the other end of the closet. I instantly recognized it as the bag she'd had at the bookstore that morning. Just as I started toward it, I heard noise coming from the bedroom. In a flash I turned off the light and froze. I recognized Lawrence's voice, but there was also a woman's.

What was he doing back?

And I had worried about being found behind the bush. Hanging out in Ellen's closet would surely be considered trespassing, attempted burglary and God knew what else. I didn't need a fortune-teller to tell me there would be handcuffs in my future, along with a trip to the police station. I could just imagine the delight in Detective Heather's eyes when she realized she finally had a reason to arrest me.

I could make out only every third word or so. Lawrence seemed to be giving instructions to the woman. Instinctively I moved all the way to the back and hid under a long evening dress. I was just in time, too, because Lawrence and the woman came into the closet. The dress was sheer enough for me to see the light when it went on. I was afraid to breathe.

By now I'd figured out that the woman was the housekeeper, and Lawrence was telling her to get some boxes and pack up some of Ellen's clothes. So he wasn't as sentimental as I was, after all. The hangers scraped on the rod as he pushed things back and forth. The noise was getting louder, and it was obvious he was getting closer. One of the shortcomings of hitting middle age was that I couldn't fold myself up quite so small anymore, and I realized my feet were sticking out below the dress. I was really going to have to take up yoga or something.

I could see Lawrence's silhouette through the dress. I prayed he wouldn't look down as I twisted my feet sideways to hide them. It seemed like forever that he and the woman stood there, deciding what to pack up. Then, typical Lawrence, he ended the discussion abruptly and they headed back into the bedroom. I waited until there had been silence for a while before I made a move.

To my relief, the bedroom was empty, but when I peeked out into the hall, Lawrence was giving more directions to the housekeeper. The only good thing was that his back was to me. I heard what sounded like a coughing fit, coming from somewhere across the house. It wasn't much help now.

I slipped back into the room, feeling trapped. A wave of panic made my head start to swirl, but I ordered it away with a few deep breaths. I scanned the room for a way to escape. The windows along the back seemed to be the only way out. Most of them didn't open, and when I found one that did, there was a screen to contend with. Climbing out wasn't that easy, either. Even though it was a one-story house, there was still a bit of a drop, and I landed on my butt. Then I had to put the screen back in place and hope that nobody noticed the open window anytime soon. All the climbing around left me feeling a little creaky.

Now that I was in the backyard, it seemed as if I was almost home free. I crouched low to get below the window and inched my way across the side of the house. Then suddenly I remembered the date book. Some detective I was. In my panic to escape, I'd forgotten about it. While berating myself for not checking the tote bag on my way out, I considered going back. But before I could make a move, I heard loud voices coming through one of the windows.

I recognized Lawrence's voice, and Natalie's and CeeCee's.

Apparently I wasn't the only one who had made a side trip. Lawrence had found CeeCee wandering around. She claimed she was looking for the bathroom, but I knew she was looking for another chance to go through the home office to find the file that I was sure Natalie already had.

Natalie apologized to Lawrence, saying she'd been on a business call. He insisted that she make sure everyone stayed in the crochet room, then said he was leaving again.

I race-crawled the rest of the way to the little patio off the crochet room, wondering whether I should tell CeeCee that Natalie had what she was looking for. But I decided against it. I wasn't sure who the good guys or the bad guys were, and it would require way too much explaining.

When I stood up, I realized there were grass stains on my knees. I finger-combed my hair and hoped there weren't any smudges on my face. Then I slipped inside just as Natalie, with CeeCee in tow, came into the room through the other door. I grabbed the puffy beige afghan off the love seat and used it to block the front of my pants as I pretended to admire it. Natalie gave me a strange look, but it was nothing compared to the one I got from Dinah. She looked as if her eyes were about to pop out of her head.

"So, how many squares do we have?" I said in my best nothing-is-going-on voice.

CHAPTER 9

"Your friend Dinah called," Rayaad said when she found me reading in one of the big overstuffed chairs in the back of the bookstore. "She said she had some bad news, and she'd be in her office after two."

"Bad news? Did she say what it was?" I put down the book and sat up.

Rayaad shook her head. "She didn't give any details, sorry."

I had told Rayaad to take messages so that I could read some of Will Hunter's book. It was surprisingly poetic as he described growing up in Texas. I still found it hard to believe he'd written it, but at the same time I thought a ghostwriter would have had a more matter-of-fact style. I'd just gotten to the part in which a tornado was headed for their town, and Will and his brother had played hooky from school and were wandering out in an open field.

So far it had been a quiet day, and the event area sat empty. Yesterday's meeting at the Sheridans' house had turned out to be a disappointment. Ellen had left far fewer finished squares than we'd expected.

And, taking Lawrence's orders seriously, Natalie had practically stood guard over us for the remainder of the visit, so I'd had no chance to go back and look for the date book.

I stuck a bookmark in Will's book and checked my watch. Blondie needed to be picked up from the groomer, and I decided I might as well meet Dinah and hear the bad news in person. I'd even bring lunch. I told Rayaad I was leaving for an hour or so. Since Mrs. Shedd knew I was more likely to work extra time than leave early, she let me keep my own hours.

Dinah worked at Walter Beasley Community College, which was set on four hundred acres of land draped over soft hills. It featured a whole area devoted to agriculture. There was an equestrian area, a dairy barn and fields of crops. Black steers grazed on the golden hills on the outskirts of the campus, right next to a new apartment complex. I guessed the people who lived there wouldn't be opening their windows to let in the fresh air.

I parked at a metered spot that was a healthy walk from Dinah's office. After my difficulty climbing out of the window at the Sheridans' house, I was determined to get more exercise. Blondie thought longer was better when it came to walks, anyway. Her strawberry blond terrier fur was all fluffed out as she trotted along beside me, and she seemed to have a dog smile.

The clock in the tower had just finished striking two when we walked up the stairs to Dinah's office. She was at her desk, talking to a student wearing a sideways baseball cap. Her three office mates were busy at their desks. Dinah saw us and pointed to a chair against the wall. The office was too small for privacy, and I heard her whole interchange with the student.

"So, I'm here," the boy announced, rocking his head

with attitude. "What did you wanna see me about?" He slumped on his elbow and leaned on her desk. He was obviously one of the new freshmen Dinah talked about with so much consternation.

"Jason, I could tell you all about good manners and how it's rude to wear a hat inside and lean all over my desk, but I'm just going to get to the point."

Jason's baggy jeans were supposed to be some kind of fashion statement. Really, he looked like some cartoon character with weird proportions. I truly wished I could look over his shoulder when he was, say, my age, and showed his kids a photo of him in his college days. I'm guessing they would laugh their pants off.

"C'mon, Ms. Lyons, nobody takes their hat off. It's the look."

Dinah held up her hand. "Beasley lets everybody in, but not everybody gets past their first semester. When it comes to my classroom, I am the queen. My rules, with no arguments. You wear the hat, you have to leave. You aren't in class, you flunk. Got it?"

Jason groaned. "Like, what do I need English for, anyway?" He unslouched himself, got up and left, mumbling about the unfairness of it all as he shuffled out.

Dinah shook her head in exasperation. Her eyes brightened when I held up the bag of sub sandwiches.

"Okay. What's the bad news?" I said before I reached her desk. Suddenly three pairs of eyes looked up from their work and focused on me.

Dinah patted Blondie and smiled at me. "I think it's time to take a walk."

Once we got outside, Dinah gestured back toward the low building that housed her office. "Too many ears in there." Due to the chronic lack of funds, her building, like most of Beasley, was old and looked a little frayed along the edges. Despite my urging her to spill the news now that we were outside, she refused. Nobody could say Dinah didn't know how to build up suspense. It made her a great teacher, and if Jason ever got past his love affair with his hat, he'd realize that.

We took our picnic to the horticulture department. It was a beautiful area full of plants and flowers. There was something iridescent about the light, and it was favored by photographers. Even now, as we settled on a bench near a bamboo forest, a professional type was taking photos of a family along with their dog. Blondie did her berserk dog dance from behind my legs.

"What's with her?" Dinah asked. Dinah was a cat person and liked independent pets, and wasn't into being tied down to walks and tummy rubs. I didn't want to go into Blondie's background again. What was the point of repeating the story about how I'd gotten her from a shelter after she had been returned twice due to her unusual personality? She was unpredictable, except she loved to go for walks and eat cheese, and if she saw another dog, she always went nuts.

Peter had voted that I take her back, but I'd nixed it. I related to her. We were both confused and abandoned.

"Forget about the dog, and tell me the bad stuff." I couldn't believe I was actually begging to hear bad news.

Dinah looked around. There was nobody even close. "Detective Heather stopped by my office this morning. She made some excuse that she was thinking of taking some English class, but then she made an awkward segue to having some questions about my statement at the murder scene."

"Like what?" I asked.

"Like, nothing. She really wanted to ask me about you, and specifically about your financial situation. She wondered if you were hard up for money because of being pushed out of the business by Ellen. She knew you went to see Natalie Shaw and thought you were trying to become the Pink in the company name."

"You mean the P," I said, reminding her that it was now PSS PR.

"This is no time for jokes, Molly. She is seriously looking for a motive she can stick on you."

"I wouldn't even know how to strangle anyone," I said. In a moment of weakness, Barry had told me he'd found out that had been the cause of death, even though the medical examiner wasn't sure how it had been done, since there weren't any bruises or marks on her neck. Apparently they could tell by the internal damage to her neck and these red marks that showed up in her eyes that she'd been strangled. She'd been hit on the head with the poker after she was already dead. But, like the ransacking, it was just a cover-up.

"There are so many other suspects; she ought to be checking them out. Like Lawrence Sheridan—he probably got a big insurance payout and his freedom without a messy divorce."

"You know I'm with you on that one, but there's more bad news," Dinah said. "Detective Gilmore talked to him. You won't believe what she said. She said he was charming and helpful."

"Hard to believe she talked to the same guy who looked right through you at his front door," I said, incredulous.

Dinah shrugged. "That's life. I think when you're in your early thirties and you have hot blond hair and enough curves for a roller coaster, you get a different response."

"I guess that means we can count him out as far as she's concerned. I wonder if she knows he collects dog fur."

"Huh?" Dinah said with a chuckle.

"It turns out he goes to the same groomer I do. When I picked up Blondie this morning, the groomer showed me a bag of black fur. She said she always saves Felix's clippings, but Lawrence had forgotten to take them the last time."

"What would he do with a bag of dog hair?" Dinah asked. "Throw it on his carpet to see if his vacuum cleaner works?"

"Like he really does his own vacuuming," I said, shaking

my head at the mental picture. "How can Detective Heather miss that Natalie is now running the publicity firm? I think that makes her look very suspicious. On top of which, she could have been Lawrence's overnight guest. Remember, she was there when we got to the Sheridans' house. And something is going on with CeeCee and her file. What if Ellen was blackmailing her with whatever is in it? Maybe the ransacking was a cover-up, but not the cover-up Detective Heather thinks."

Dinah seemed confused.

"CeeCee could have thrown the stuff around in the living room as a cover-up, but the mess in the home office could have come from her trying to find the file," I explained. "Too bad Detective Heather doesn't know what I know about the file. Maybe she'd investigate CeeCee."

"Maybe you could start a rumor that CeeCee had the hots for Barry," Dinah said, and I rolled my eyes.

When we finished our sandwiches, we parted company— Dinah had papers to grade and I had Will Hunter's book to finish. I wanted to find out what happened when the tornado hit, and it was a lot better than thinking about Detective Heather's continued efforts to put me in jail. I dropped Blondie off at home and went back to the bookstore.

"LET ME TAKE YOU AWAY. . . ."

I jumped at the sound of the male voice, lost in Will and his brother's efforts to dig through the rubble and find their German shepherd. When I looked up and saw that it was Barry, I came out of my mental fog.

"From all this," Barry finished, gesturing around the bookstore office. He took my arm and pulled me out of the chair. "You're done here, right?" I glanced at the clock and noticed that it was well past the official end of my day. I nodded.

"Good, because I have plans. Jeffrey is at a drama club

event. One of the other parents is going to bring him home, so my evening is free. I made reservations at Marceline's at Malibu," he said, watching for my reaction. Marceline's was much more expensive than the usual places we frequented. Charlie and I had gone there often, but it had always been a business-expense dinner. After letting the name of the restaurant sink in, he mentioned something about there being time for *dessert* at my place.

"No talk of murder or bodies, or kids who change their name to something stupid. Just you and me and the moonlight," he said, giving me his magnetic stare that was so hot, it made me blush.

I started to feel all warm and fuzzy at his romantic gesture; then I realized he'd done it again, just shown up with no warning and announced our plans. "It sounds lovely, but you should have called. I'm not dressed right." I pointed out my khaki pants, white shirt and black vest. Barry was wearing nice jeans, a soft beige T-shirt and a black sport coat. He looked great.

"It's the beach—it's casual," he said, taking my hand. "Have you seen the moon?" Before I could answer, he'd led me outside.

"Wow," was all I could say when I saw the huge yellow ball lifting in the eastern sky. Barry held me against him and nuzzled my neck.

"It sounds really nice, but you can't just show up and expect me to go. I might have plans."

"Do you?" he asked. "You have some other guy hidden somewhere?" he teased.

I shook my head. "Well, no."

"There you go. You're free and I'm free. I know you like the restaurant, and getting a reservation there on the weekend—not going to happen." He squeezed me close. "So, get your jacket, and let's go."

When I didn't move, he said that if it would make me happy, he would call in the future. That cinched the deal.

We dropped the greenmobile in my driveway.

"What's with the truck?" I asked, climbing in.

"It's a loaner. The Tahoe is in the shop," Barry said, as we took off for the beach.

Marceline's at Malibu was an entertainment industry favorite, but far enough out of the way that it didn't attract many paparazzi unless word got out that somebody big was making an appearance. There were only two lanky guys with cameras hanging around the front when we arrived. They ignored us, and we went inside.

The restaurant was just above the beach; the inside was nice, but the outside was truly special and Barry got us seated on the deck. Though the evening had turned chilly, heat lamps offered islands of warmth and potted ficus trees strung with little white lights were placed among the tables to give the illusion of privacy. The host led us to a table next to two of the lacy trees.

As I was about to sit at the white-clothed table, I glanced through the greenery to the table behind us. I did a double take. There were three people seated around it, and I thought I recognized Natalie and Lawrence. Then I dismissed it: When you're thinking about pink elephants, you think you see them everywhere. Except that when I looked again, it wasn't my imagination: It was Lawrence and Natalie. There was no mistaking his thick graying hair and arrogant expression, or her chin-length brown hair and big lips. Natalie wore a suit, which made me think it was a business dinner.

I didn't mean to stare, but I couldn't help myself. Barry followed my gaze, but since he'd never seen either of them before, he didn't understand my interest.

"What's going on?" he asked as I finally sat down.

He didn't look happy when I explained who our neighbors were.

"Maybe we should move." He lifted his hand to get the host back.

"No way," I said, pulling his arm down. "Besides, all the tables are full."

"Fine. Then just ignore them." Barry opened his menu and began to study it. "The filet sounds good." He waited for some reaction from me. When I didn't say anything, he looked around his menu and saw that I had put mine down and was leaning back in my chair to hear what was going on. He waved his hand in front of my face and pointed at himself. "You're having dinner with me, remember?"

I smiled and sat forward. He was right, and it was very sweet of him to spring for such a fancy place when it wasn't a business deduction. I picked up my menu and began to consider the options.

I didn't mean to keep eavesdropping, but the wind carried their voices right into my ears. I kept staring at the description of Fettuccine Marceline without it registering. The man with them was obviously a client of the public-relations firm. I knew the drill. When you were afraid of losing a client, you wined them and dined them and promised them the moon, whether or not you could really deliver. The man's cell phone rang, and he excused himself.

Once Natalie and Lawrence were alone, their conversation grew more interesting. Out of the corner of my eye, I saw that they were leaning closer to each other.

"We've come this far; don't fall apart now," Lawrence said. Natalie took out a tissue and dabbed at her eye.

"You're right, L.S. I don't know what I would have done without you." She reached for his hand, and I fought the urge to gasp.

Without realizing it, I was leaning farther and farther back in my chair. The front legs had left the ground. Just as I was about to go over backward, which certainly would have gotten their attention and everybody else's, Barry grabbed my arm and pulled me back.

"C'mon, Sherlock, let's order dinner." He reached across the table and stroked my forearm, while reminding me of his plans for dessert. Nobody could say Barry wasn't good with his hands, and he got my attention—temporarily, anyway.

Barry looked happier when he saw Lawrence and Natalie head toward the exit after their companion returned. "Now are you all mine?"

"Omigod, you should have heard what they were saying. Lawrence said something about her not falling apart because they'd come this far. And then she said she couldn't have done it without him, or something like that. And she grabbed his hand. You should tell Detective Heather what they were saying." I stopped and checked his expression. "Okay, that's not going to happen, is it?" Barry shook his head as an answer. "Right. You can't get involved," I grumbled.

The waiter brought the glasses of wine we'd ordered, and Barry proposed a toast that from now on our conversation should exclude anything to do with Ellen's murder.

"It's kind of hard to drop the subject when Detective Heather is trying to find ways to make me look guilty."

He looked frustrated. "She's not trying to make you look guilty."

"Well, she certainly isn't looking for any other suspects." I told him how she had found Lawrence so charming. He didn't seem surprised.

"She probably flirted with him to catch him off guard."

"Isn't that against some police rules?"

Barry grinned. "Not that I know of. I've heard of female uniforms who flirt with suspects to get them into the backseats of their cruisers. It's better than threats."

"I don't know. It still doesn't sound right to me. Maybe she's interested in Lawrence."

"No way," he said a little too forcefully.

"You sound jealous," I teased. Barry just groaned.

Barry got his wish, and when the food arrived, our conversation turned to more pleasant topics. When we'd finished, he suggested a walk along the beach.

The moonlight made the sand look blue, and it was bright enough to make shadows. Barry's arm felt protective around my shoulders as we walked just beyond the lights of the restaurant.

Much as I wanted to focus on the magic of the beach and the feeling of Barry's body heat mixing with mine, my mind went back to Natalie and Lawrence in the restaurant.

"You're a guy," I said.

Barry chuckled. "Last time I looked. Why?"

"You saw Lawrence and Natalie. For a moment or so, anyway. From a guy's point of view, don't you think they were acting like a couple?"

I could feel Barry's body tense.

"Remember the romantic-evening concept? No kids, no murders, no Lawrence-is-a-suspect," he muttered.

"He spent the night with someone," I blurted out. "There were water glasses on both sides of the bed." Barry stopped walking, and even without looking, I could feel his gaze focusing on me.

"And how do you know that?"

I considered how to answer. The sand felt cold on my bare feet, and the ocean shimmered in the distance. I just didn't think telling him about my snooping around the house and hiding in the closet was going to work.

"You don't have to answer. I don't want to know," Barry said quickly. "It's only going to upset me, isn't it?"

I started to say something, but Barry muttered something about having a better idea; then he turned toward me, took me in his arms and started kissing me. Barry was an exceptional kisser. They were long, slow and deep. He never cut corners or, like some people, treated kisses like just a quick stop before the main event. As he leaned in to me, I let myself be carried away, and all thoughts of Natalie and Lawrence disappeared.

"Enough with the walking," Barry said hoarsely when he finally released me. We were both a little breathless, and it wasn't from the exercise. He held on to my hand as we headed back to the car. "Time for dessert."

At first we drove in silence. I was nestled against him as he turned onto Topanga Canyon. The moonlight illuminated the jagged, empty mountain alongside the road. There was something wild about the area just in from the beach, and it looked as if we were a million miles from civilization.

By the time we drove through the town of Topanga, with its mixture of hippie shops and traditional stores, I sensed that Barry had something on his mind.

"Okay, I can't take it anymore. How did you know about the water glasses?"

"Are you sure you want to know?" I asked.

"It's going to upset me, isn't it?" he said.

"Probably."

"Tell me anyway," he said in a resigned tone.

I had to work my way up to the snooping part. I left out hiding behind the bush; that would have set Barry off right away. I told him about the group's going there for the squares and described in great detail all the things in Ellen's crochet room.

"You're stalling, aren't you?"

"Maybe a little."

"So I'm really not going to like this." Barry sighed. "Just go for it. Tell me the bad part."

And I did. All of it. Looking around Lawrence's bedroom, hiding in the closet. I didn't have to see Barry's face to know he was probably making all kinds of exasperated expressions.

"How did you escape?"

I thought he would choke when I said I'd climbed out of a window.

"Molly, how did you manage to take something as benign and nice as crocheting and turn it into trouble?" He blew out a puff of air. "Never mind. But you have to promise me you won't ever do anything like that again. Do you know how much trouble you would have been in if he had found you?" I was sure Barry would have thrown up his hands if he hadn't been driving.

I looked out the window. We'd passed through the main part of the canyon and begun our descent into the Valley. As we went around hairpin curves, the lights spread before us. I recognized the main north–south streets by the stripes of white headlights heading in and by the red line of tail-lights going out. Way in the distance, nestled against the north mountain, the lights of Porter Ranch shimmered.

Barry was waiting for my answer. This was my problem with our relationship. I didn't want to have to answer to him or to anyone. I didn't want to promise that I would or wouldn't do anything. But I also liked him, so I took the coward's way out. I put my hand on his thigh. When he sort of groaned/moaned in surprise and pleasure, I moved my hand up just a little. Not enough to really touch anything, but just enough to make him wish I would.

Suddenly he pressed the accelerator, and the truck jumped forward. We made the last part of the journey in record time, with no more questions or concerns about my detective work.

Barry was all hands-on, flirty and playful, as we walked across my back patio. I was surprised to see the lights on in the kitchen. Barry ignored my concern about the lights, nuzzling my neck and making some very specific promises of nice things he planned to do to me. The door pushed open when I leaned against the handle.

"Hi, Mom."

I looked down the length of the kitchen. My younger son, Samuel, was making a grilled cheese sandwich on the stove. His gaze went to Barry, and his expression changed to the hangdog look I'd told Barry about.

Barry dropped his hands and stepped away from me. We were like two teenagers caught by our parents.

"I have news," Samuel said to me, clearly ignoring Barry's presence altogether. Samuel was a couple of inches shorter than Peter, with a more solid build. He had sandy hair like Charlie's, though unlike his father, Samuel had a ponytail. He wore jeans and a black T-shirt with an open gray flannel shirt over it.

He pointed to the bouquet of stargazers and eucalyptus branches. The heavy, sweet scent of the flowers mixed with the clean scent of the leaves. I couldn't help but smile at how Samuel had remembered I liked flowers that had fragrance.

"And . . ." He pointed toward the bottle of sparkling lemonade chilling in an ice bucket. After Charlie died, Samuel had come close to developing a problem with alcohol, and had handled it by simply giving up drinking altogether. "I thought we could toast." He glanced in Barry's direction. "You're welcome to join us."

That may have been what he said, but his tone implied just the opposite. Samuel had never been as openly hostile to Barry as Peter had been. But he was never genuinely friendly, either. He had taken Charlie's death harder than any of us. To him, my seeing Barry was cheating. And it forced Samuel to face the fact that his father was never coming back.

Barry sighed, and I could read his mind. He knew dessert had gotten cancelled.

"You and your mother toast your news. I was just bringing her home." Barry kissed me on the check and headed back to the door. "I'll call you later."

As soon as Barry was gone, Samuel brightened. He was bursting with pride as he told me he'd gotten a music gig.

CHAPTER 10

"THE KNITTERS GOT MEREDITH," ADELE SAID IN a panicky voice as the rest of us started to set up our crocheting supplies on the event table.

"What are you talking about, dear?" CeeCee said, giving Adele a concerned look. She wasn't a fan of knitting, but she wasn't as rabid about it as Adele.

Adele held up a note written on yellow legal-size paper, and a plastic bag with three red-and-white squares with black borders. "Rayaad gave me this when I came in."

I looked a little closer, wondering why Rayaad had given it to Adele rather than to me. More likely Adele had seen it and just taken it.

"Meredith said she was dropping out of the group because Ellen brought her in and it just doesn't feel right without her. That's what the note says, but I'm betting she went with the Encino twins and joined their knitting group."

CeeCee looked at Adele, aghast. "Oh, dear, that does leave us even more in the lurch." CeeCee set a box on the table. She added Meredith's squares and then showed the contents to all of us. It was pretty sad.

I handed her a black-bordered kelly green square I'd done in single crochet, and Dinah gave her a similar one in yellow and black, but it made the amount look only a little less sad.

"Ladies, we're in trouble," CeeCee said.

Adele noticed something white and puffy sticking out of CeeCee's tote bag and pulled it out. "It's a blanket I made for a friend's grandbaby. I was going to show it to you."

Adele shook her head. "You shouldn't be working on baby blankets when we need squares."

CeeCee sighed. "Some of us can do both." She presented five perfectly done three-color granny squares.

Adele, taking it as a challenge, whipped out another of her floppy-flowered squares, explaining that hers took more work and she had a full-time job—made worse by having to deal with story time. She stood with her hand on her hip. "You don't have to deal with kids giving you a hard time every chance they get. Can you believe one of them thought this was a costume?" she said, pointing at her crimson peasant blouse and full skirt made of strips of different patterns. "What kind of a costume would it be, anyway?"

Nobody answered, but I had a feeling we were all thinking the same thing: *Clown*.

"With their miniature-size couture clothes, all those kids know about are designers. They need to learn about style," Adele grumbled.

Sheila was working on a royal blue square that began with a flower motif and then became square-shaped with rows of spaces and double-crochet columns. Her stitches had become so tight, she had to use her hook like a shovel to dig into each of them. Her shoulders looked hunched. "Okay, I'm guilty. I should have been working on squares, but I made this." She laid down the square and took something from her bag. As she unfolded it, all of us oohed and aahed. It wasn't just a magnificent scarf. It was a work of art. Sheila smiled shyly at our responses and explained how she had used more than one strand of yarn. The one constant throughout the piece was the variegated blue ribbon yarn, but she had mixed it with a different shade of green eyelash yarn in each section. The effect reminded me of an impressionist painting. To finish the piece, she had added fringe made of strands of tiny wooden beads.

"*You* made this?" Adele said, holding it up.

Sheila nodded.

"But how did you manage to keep the stitches so loose?" CeeCee asked, touching the scarf appreciatively.

"I'm not as nervous when I crochet at home, and I used this." She held up a crochet hook that looked like a tiny baseball bat.

Dinah tried the scarf on, and it looked great. Sheila was certainly a surprise. She always seemed to be having trouble just making a square. Who knew she was so artistic with color?

Adele pulled some place mats out of her bag. "As long as everybody is showing off what they made"—Adele laid them on the table—"I made a whole set." They were a hot pink and electric purple combination, which made me wonder about Adele's home color scheme.

"Maybe we should try and get Meredith back. I know where those knitters meet," Adele said. She looked a little disappointed that we hadn't been as excited about her place mats as we were about Sheila's scarf.

CeeCee shook her head. "Dear, we have to let her go. If she wants to join the knitters, so be it. I never felt she was a committed crocheter anyway. She only came because of Ellen."

Adele grumbled a few times and then, once again trying to hold on to the mantle of leader, suggested we all stop talking about the squares and start making some.

For a few minutes all was quiet except for the pop music over the loudspeaker and Rayaad announcing there were fresh peanut butter cookies in the café. But only for a few minutes.

"See how stealthy crocheting is," Adele said to no one in particular. "No annoying clacking needles to break the peace."

"Did I tell you that the relative of the gym member who works at the police's West Valley Division said that Ellen had a big life insurance policy? Lawrence is going to get a bundle," Sheila offered.

It was frustrating that she knew more than I did, considering I had someone on the inside.

"Do you think Lawrence was having an affair before Ellen died?" I asked.

CeeCee blinked at me. "You don't know, dear? I thought that since Ellen was your husband's partner, you probably knew all the dirt."

"Ellen and I were just cordial." That was really an overstatement. Most of the times when I'd been with Charlie and seen Ellen, she barely acknowledged me. "And Charlie's relationship with her was just business."

"Let me tell you, Lawrence got around. It got worse after he became a TV producer. Ellen confided in me because of Bill."

At the mention of her late husband, CeeCee's eyes welled up with tears. "I know everybody thought Bill and I were the perfect couple. Ellen kept the image going. It wasn't easy for him, being Mr. CeeCee Collins all those years. He was a world-renowned dentist, but nobody ever thought about that. You know, that opera singer Maria Brava flew thousands of miles so he could clean her teeth. But even so, all everyone did was ask about me. So I couldn't really blame him for having a fling or two with some little nobody who wanted to hear about just him."

"Men are skunks," Dinah said. CeeCee looked a little miffed at losing the floor as Dinah continued. "Jeremy wasn't a world-renowned dentist. More like a world-renowned jerk. After being married for twenty-five years, he had one of those midlife hissy fits. He walked out on me and the kids—though by then they were mostly grown. He took off with the little nobody he'd been having an affair with, and started a whole new family."

"I had no idea, dear," CeeCee said with a sympathetic pat. "Of course, Bill never left me."

There was just enough emphasis on the *left me* for it to be one of CeeCee's sweet-toned barbs. Dinah gave her a dirty look but didn't say anything. She knew when it was best to just leave things alone.

All this talk of cheating husbands made me think of Charlie. As far as I knew, he had never strayed, and I realized I didn't want to know now if he had. It was better to keep his memory intact.

Sheila stared down at her crocheting, her brown hair falling forward to hide her round face. She'd come to an impasse with the stitches. No way would her hook go in. Her only choice was to unravel them and start again. Unlike knitting, which was difficult to undo, crochet came apart with ease, making it much easier to correct a mistake. At last Sheila was just staring at a pile of curly blue yarn in her lap. I noticed a splotch of water hit the yarn, and when she looked up, she was crying. Not the theatrical tears like CeeCee turned on, which always seemed more for effect than genuine and which never mussed her makeup. Sheila's eyes were already on the way to puffy and red, and so was her nose.

"Okay, here it is. The reason I had so much time to make the scarf is, I broke up with my boyfriend. Well, he broke up with me."

Sheila, who had never talked much, suddenly started pouring out her heart. "My boyfriend did this intervention thing. He tricked me into going to some doctor he knew

who wanted to prescribe a bunch of drugs for my nerves."
She glanced at all of us. "You know how it is. They rave on
about some new pill being so wonderful, and then six
months later, you find out that it causes warts. Besides, I
want to conquer my nerves through natural means, like
meditation or crochet. Anyway, when I told him I wouldn't
do the meds, he said he couldn't stay with someone who
wouldn't help themselves." A tear rolled down her cheek.

To my surprise, Adele went over and hugged her.

"We're not all as lucky as Molly," Dinah began. Though
I tried to stop her, Dinah told them all about Barry and that
the *worst* thing about him was that he kept trying to get me
to make a commitment. "On top of that, he's great looking
and has a regular job."

"Pink's not the only lucky one. My man isn't a skunk,
either. In fact, he's a total hunk." Adele's face was all ani-
mated, and she was obviously anxious to give details. But
we were spared by an interruption.

"Ladies," Natalie Shaw said, rushing up to the table. She
was dressed in her usual business attire and seemed harried.
"I was going to call you," she went on, gesturing at me.
Both Adele and CeeCee gave out little gasps, apparently upset that Natalie thought I was in charge. "But I had a breakfast meeting over at the deli, so I thought why not just come
over and see the blanket in person." She took out a digital
camera. "I need to get a photo of it for the publicity."

She glanced around the table and looked a little puzzled
when all she saw were some loud place mats, a baby blanket, a dreamy blue and green scarf and each of us working
on a single square.

"I got a call from the chair of the Hearts and Barks auction committee, and she wants to bump up the blanket from
silent auction to live. They already put a special blurb
about it on their Web site. She thinks it has sentimental
value as Ellen's last contribution." She glanced up and
down the table again. "Where is it?"

For once, neither Adele nor CeeCee rushed to take charge and give an answer. Finally Sheila spoke up. "You don't want to take a photo of it yet. The squares still need to be put together, and a lot of them have yarn stragglers," she explained.

"It's close to finished, isn't it? Maybe you could lay out the squares on the table and just fold the stragglers under. I'm writing a press release, too. Something touching that will tug at the heartstrings." Natalie looked at all of us. "So?"

I had to do something. No way could we display the squares we had. If Natalie saw how far we were from finished, she would have no confidence in our being able to complete the blanket. I didn't want her to be upset about the afghan and let it color her feelings about Will Hunter's author event.

I had an idea.

I encouraged CeeCee to tell Natalie a story she'd told us about a dog with short brown fur that had been abandoned on the freeway and was running between cars. Someone from Hearts and Barks had seen her, and with the help of the highway patrol had gotten the traffic to stop long enough to get her off the freeway, but not before the dog had been hit.

"The poor dear. One of her legs was so badly injured, it had to be amputated," CeeCee said with a catch in her voice. "The Hearts and Barks people named her Miracle and paid all her vet bills and even sent volunteers to visit Miracle until she recovered. Then a nice woman in Chatsworth kept her in foster care and helped her adjust to three legs."

"What happened after that?" Natalie asked, clearly touched by the story.

"Hearts and Barks found just the right family for Miracle, and hopefully she'll live happily ever after in Sherman Oaks," CeeCee said.

"You could include that story in your press release. It would show the great work the charity does, and then you could mention something about how much Ellen supported them and this blanket is a final gesture from her," I said, fighting back a tear. Even though I'd already heard the story, it got me again.

Natalie nodded with approval and turned to me. "I like the way you think." She scribbled down some notes and then looked up. "But I still need to see the blanket. How can I describe something I've never seen?"

"I know. CeeCee made a diagram of it," I said, trying to sound optimistic. "That should give you some idea what it's going to look like." I gestured to CeeCee to bring it out.

"Of course, dear," CeeCee said, rummaging through her tote bag and taking out the sheet with the squares. In the meantime she'd done some work to the design, adding some detail of the motifs and colors of the finished squares. She'd filled in the blank ones with some color and given all of them black borders. The unfinished squares far outnumbered the completed ones, but thanks to the colors, the afghan looked good on paper.

CeeCee had four all-black squares drawn in the corners. She'd glued red paper hearts on two and a white dog and a white cat on the other two. CeeCee explained that it had originally been just dogs, but cats had been added. The organization didn't want to change its name, so the cats were silent partners.

"This can work for me. At least it gives me an idea of what I'm writing about," Natalie said, brightening. "I'll skip the picture and just build up the anticipation, saying that the blanket won't be unveiled until the auction."

"Of course, you'll mention that I've made many of the squares in the blanket. I don't have to tell you, a celebrity name adds value," CeeCee said sweetly. "You probably should include that I'm carrying on the banner for Ellen and leading the group." Natalie nodded and reminded

CeeCee that they were meeting for dinner at The Palm. They talked back and forth about what time. So Natalie was trying the wine-and-dine-to-keep-the-client maneuver on CeeCee. I bet they were going to discuss the contents of the file CeeCee was so concerned about and that I was sure Natalie had found.

"Be sure to mention that Shedd and Royal Books and More sponsored the blanket. We provided the yarn and a place for the meetings," I said. Why not get a plug for the bookstore?

Adele's face was getting stormier by the second. CeeCee had taken all the credit for the group, with no mention that Adele was coleader. Just when I thought Adele was going to blow, CeeCee gave her a cease-and-desist stare.

I didn't want to waste the opportunity, and I pitched Natalie again on the Will Hunter event.

"You know I won't make a decision until I actually see how the other one goes. When is it again?" I repeated the date and time and promised to call her the afternoon of, to remind her. She nodded at me, pleased. "I like the way you take care of things. We should talk. I think we might be able to put something together where you do some work for PSS PR on a consultant basis. I certainly need some help."

I was taken aback by the offer and wondered whether she really had too much work or whether it was some kind of bribe. Maybe Natalie had seen me at the restaurant and was worried about what I'd heard and seen. I told her I appreciated the thought. Since CeeCee still needed the diagram, I walked Natalie to the front and made her a copy before she left.

On my way back to the table, I noticed a bubble of white-blond curls peeking above a nearby bookcase in the auto repair section. I walked into the aisle and found Detective Heather engrossed in *How to Do Your Own Lube and Oil*.

"Can I help you find something?" I did my best to keep the edge out of my voice, but it snuck in anyway.

"No need," she said, putting the book down. "I already found everything I was looking for."

Was it my imagination, or did she have a little self-satisfied smirk?

AN HOUR LATER DINAH AND I WERE SITTING AT a table at a small French café down the block from the bookstore. The group had called it a day, but not without a face-off between Adele and CeeCee over CeeCee's comments to Natalie about heading the group. CeeCee had managed to subdue Adele by telling her that she had said it to get more attention for the group's afghan.

"Adele, dear, whether you like it or not, my name connected with a project means something, and yours does not."

Adele for once had no comeback. Then the two of them had launched into a rah-rah speech aimed at the rest of us about working on squares every possible minute.

Dinah and I ordered lunch. My head was still reeling from seeing Detective Heather.

"There's nothing you can do," Dinah said. "The bookstore is a public place, and she was looking at a book."

"Right. Miss Blond Bombshell is going to do her own lube and oil. Please. She was spying, listening. What do you think she heard?"

Dinah looked down at her cup of espresso. "I don't think you want to know."

"C'mon, that's what I always tell Barry."

"Okay, she probably heard everything, including Natalie's comment about offering you work, and your sounding anxious about Will Hunter's book thing. . . ." Dinah sighed and shook her head. "And my spiel about Barry being the perfect guy."

"Yikes. I didn't realize it was that bad. We've got to hurry up and find out who really did it."

"We could try to get everybody's alibi," Dinah offered.

"Lawrence would never talk to us, and we'd ruffle too many feathers with the others. There has to be something else we can do," I said, taking a last sip of my red-eye. "Maybe we can find out CeeCee's secret."

CHAPTER 11

IT WAS NO PROBLEM GETTING INVITED TO CEE-
Cee's. Now that the afghan was the star of the auction and
her name was connected with it, she was frantic about its
being finished and fantastic. All I had to do was ask her to
teach Dinah and me to make granny squares, and promise I
would bring cake.

"Oh, yes, dear, let's make it tomorrow," CeeCee said in
her trademark cheery voice. "Three-colored granny squares
would be so much better than those plain Janes you two have
been making. And I can't wait to taste your pound cake. Did
you say there would be icing?"

The aforementioned cake, safely encased in a plastic
carrier, sat on the backseat as we drove up to CeeCee's
house. It was located just on the Woodland Hills side of the
border with Tarzana, along the ridge of Corbin Canyon.
Though it was only a few blocks from the level area where
Ellen's house and mine were, it had a very different feel.

"Wow, not what I expected," Dinah said, looking at the
wrought-iron fence across the front of the property. We

passed between two stone pillars and started up a stone walkway. The trees were so thick, it was almost like a forest, and only after we got a few feet in did we see the stone cottage. Beyond it the land went down into a ravine. All the trees made it look dark and mysterious. A rabbit ran in front of us as we proceeded toward the house, and I noticed several bird feeders hanging from the trees. I bet there were coyotes at night.

"You're not planning to do a repeat of the sneak-around-and-cough move, are you?" Dinah asked.

"No, of course not, though I have to admit the sneaking around was exciting. The adrenaline high lasted all afternoon," I said, imagining Barry's expression if he heard me say that. "I found this book at the bookstore—*The Average Joe's Guide to Criminal Investigation*. There was a whole section on questioning and how to tell if people are lying by looking at which way their eyes move. The book recommends making people comfortable first by talking about other things. And then you just direct the conversation and slip in what you want to know, and if you understand the eye thing, you can tell if they're lying."

"Is that what we're going to do with CeeCee?" Dinah asked.

"It seems like a good plan," I said as we approached the door. "The book made it sound like a sure thing."

We reached the door, but before I knocked, it opened. I was suddenly face-to-face with an attractive man with thick white hair and lively blue eyes. It took a moment for me to recognize Tony Bonnard, aka Dr. Kevin McCoy, the original heartthrob on the long-running soap opera *My Family and Friends*.

Gradually I began to notice that his shaggy hair was carefully styled and his face had the well-cared-for look given by night cream and facials. What I saw of his body was no slouch, either. Nice broad shoulders and a ripple of biceps showed under the sleeves of his navy blue polo shirt. He obviously hung out at the gym when he wasn't doing his make-believe medical things.

"Cees, you've got company. A couple of hot chicks . . . and they've got cake."

Oh, ugh. Did he really call us chicks?

Dinah and I rolled our eyes at each other.

CeeCee appeared with a puzzled expression. When she saw that it was us, she almost doubled over with laugher.

Okay, come on, calling us chicks *wasn't that ridiculous.*

"This is Molly," she said, indicating me.

Tony's eyes suddenly registered extra interest. "She's the one you told me about?"

CeeCee shot him an annoyed stare, and he stopped talking. I took a wild guess and figured it had something to do with my being a murder suspect.

When CeeCee introduced Dinah to him, they exchanged a few flirty glances and Dinah suggested he stay for cake.

"Sounds good, but I've to get to the set." Just then there was some clattering noise from inside.

"Oh, no, here come the girls," CeeCee said. "Somebody grab them."

The "girls" turned out to be a pair of Yorkshire terriers, who came tearing through the entrance hall, yapping and barking as they ran. They were fast as lightening, but Tony managed to capture them before they ran out the door. Not happy at having their travels aborted, they yipped and barked even more, if that was possible. He passed them on to CeeCee and made a quick departure.

"Come in, come in," CeeCee said impatiently. When the door was safely shut, she released the squirming dogs. They immediately began a frantic sniff search of Dinah's shoes and mine.

"Tony's got a lot of lines today. His character has a big scene with his son, who has just come home after changing from John to Joan." CeeCee laughed her musical laugh. "Typical soap opera."

"I didn't know you were seeing anyone. I thought you told us you were single," I said, realizing that I really knew very little beyond the obvious about CeeCee.

"Actually, I said I wasn't married, which to me means single. I don't subscribe to this new definition of single, meaning you're not dating anyone. If it's even called dating anymore," she said with a dismissive wave.

Dinah spoke up. "I think it's called being part of a couple or in a relationship. But technically aren't you considered widowed?"

"I hate that label, dear. It sounds like I should be wearing a veil and pulling out my hair or something." I was with CeeCee on that and nodded in agreement as she continued. "Tony and I are seeing each other, but we've been trying to keep a low profile. You know how it is these days, with the paparazzi everywhere you go. I don't want someone shooting pictures every time we go out to a deli."

I just nodded, but I honestly doubted she had to worry about photographers popping out of the bushes. They weren't exactly Brad Pitt and Angelina Jolie.

"I'd appreciate it if you two would keep it to yourselves. I'd rather avoid having gossip items showing up in the tabloids." We were still standing in the entrance hall. The dogs had smelled the cake and were sitting under it, looking up.

"I'll just put the cake on the table and give you the grand tour." CeeCee took it out of my arms, and the dogs trotted after her as she left the room.

The idea of getting a house tour amused me. When I'd gone with Charlie to any of his celebrity clients' houses, they always wanted to give a tour as if it was some kind of exhibit. The tours covered only the public areas they wanted to show off. Nobody ever took you into their bedroom or into the bathroom with the socks on the floor.

"I can't wait to taste the cake. It looks wonderful,"

CeeCee said when she returned without the dogs in tow. Apparently they had chosen to stay with the cake.

"This is the living room." CeeCee started down the hall and pointed to a room off to the side. Dinah and I looked in. I was about to make an automatic what-a-lovely-room kind of comment, but when I actually saw it, I was speechless.

"That looks just like . . ." Dinah started.

"The living room on *The CeeCee Collins Show*," CeeCee said, finishing Dinah's sentence. "I liked the set so much, I had the designer make a replica here." She pointed to the floral-print sofa and matching easy chairs. There were big table lamps with white shades and a coffee table with a bowl of pears made of marble.

"You know, the show was really groundbreaking for its time. Single woman inherits a family." She shrugged. "Now it seems like old news."

As everybody else did, she skipped over the bedrooms and bathrooms and took us to the den. The cream-colored sectional sofa and the floor lamp shaped like a woman holding a torch were straight out of the show. But she had added a flat-screen TV on the wall and all kinds of examples of her handiwork and other personal items. I practically drooled over the afghan draped across the couch arm. It was made of squares with a sunflower motif and was gorgeous.

"That was one of the first things I crocheted," she said as I examined it.

Dinah walked over to the fireplace. The mantel was decorated with six gold statuettes representing different TV awards. "You won all these?"

CeeCee smiled and nodded and waited until we noticed the wall of photos. There were rows and rows of framed eight-by-tens with pictures of CeeCee with everybody from Elvis Presley to Al Gore.

When CeeCee was satisfied that we were suitably impressed, we moved on to the kitchen, which was too
adorable to be true and looked as though not much cooking
went on in it. Our last stop was the dining room, where she
suggested we do our crocheting. I recognized it from the
show, too. The TV family had always had their powwows
around the dark wood trestle table. Only the lacy crocheted
runner and the bowl of oranges were new. The Yorkies ran
around CeeCee's feet, barking with excitement as she took
the plastic top off the cake carrier.

She had snagged a bit of icing off the cover and tasted
it. Her eyes went heavenward. "Oh, but that's good. You
made this from scratch?"

"It's the only way I bake." I explained that cake mixes
never worked for me, but CeeCee didn't seem to be listening. She was already getting plates and silverware. Though
nobody had said anything, apparently it was cake before
crochet. I had to admit, the cake did look pretty good. The
strawberry halves were still in place along the top and the
buttercream icing might not have that swirly gloss the stuff
out of the can did, but it more than made up for it in taste.

Dinah was curious about how I'd learned to make it, and
I explained it was the first cake I had learned to bake. "I always call it Helen's Pound Cake, since that was my grandmother's name and she's the one who taught me."

CeeCee did the honors, and as soon as she'd served us,
she started on hers with relish. Between bites she raved. "It
practically melts in your mouth. That icing is heavenly, and
the strawberries give just the right contrast to the sweetness
and creamy texture. I'd ask for the recipe, but I don't bake.
If I need a cake, I'll just ask you for it, okay?"

Dinah and I rolled our eyes at each other. The Yorkies
had jumped onto the chair behind CeeCee, and their heads
were poking out from under her arms. It looked as though
they knew the drill. "Oh, Tallulah and Marlena, you girls
are so naughty," she said, giving each of them a bite of

cake. I suppose I should have taken it as a compliment that they both licked their lips and went looking for more.

I gave Dinah a secret little nod, hoping she'd realize I was going to start trying to direct the conversation as the criminal investigation book suggested. She winked back.

"What are you going to do for publicity now that you've left Pink Sheridan—excuse me, Pink Sheridan Shaw?" I asked.

"Actually, it's PSS PR now," CeeCee corrected. "Though I still don't know if you're supposed to say the letters or say the sound." She wrinkled her nose. "*PSS PR* sounds like someone saying *whisper* with a lisp." CeeCee scraped the icing off her plate and licked her fork. "It looks like Natalie finally got what she wanted."

"You mean taking over for Ellen?" I asked.

CeeCee looked at me. "I thought you knew how Ellen operated." She cut another piece of cake and put it on her plate. "I was with Ellen for years, and I saw her do the same thing over and over. She would hire someone like Natalie who was ambitious and a hard worker. She'd dangle the promise of making the person a partner in the firm and then get them to work cheap. Ellen always maintained the relationships with her clients and directed things, but the person in Natalie's position did most of the work. Everything was fine for a while, but eventually they'd start asking about the promised promotion. That's when they'd get fired and she'd hire a new person. Natalie is the first one who actually got her name on the firm, even if it's only an initial."

Something about what CeeCee was saying rang a bell. Charlie had complained that he didn't like some of the ways Ellen did business. He had never gone into detail, but I guessed this was the kind of thing he'd been talking about. She and Charlie had been so different; it was amazing they'd managed to stay partners all those years.

"Natalie must really be thrilled," I said. "So, are you going to hire another firm?"

"Actually, dear, I'm thinking of staying with Natalie. I have the face cream thing coming up, and it doesn't seem like a good time to make a change. Plus, Lawrence is going to be involved now, too."

I tried to contain my excitement. I had moved the conversation just where I wanted it. CeeCee was all primed and ready for me to get her to talk.

"It's probably a good idea to stay with Natalie. I'm sure you have secrets that need to be handled," I said.

"Secrets? What makes you think I have secrets?" CeeCee asked, suddenly wary. "And why are you so interested in what I'm doing for publicity?"

Maybe she wasn't as primed as I'd thought. I was suddenly speechless, but Dinah came in for a save.

"Remember, Molly might be working with Natalie?" Dinah said, winking at me.

"Right. And I . . . I . . ." I struggled to think of where to go from there. I suddenly remembered something Charlie had used with new clients, and it seemed perfect for now. "And if there's anything you want to keep out of the media, you probably ought to tell me in the event she has me work on your account."

"Okay, then, there is one thing you might help me with."

Omigod, thank you, Average Joe's Guide. She's going to tell me what it is. I tried to keep my excitement from showing.

"You probably don't understand, because when you shop at one of those warehouse stores, nobody cares. But when CeeCee Collins is seen pushing a cart with fifty rolls of toilet paper, people look. I know they think I should be dashing out of a limo on Rodeo Drive, but I'm just a real person like everybody else, looking to save a few bucks. Someone took a picture of me with their cell phone, dear, and I'm afraid it's going to end up in the tabloids. I was thinking, is there was a way you could put out some kind of media release that gave me some other reason for shopping there? Like maybe I was undercover, studying for an up-coming part?"

All my anticipation fizzled. No need to worry about which way her eyes were supposed to glance if she was lying. I knew she was telling the truth. Just not the truth I wanted to hear. But CeeCee was right about the tabloid thing. She might not be Angelina Jolie, but a photo of her pushing a cart full of toilet paper was just the kind of thing someone would run. CeeCee seemed disappointed when I suggested she talk to Natalie about it. Then she cut herself another sliver of cake. She gave the girls their share and polished off the rest, then began to clear the table.

"I suppose you want to take the rest home with you?" She looked at the more-than-half that was left.

"Why don't you keep it?" I offered. She was on her way to the kitchen with it before I had finished the sentence.

A few minutes later she returned with my empty cake carrier and set it on the table. After that she became all cro-chet business, and I realized any chance of getting her to tell me about the secret in the file was lost.

We took out our hooks and yarn. I had brought some green sueded yarn for the middle of each square, some blue fuzzy stuff for the next part and finally some black worsted for the final rounds. CeeCee didn't look pleased with my selection.

"Dear, it's not a good idea to mix yarn types in a square. Only a master like Ellen could pull it off, and the only rea-son she did it was because the yarn in the middle was from her daughter's Siamese cat."

"What?" I said. "Yarn from her cat? How do you do that?"

CeeCee explained that there were places that spun the yarn for you. You just sent them the fur, and they sent you back balls of yarn. "I did it once. My husband had a golden retriever he adored, and I thought something made from the dog's fur would make a nice present." She left and returned with a small lap blanket. Sure enough, it was

golden retriever–colored, and the texture resembled mohair. CeeCee pointed out all the fluff around the yarn and
called it a halo.

All of a sudden I understood the bag of poodle fur at the
groomer's.

"But we're getting off the subject," CeeCee said. She put
the throw off to the side, along with our yarn and hooks,
gave us each two colors of cotton yarn and a G hook, and
announced we were going to make granny-square washcloths.

"I like the idea of making something instead of just a
sample."

I was very excited about the prospect of learning to
make a granny square. I'd always loved them, but imagined
them as complicated to make and something I could never
learn.

CeeCee had us all begin making the start of a square together. She made a short chain and joined it with a slip
stitch, and we followed.

CeeCee poked her finger through the center to demonstrate. "This is where people get confused. They have a
knitter's frame of mind. You know, stitches that go back
and forth in rows, and if there's a hole, it's because you
dropped a stitch. I think Adele may be a little too militant
about it, but she's right. Crochet wins over knitting in my
book, too."

To start the next round, CeeCee told us to chain three,
which would count as the first double crochet. "Now make
two double crochets in the ring," she said.

We both looked at her, confused.

"This is the great freedom of crochet." She yarned over
and slipped the hook into the middle of the circle, yarned
over again and made a double crochet. After having us
make another double crochet, we chained two and made
another section of three double crochets by going into the
middle of the circle. It seemed to defy logic, and when I

looked at my work, I couldn't see anything but a bunch of loops and couldn't understand how that was going to become a granny square. "Are you sure this is right?" I said, holding it up

"Have faith, dear. Sometimes you just have to follow the directions one stitch at a time for a while until you realize what you are doing." She had us change colors for the next round, and I followed her directions of double crochets and chain ones and twos. We went back to the first color and added on another round. And so it went until we completed five rounds and she pronounced them done. I held mine up to admire it, but it looked lopsided. Dinah displayed hers, and it looked just like CeeCee's.

"Well-done," CeeCee said to Dinah, looking at her work. "Nice, even stitches and four good corners."

After raving on far too long about what a perfect job Dinah had done, CeeCee turned to mine.

"I'm sure you'll get in right in time, dear." CeeCee took my sad crooked square and examined it. She pointed out how I'd skipped one of the sets of three double crochets in the first round. I didn't get points for making four corners in the rest of the rounds.

I know I shouldn't have felt this way. I am a mature woman with grown sons, but it took me right back to third grade, when we did needlepoint and Mrs. Krieger hung up everybody's but mine. As much as I had thought I loved crochet, I suddenly felt like it wasn't for me. Okay, and I was jealous that Dinah had done so well. It only looked as though she was gloating.

"But," CeeCee said, pulling on the cotton yarn, "the good thing is, crochet is easy to take out." When she had taken my whole square apart, she handed me back a pile of two colors of kinky cotton yarn and had me try again.

This time I got it right, though my square did look a little loopy and wasn't as good as Dinah's. But when I held it at arm's length, the pattern was recognizable. For a moment I forgot all about dead bodies, book signings and being a possible murder suspect. I had made my first granny square.

We wove in the loose threads, and then we each had a nice washcloth to show for our trouble. Mine was never going to touch water. It was getting framed and hung up, or at least stuck up with a push pin.

When CeeCee and the girls finally walked us to the door, she pressed some skeins of yarn on us, along with written instructions on how to make granny squares, and encouraged us to get busy.

I felt slightly dismayed as we got in the car. "I'm thrilled about the granny square, but we zeroed out in the info department."

"Not really," Dinah said with a chuckle. "We did find out she's got a thing for cake."

CHAPTER 12

"THAT'S IT. I GIVE UP," I SAID OUT LOUD, EVEN though the only one who heard me was Blondie. I examined the granny square again, trying to figure out where I'd gone wrong. It looked like a jumble of loops, and I couldn't pick out the individual stitches. The only thing I knew for sure was that one corner was smaller than the others. Blondie looked up when I spoke, and when she realized there wasn't a walk or treat involved, she put her head back down.

I had been staring at my work too long and felt all tense. There was no choice but to unravel it and start again. I only hoped that the other members of the Tarzana Hookers could work faster than I could.

The phone interrupted my efforts to stretch the kinks out of my neck.

I smiled when I heard Barry's deep voice. His schedule and mine had been at odds, and we hadn't seen each other for what felt like forever but was more like a few days. We hadn't talked much, either, because every time he called, it

sounded as though Jeffrey was standing next to him. I half
expected him to call me Mrs. Pink.

This time, however, it was clear that Barry didn't have a
thirteen-year-old audience.

"Where are you?" I asked.

"Just leaving work," he said evasively. "I don't think
you want a full description."

"Actually, I do," I said, but Barry groaned in response.
He was getting used to my need to know. I had chipped
away at his reluctance to talk and found out bits and pieces
about him. Like that he'd grown up in North Hollywood
and decided to go into police work when his parents' convenience store was robbed for the fourth time and the police never could find the guys who did it. He took his job
seriously and worked hard to solve his cases.

I had been able to find out very little about his ex-wife.
He didn't bad-mouth her, and he seemed to feel that his divorce was a sign of failure, though it sounded as though
he'd gone above and beyond in trying to make it work. At
her insistence, he'd given up his LAPD job and they'd
moved back East to a rural area of Pennsylvania. He had
ended up working for an uncle of his wife's, doing some
kind of paper-pushing job that wasn't him. It had taken him
less than a year to figure out that the job and the marriage
were over. The one thing Barry and his ex had in common
was wanting the best for Jeffrey, which apparently now
meant his living with Barry.

"Since you're so hot to know, I just left the morgue,"
Barry said at last. "But now the reason for the call. You
might remember that we have some unfinished dessert
business from the other night." If it were possible, there
was a wink in his voice. "And I happen to have a free evening. How about I pick up a pizza and we stay in?" His
voice was heavy with suggestion.

It sounded appealing. Not only had I been hovering

over the granny squares, but I had spent the day trying to make sure there were no problems with the upcoming author event. If Natalie was going to use it as a test, I wanted it to be perfect.

Thankfully, Debbee Stewart, the author of *Hook Down the Pounds*, seemed like a smart speaker. She was experienced at being in front of an audience and had no demands beyond suggesting that, since she was going to do a demonstration, we have balls of string and crochet hooks available for purchase.

"There's just one problem," I said to Barry. "I already have some plans."

Barry made kind of an *oof* sound. Like he was surprised, disappointed and maybe a little jealous.

"Samuel's playing tonight, and I thought I'd sneak a peek."

Barry's sigh of relief was audible. "So he invited you?"

"Not exactly." That was an understatement. Samuel hadn't even told me where he was playing or when. But, when he'd gone through his old room to look for publicity photos, he'd left a copy of a schedule. The heading read VALLEY PROMENADE. Underneath, there was a schedule of days and times. Actually, what Samuel had said was that he didn't want anybody to come until he'd worked out the kinks.

But I was his mother. I didn't care if his act had kinks. I knew how much this meant to him. I explained to Barry that I planned to stay in the back and not even let Samuel know I was there.

"I'll come along, if it's okay. I really want to see you." There was just a little note of disappointment that it wasn't going to be exactly the way he had in mind.

"What about Columbia–Jeffrey?"

"I can't control what he calls himself at school, but to me he is Jeffrey—plain Jeffrey—and he has a rehearsal."

"So, then, you have to drop him off and pick him up?"

"Right. That was why I had the pizza-and-staying-in plan." He sighed. "It used to be so easy."

"Lots of things used to be easy," I said with a laugh, and told him he was welcome to come along. Barry said he'd pick me up once he'd delivered Jeffrey, and he hinted that we might still be able to work in "dessert."

Barry looked agitated when he arrived. "Somebody at school told Jeffrey about a commercial audition, and now he wants to go. And if he does, he needs eight-by-ten photos. Do you think he's deliberately trying to annoy me?"

I was following him out to his Tahoe parked in the driveway. "No. From what I saw of him, I think he really wants to be an actor. Annoying you is just a bonus." Barry beeped the door open, and we got in.

Barry didn't look happy with my answer. "But it's a horrible plan."

"Yes, but it's his plan. I think you need to face the fact that Jeffrey has his own mind."

"You're lucky your kids are grown and on their own," Barry said as we headed to his car. "You don't have to worry anymore."

"Ha," I laughed. "There is no retirement from the job of mother. And worry is part of the job description."

The Valley Promenade was an outdoor mall made up to look like the downtown of an idyllic small town. Part shopping center, part destination, it was a superpopular spot in Woodland Hills. Barry parked the SUV, and we walked into pretend-land. It was shaped like a square so that the outside world didn't intrude and also so that they had good control of the crowd filling the walkway.

"Where's he playing?" Barry gestured toward the array of restaurants mixed in with the small stores. I shrugged and told him I wasn't sure, and planned to just make the rounds until I found Samuel.

Barry slipped his arm around me as we started toward the first place. I was suddenly very glad to be there with him. "I wonder if there will be a stage and spotlights. This means a lot to Samuel. It's his first actual paying gig, if you don't count some stuff he did in college."

Our first stop was the Promenade's attempt at a French café. It had the look, with the white-tiled floor, dark wood walls and baskets full of baguettes. In the bar area, a woman in a sequined gown sang in French while a man played the piano.

I looked at both of them and was relieved that the one in sequins wasn't Samuel. The guy at the piano wasn't him, either.

"Want to eat here?" Barry asked, eyeing a mound of perfectly prepared *pommes frites*. I shook my head.

"Not until I find Samuel." Barry looked disappointed, and I heard his stomach rumble.

"Sorry. I missed lunch," he said, watching wistfully as the paper cone of french fries was delivered to a table.

We walked past a lingerie store and a fancy kids' store set on a little side street. At the end there was a California-style restaurant. It was all done in wicker, with dimmed lights and a menu heavy on fancy lettuces and avocado. There was a strolling guitar player—not Samuel.

"What does he play?" Barry asked as we skirted the edge of the grassy park in the center.

"He's multitalented. Guitar, piano, dulcimer, harmonica. He writes songs, too, though I expect he'd be doing covers here."

"Spoken like a proud mother. I wish I could feel as enthused about Jeffrey's ambitions."

"Just wait until he performs whatever he's rehearsing. You'll probably be there with a video camera, pointing and yelling, 'That's my son.' "

He considered what I said. "I'd be a lot more likely to

do the yelling part if it was some kind of Junior Forensics event."

"You're certainly stubborn."

"I like to think it's just being right." He smiled just enough to let me know he was joking.

We stopped and surveyed the area for other possibilities. "That has to be it," I said, pointing toward Montifiore's. It was the only place left that looked as though it might have entertainment. I started toward it, feeling a growing sense of excitement. The wonderful smell of garlic mixed with tomatoes filled the air as we approached the open door. Inside, the smell was stronger, and my stomach gurgled in response. Barry was getting to that desperate kind of hunger, and I was afraid he was going to snatch a meatball off a waiter's tray as we walked through the entrance area. It was filled with people waiting for tables, and the waiters had a hard time navigating their way through the crowd with trays of food.

"I'll just watch him for a little bit, and then we can eat," I said as we pushed through the crowd toward the bar. I could hear music, but most of it was drowned out by noise.

There wasn't really a stage, just an area off to the side cleared of tables. And even though they were Frank Sinatra songs, it certainly wasn't Frank, nor was it Samuel.

"But I'm sure this was the place I saw written down, and I know I'm right about the time." We had gone outside, and I was looking around, a touch frantic. The stores were all closing, making the restaurants stand out even more.

"Could I have been wrong?" I glanced around the square, feeling hopeless.

Barry took my hand. "We'll figure it out. And probably a lot better after we've eaten. I'll put in our name." I agreed. We would think better if our stomachs stopped rumbling. I had noticed Barry looking at his watch with a worried look. We were running out of time, too.

Barry came back from the hostess's stand looking

gloomy, and I understood why, when he gave me the wait time.

"They can't be serious. Forty minutes! No Samuel and no food," I said, hoping I didn't sound as whiny as I felt.

"She said forty minutes or less," Barry said, trying to console me. Both of our moods had taken a tumble. To try to get his mind off his hunger, I asked how Barry's day had gone. He gave me that look that meant he didn't want to talk about it. But, then, he'd said his last stop was the morgue. I could see his point. He grumbled a little more about Jeffrey and then asked what was up with me. Glad for the diversion, I filled him in on my efforts to make sure the upcoming book signing came off perfectly.

"Then Natalie won't dare turn me down," I said, beginning to cheer up now that my mind was off my empty stomach. "And did I tell you that she mentioned giving me some work? You know, like as a consultant. CeeCee said I'd be the P in the name again."

I was surprised when Barry's expression darkened. "Do you really think pushing for the Will Hunter book thing is such a good idea?" He shook his head. "And working for Pink Sheridan?"

"Sure. Why not? The Will Hunter book signing would be a coup for the bookstore, and doing some work for Natalie—it would be a nice ironic twist to Ellen's pushing me out of the company."

Barry measured his words. "To some people it might seem that you gained an awful lot from Ellen Sheridan's murder. If you mix that with being found hanging over her body . . ."

"Omigod, you've been talking to Detective Heather."

"I'm just saying, it might be better to back away from the book signing and consulting work."

"You *have* been checking up on things behind the scenes, haven't you?" All along, Barry had been telling me the best thing was for him to stay out of it. And all along, he had been telling me I had nothing to worry about because Detective Heather was a good detective who would find the real killer.

"Let's just say I've been keeping my ears open, and Heather and her partner haven't come up with any more likely suspects than . . ."

"Me," I squealed. "That's ridiculous. There are so many others, like Lawrence Sheridan. You said yourself you'd look at him first. Or CeeCee. I think Ellen was blackmailing her, or at least making it so she couldn't leave the firm. And if Heather really wants to see who has gained the most through Ellen's death, try Natalie Shaw. She went from being Ellen's slave to taking charge of the business. I'm not going to back off from the book signing. I worked too hard to get this far, and Mrs. Shedd thinks it's a done deal."

"And why is that?" Barry asked, his eyes beginning to take on that hopeless sort of look.

"Maybe I implied I was pretty sure it was going to happen."

By now Barry had begun shaking his head again. "You are hand delivering a motive. Are you worried about money or losing your job? If you need something—"

"Detective Heather again?" I said, interrupting.

He measured his words. "Well, you do have a big house in the high-rent district, and a not-so-big job that could be shaky if you don't bring in business."

Finally what Barry was saying sunk in. Even leaving aside Detective Heather's desire to get me out of the way, I could see how someone might think I looked guilty.

"I wasn't going to tell you this," Barry began. "But Heather wanted to arrest you at the scene. I talked her out of it. I convinced her she would look foolish."

"And?"

"Now she says it was a mistake to listen to me."

I felt a gush of warmth for Barry. "I didn't know you did that."

"Did you really think I would just walk away and leave you in handcuffs?"

"It kind of looked that way."

He brushed some hair from my face and gave me one of his smoldering looks, which suddenly made me regret that we hadn't followed through with his plans for the evening. "I'm always there for you," he said in a low voice.

If this had been a movie, the music would have swelled. Instead my stomach let out a loud, embarrassing gurgle.

"That's it. I'm going to check on our progress," he said, moving toward the hostess's stand. He came back, his eyes flashing. "They're still saying forty minutes. C'mon." He grabbed my hand, and we went outside. "I think there are some food stands in the middle. We can grab a slice of pizza or something."

But first we had to get there. The area was thick with people, heavy on teenagers.

"Don't any of these kids have homework?" Barry grumbled as we threaded our way through the crowd. I explained seeing a sign talking about some kind of fund-raiser.

Finally past them, we reached a wide walkway surrounded by the hilly park area. It had a carnival atmosphere. There were little lights in all the trees. Carts were selling jewelry and food items, and there was entertainment. I stopped short. There was a guy juggling power tools, someone else doing magic on a folding table—and Samuel. He sat at a portable keyboard, next to a table with CDs for sale manned by a pretty light-haired woman I didn't recognize.

Samuel looked like he was playing his heart out, but the crowd shuffled by with barely a glance at him or at the hat lying on the ground with some money in it.

Barry came up behind me and followed my gaze.

"You found him," he said. "See, I knew you didn't screw up. You had the right day and place." He rambled on while I just stared. Of all the things I had hoped for Samuel's premiere engagement, the very least was that it would have a roof.

Barry handed me a slice of pizza and suggested that we walk and eat. He had to rush to pick up Jeffrey. Once again dessert got cancelled.

CHAPTER 13

"I BELIEVE THE CORRECT TITLE IS 'OPEN-AIR EN-tertainer,'" Dinah said. "Those places are very picky about who they give the space to. One of my students wrote a composition about trying to get a spot doing the three-card monte trick. Of course they turned him down. I'm sure they knew it was just a con. But he saw a lot of other people audition, including several he thought were 'downright audibly awesome,' to quote what he thought was a really cute phrase, but they still didn't get hired."

"That makes me feel a little better, but not much. I don't want to seem old and stodgy, but how could Samuel be so excited about being a street musician? What kind of step in his career is that?"

I had told Dinah that somehow I'd gotten the position as main suspect, along with the few other tidbits Barry had let slip. Through his partner, Barry had found out that the detectives were sure Ellen had known her killer and that it was a disorganized crime, which meant it hadn't been planned out first. Neither of those facts helped me.

I berated myself again for not checking the tote bag for the appointment book in my rush to get out of the closet. If I'd seen it, I'd know whom she'd had lunch with. It was frustrating knowing where the book might be and not being able to check or even tell anybody to look there. It would involve too many questions about how I knew.

Dinah and I had both agreed that the best way to keep me from panicking about my upgraded suspect status was by focusing on Samuel's gig.

"You never know, he could be heard by some big agent," Dinah said.

"Like Peter?" I looked heavenward. "He would have a fit if he saw his brother playing for money in a hat."

"I think they get an actual salary from the place, plus the tips." She patted my arm. "Okay, it isn't the best situation, but he's grown and all that."

Dinah and I had gotten together to crochet granny squares. I'd thought she could help me figure out what I was doing wrong, but it turned out that, away from CeeCee's directions, Dinah was as lost as I was. I know I shouldn't have been happy, but it made me feel vindicated when hers turned out lopsided, too.

"Right," I said, unraveling the yarn once again. "I suppose I should be grateful for that and happy that he is following his dream. Maybe if there wasn't the hat for money, it wouldn't look so bad. I feel awful for not being happy for him."

Dinah nodded. "You think it gets easier when they're grown, but there are just different problems. Since my two moved cross-country, I don't get a play-by-play anymore. Much as I hate to admit it, I miss it."

I'd had enough of dissecting the situation with Samuel. Dinah was right. He was a man and making his own choices. If playing on a phony street was what he wanted, I would just keep my mouth shut and support him.

"What ever happened with Mr. Online?" I asked, changing the subject. Once he and Dinah had moved on to live voice, he'd suggested they meet.

Ever-talkative Dinah suddenly went silent. She focused on her lopsided granny square like her life depended on it. "I was hoping you wouldn't ask, so I wouldn't have to tell."

"Uh-oh."

"Right answer," she said. "We arranged to meet at Starbucks. He still had the great voice in person and he wasn't too bad looking, a little short on hair, but who cares. We seemed to be getting along pretty well, and he suggested we go to the theater on the weekend. That's when it all fell apart. First he asked if I could get the tickets, and he'd pay me back. He said he was just having a little cash-flow problem. Then he asked if I could lend him forty bucks until the weekend, too."

"Oops, kind of had *deadbeat* written on his forehead, huh?"

"Not everybody gets someone like Barry Greenberg dropped in her lap." Dinah looked at me and shook her head. She couldn't understand why I kept him at a distance.

"I like him, I really do, but I just want to keep my options open. What did you do with Mr. Deadbeat?"

"I told him I was having a cash-flow problem, too, and left." She looked down at her granny square. The center was a nice yellow, the next round a medium blue and the one beyond that a darker blue. She had done the final two rounds in black, but the whole thing was lopsided. She held it up. "Whatever I'm doing wrong, at least I'm consistent. All CeeCee would have to do is look at this, and she'd know right away how to fix this."

I called CeeCee and explained our problem.

"It really isn't a good time," she said when I suggested we come over.

"It would just take a minute, and without some help, we can't make squares for the blanket."

"Oh, dear." She sounded harried. "That is a problem. Okay, but you must come over right now. I mean, pick up your things this instant and head for the door."

We did exactly as CeeCee requested and tried to park in front of her house a few minutes later. I say "tried to" because the whole area was filled with trucks and cars, and we had to park half a block down. There was a lot of activity, with furniture and people going in and out. We threaded through them and headed up the stone walkway. No need to knock—the door was open. The sound of muffled barking came from somewhere in the distance. My guess was that the "girls" were locked up somewhere and not happy about it.

CeeCee met us in the front hall. "Be careful with that sofa," she snapped at a pair of men in jeans and bandanas who were moving said couch out the door and just missed smashing it into the doorjamb.

"What's going on?" I said. There was all kinds of activity inside, too. Another man in jeans and a bandana was on the floor taping down cables that were coming from outside, and a similarly dressed man was carrying industrial-type lights into the living room.

"This is all for the shoot of the 'before' part of the face cream infomercial." CeeCee glanced nervously toward a coffee table another set of movers was hoisting to remove. "Be careful there. That's irreplaceable." I noticed the movers didn't seem happy with her comments.

A slightly better-dressed woman with a clipboard came up to CeeCee. "I appreciate your concern, ma'am, but don't worry. Nothing will be damaged, and if it is, we'll make sure it's fixed."

CeeCee didn't seem placated, and the woman sighed and grimaced. "Generally the owners aren't here when we're setting up, ma'am."

"Well, that doesn't matter to me. I am here, and I am concerned. Those young men handled my couch recklessly. And I'd appreciate it if you'd stop calling me *ma'am*. *Ms. Collins* will do just fine."

The woman swallowed her annoyance and put on an artificial smile. "Let's move you and your friends into the other room. I'm sure you'll all be more comfortable there." To ensure that we moved, the woman took CeeCee's elbow in a studied gracious manner and steered all of us into the dining room. "The makeup person will be along any minute. Why don't you wait in here?"

The dining room looked the same, and CeeCee sank into one of the chairs and indicated for us to sit, too. "I've been on lots of locations and never thought twice about the owners' furniture and house. It's a little different when it's your place and your things.

"Okay, let's see what's going on," CeeCee said as we brought out our poor, misshapen granny squares. The worry went out of her face, and she laughed her musical laugh. "Oh, my dear, you did make a mess. They can't be fixed. You'll have to unravel and start again. Do it quickly," she said, looking toward the hall.

Two women came in, carrying a bunch of supplies. They continued into the kitchen. CeeCee followed them, and we followed her. The women set up plates, cups and coffee. Another woman came in, carrying a box of donuts and jugs of orange juice. As soon as the women set their things down, they all headed back out, taking no notice of us.

As if in a trance, CeeCee headed right for the donuts and lifted the lid on the box. "They've got Bavarian cream–filled," she gushed. When she turned back toward us, she had a donut along with plastic silverware on a plate. "Go on. Help yourself. It's for the cast and crew, but they always bring way more than they need."

We passed on the snacks, but CeeCee fixed herself a cup

of coffee with double cream and sugar before we all went
back to the dining room table.

"I always buy the fat-free half-and-half," CeeCee said,
taking sip of the coffee.

Fat-free half-and-half? That was an oxymoron if I'd
ever heard one. Personally, I only bought the real stuff.

CeeCee cut into the donut with the plastic knife and
fork, and the cream oozed out. She took a bite and smiled
at the taste. "You don't know what you're missing," she
said. That's where she was wrong. I knew exactly what I
was missing—somewhere around a zillion calories and a
sugar overload. Between bites, she explained that we'd left
out some stitches in beginning of our squares, and she told
us to start on new ones quickly. The pressure made me nervous, and I had trouble joining the beginning chain.

CeeCee watched us both and waved her hand. "There's
your mistake," she said, stopping me when I left out one of
the chain twos in an early round. She caught Dinah as she
finished the first round with only three sides. CeeCee gestured for us to work quickly, and we'd gotten to the third
round with no apparent errors when the woman with the
clipboard returned.

"Makeup's ready," she said to CeeCee. We followed
along as she led CeeCee to her own front door. A trailer
was parked in the driveway, which appeared to be our destination. We followed, still hanging on to our squares-in-
progress and crochet hooks.

Natalie Shaw arrived along with a man and woman,
and stopped the procession. She hugged CeeCee and nodded a greeting to Dinah and me before introducing Jeff
Rogers, a human-interest columnist for the *Valley News*,
and his photographer.

So CeeCee had definitely changed her mind about terminating. I wondered how Natalie had gotten her to stay.
Was it really the promise of doing a great job, or did it have
something to do with the file CeeCee wanted so much and

which Natalie apparently had seen? Whatever was going on, it seemed to be taking a toll on Natalie. She had lost the confident, in-charge look I'd noticed at the funeral. Each time I'd seen her since, she'd looked a little more harried. Though she was dressed in a power suit and heels, with not a strand of her chin-length brown hair out of place, there were circles under her eyes even her perfectly done makeup couldn't hide.

What was the old saying about getting what you want and wanting it when you get it? Maybe, as much as Natalie might have wanted to be in charge, the actuality of it had turned out to be a bigger bite than she could chew.

Natalie was staying close to Jeff Rogers, as if she was afraid he would bolt if given the chance. It quickly became apparent that the hook for the interview was "CeeCee Collins: The Legend Continues." Calling CeeCee a legend seemed a little over the top, but it wasn't my business, though Jeff Rogers seemed to be having some trouble with it, too.

"Ms. Collins, your sitcom was groundbreaking. Am I to understand this face cream is going to be the same?"

The woman with the clipboard was moving us en masse to the trailer. CeeCee was definitely in her element and enjoying every second of having an entourage and being the center of attention.

Natalie didn't look happy. This interview obviously wasn't going as she had hoped. When we had all been herded into the trailer, she suddenly looked less worried. "If you are looking for human interest, what could be more human or more interesting than CeeCee's charity work?"

CeeCee listened to what Natalie was saying, but clearly hadn't a clue what she was talking about.

"Your crochet group," Natalie prodded.

Finally it clicked in. "Oh, yes, dear," CeeCee trilled. "I've taken over leading the Tarzana Hookers. We hook for charity," she said with her trademark giggle.

Jeff Rogers looked more interested, particularly when CeeCee explained whom she was taking over for and what had happened to her. He was taking furious notes and more than once had checked to make sure his tape recorder was working.

"Hearts and Barks was Ellen's favorite charity. They're expecting the blanket to fetch a high price, partly because of the sentimental value and partly because my name is connected with it. Of course, with Ellen gone, I'm the master crocheter on the project."

Nobody could accuse CeeCee of being humble.

"I suppose the blanket's connection to a murder would generate some interest. Have they any leads on who did it?" the columnist asked.

I held my breath, but nobody looked my way. Natalie sensed the direction of the interview and stepped in.

"These are two of the crocheters on the project." She pushed us close to CeeCee, and we held up our partially completed squares. My hook clattered to the ground, and I bent to pick it up. When I stood, the photographer was aiming her camera at us.

I was curious about how they would do the makeup for the "before" section of the infomercial, but never got to find out. Once they'd gotten our photograph, Dinah and I were quickly dismissed.

As Dinah and I headed back to my car, we passed the back of one of the trucks. CeeCee's couch was upended against the inside wall.

"CeeCee wouldn't be happy if she saw that," I said. I glanced back toward the house. "If it was making her so upset, I wonder why she let them use her house."

Dinah rubbed her fingers together. "Moola. Do you know how much they pay to use your house as a location? Down the street from me, there is a couple whose house gets used all the time, though I think it's for porn stuff. I asked one of the crew what they were shooting, and they just gave me a weird look."

"Hmm, shopping at warehouse stores and renting out her house for productions. Could she be short on cash?"

CHAPTER 14

I WAS DEEP UNDER THE WATER AND COULDN'T see where I was going. It was a scary, exciting feeling, but this noise kept interrupting. I wanted it to go away and stop ruining my dream. Gradually I began to float to the surface, but the noise continued until I realized it wasn't my dream—it was the phone. I reached for the cordless, feeling my heart rate pick up. Who ever calls in the middle of the night with good news? Through the window I could see that the night sky had just a tinge of light.

"I didn't want to scare you by ringing the doorbell," Barry said after I'd finally got my mind clear enough to say hello into the right end of the receiver.

My pulse took a bump down. "Hearing the phone ring in the middle of the night did a pretty good job on its own."

"Technically it's morning, and for me the end of a long night. Sorry to have startled you," he apologized. "I thought you'd want to see the paper, since your picture's in it."

"Where are you?" I asked, sitting up and swinging my legs over the side of the bed.

"At your front door."

Blondie and I went to the door. A worn looking Barry stood in the glow of the porch light. He was dressed in a suit, with his tie pulled loose. He naturally had a heavy beard, but this was definitely double duty. He looked like he'd had a tough night.

When he walked inside, he held up the folded-open newspaper and showed me the picture. It was actually of Dinah, CeeCee and me, and once again I looked pasty. Even without her special makeup, CeeCee knew how to pose and had angled her best side toward the camera. Dinah just appeared stunned. I reached for the paper to look at the accompanying article, but Barry held on to it.

"Donuts," he said, holding out a white bag. I glanced back toward the paper he had moved to under his arm. I reached for it again and mentioned the article this time, but he didn't hand it over.

Why did I think there was something he didn't want me to see? He pushed the bag toward me again in an enticing manner. This time I took it and looked inside. The donuts resembled round, greasy bricks.

"You weren't planning to eat these, were you?"

"I was, unless you can think of something better." There was a forced lightness to his voice that was covering something up. I asked about his night, and he gave me a vague answer about crime fighting not being a nine-to-five job. Whatever it was, judging by how he looked, it must have been extra awful.

The "something better" was scrambled eggs and sautéed mushrooms on lightly toasted and buttered egg bread, along with orange slices, courtesy of the backyard trees, mixed with strawberries and bananas. To top it off, I made a pot of smoky French-roast coffee.

"That was so good," Barry said, devouring the last crumb of his breakfast sandwich. We'd taken our plates into the living room and settled on the couch. Outside, the sky was growing into dawn's version of twilight. Blondie had gone back to her chair.

As I drank some of the strong-bodied coffee, Barry settled against me and drifted off to sleep with the newspaper still under his arm. I extracted it carefully, wondering what could possibly be worth hiding in an article about CeeCee.

The headline of Jeff Rogers's column seemed strange. What did ALL WRAPPED UP IN MURDER have to do with CeeCee and her continuing legend?

It turned out very little. Apparently Jeff had listened to our conversation about the blanket—how Ellen had started it and we were struggling to finish it—and decided that was his topic with a twist.

The main character in the piece wasn't CeeCee at all; it was the afghan. Jeff mentioned how the Tarzana Hookers had started meeting at Shedd & Royal and had decided their mission was to crochet for charity, with their first project being an afghan made of all different squares for the Hearts and Barks Fair auction. But before it was finished, the Hookers' founder and first leader, Ellen Sheridan, had been murdered.

The next section turned out to be about CeeCee, but in the context of the crocheters, and how she had stepped in to take over the group and was sharing her knowledge with new members such as the ones in the photo. I could just imagine seeing Adele when she read that part. She'd be fuchsia-faced, to match her outfit.

Jeff did a riff on how any celebrity connection added value to the donation of charity items like the blanket. But according to him, the real added value of the afghan came from its connection with Ellen Sheridan's murder. She had made a lot of the squares, and was even found with a crochet hook and yarn in her hand. The only thing that would up the value more would be if the police caught the perpetrator right around the time of the auction.

I choked on the next line. According to Detective

Heather Gilmore, lead detective on the case, they were close to making an arrest.

"Close to making an arrest," I said out loud. "You know who that means?" I squeaked.

"Now, don't go jumping to conclusions," Barry said, waking up and putting his arm around me.

"You smell nice," he said, nuzzling my hair.

"I bet they don't have jasmine shampoo in prison. I know what you're doing. You're trying to distract me."

"Not completely. Your hair really does smell nice," he said, pulling me closer. "She's probably just vamping, trying to sound good in the newspaper. But even if she means it, there's nothing to say it's you."

"Then who? You said you thought she hadn't focused on anyone else. She asked everyone about me, but she never asked me about anyone."

Barry tried to keep the shades down on his expression, but I knew him well enough to recognize the flicker of a troubled feeling.

"People do all kinds of thinks to get rid of a rival," I said. "Her way could be sending me off to jail on a murder charge."

He ruffled my hair, but I noticed that this time he didn't give me the *she's a fair and impartial detective* speech.

He glanced at his watch and sat upright.

"Gotta go. I'm driving car pool."

Before he left, I packed up a breakfast sandwich for Jeffrey, and Barry gave me a hint on his night. It involved domestic violence and a dead child. He gave no details, and I really didn't want any. Then, as I watched, he filed it away in the do-not-touch part of his mind, and the haunted look about his eyes softened. He took me in his arms at the door.

"Don't worry, babe," he murmured. The trouble was, he didn't give me any reason to follow his suggestion. He didn't let go, just pulled me closer and said he hated to leave. "We should be living together," he said, sniffing the air, which still carried the fragrance of fresh coffee and buttered toast. "It smells like home."

It felt safe and warm in his arms, and for a moment I considered what he said. But then reality kicked in, and I let go. A visitor was one thing; a housemate and his son were a whole other story. I was just beginning to get back on my feet, and I wasn't ready to tie up my life with anyone just now, even if I was beginning to think I loved him.

I thought I would get some more sleep, but before I could settle back into bed, my cell phone, the house phone and the fax machine all went off at the same time. I'm sure e-mails were piling up, too.

I had Peter on my cell and Samuel on the house phone. Both of them started talking at once. Peter insisted it was more urgent that I talk to him, and had me tell Samuel I'd call him back.

Peter was on his way to some show taping. He'd seen the article, which surprised me. I didn't know Peter did anything as retro as read the newspaper.

"Mother, I can't believe you stayed in that knitting group," he said, agitated by the column and the morning freeway traffic.

"It's crocheting," I corrected, beginning to understand Adele's annoyance at people not giving crochet its due. I explained how relaxing it was and how much I liked it, and that the charity project was worthwhile. I could practically hear Peter rolling his eyes in frustration.

"What's that about the detective saying they're close to an arrest? Who?"

"Peter, she doesn't share her information with me. I have no idea." There was no point in mentioning that I had a pretty good idea who she meant, and even half thinking about it was making me sick. In all my so-called detective work, I had come up with a number of other people who benefited from Ellen's death, but I was the only one who had been found hanging over her body. If only Ellen hadn't been so forgetful. But it wasn't forgetfulness, was it? She had been preoccupied. Everyone in the group had said she seemed upset about something. Or was it someone?

Not missing a beat, Peter cut through my vague answer. "She doesn't mean you, does she?"

"Of course not. Don't be ridiculous."

He muttered something under his breath about the morning traffic and got back on the subject. "It's time we thought about a lawyer. I know just the guy. It would be good if you met him anyway."

"Why?" I said, surprised. "In case I walk in on another dead body?"

"Don't even joke about it, Mother. I'll talk to him." Peter said he would take care of it, and I gave up. Once he set his mind on something, there was no stopping him, and much as I hated to admit it, it might not be the worst thing to have a lawyer available—just in case. Abruptly, he changed the subject to a happier topic. "I wanted to invite you to brunch next week. Samuel is coming, too, and he's bringing a date." Peter had assumed the man-of-the-family role and liked us all to get together, but always at his convenience.

I started to ask Peter whether I could bring Barry, but he cut me off. "Maybe another time," he said.

Like a half an hour after forever.

"I have a perfect idea," Peter said, sounding pleased with himself. "I'll invite the lawyer, Mason Fields, to join us. In the meantime, do you think you could try and keep a low profile—no news reports or newspaper photos?"

I couldn't help but laugh. Did he think I wanted to end up in the media? "Low-profile and anonymous sounds good to me," I said before hanging up.

I could hear the fax machine in the other room spitting out papers. Dinah and everybody I knew was faxing me the article. Dinah's came with comments. Where it reported that Detective Heather Gilmore had said she was close to an arrest, Dinah had written *in her dreams* in marker pen.

Things didn't get much better at the bookstore. Adele was waiting when I walked in.

"What's going on?" she demanded, showing me the article. I knew Adele wasn't asking about me and the potential arrest. It was all about CeeCee's comment that she was the leader of the group.

"You know CeeCee, always being theatrical. I'm sure she meant to say she was coleader with you." Was I actually trying to comfort Adele? In some strange way I felt for her, even if she was always doing whatever she could to put a chink in my job performance with the hope of getting it away from me. The crochet group was a bright spot for her, and I thought she deserved to be at least cochair. But leave it to Adele to zing me for my soft feelings.

"Pink, we should have an emergency meeting of the group. You and your friend are slowpokes in the yarn department, and we are dangerously low on squares."

"You should talk to CeeCee. I think she is still tied up with the commercial shoot," I said.

"There's no law that says she has to give her permission or even be there."

I gave Adele a dark stare and shook my head. "CeeCee has made more squares than anybody. I don't think you really want to offend her."

Adele didn't like my answer, and walked off in a huff, turning back as she did. "Oh, and Mrs. Shedd wants to see you in her office."

Mrs. Shedd was a little like Charlie in *Charlie's Angels*. None of us saw much of her, and most of our communication was by phone. I got a sinking feeling as I walked into the office, where she was going through a pile of mail.

"I can't say you're not getting attention for the bookstore, but all this in connection with a murder . . . ? Maybe we ought to change the name of the bookstore to the Notorious S and R." She looked at the newspaper again and kind of laughed, which implied she was making a joke.

She zeroed in on me with a pointed expression, and I began to tense up. Was this the part where she fired me?

"Do you think you'll have the blanket finished on time?" she asked, finally. Her question caught me off guard, and she continued while I processed the fact that she wasn't firing me. "Maybe you could call in some knitters to help out. Make it a mixed-needle-arts blanket or something. It just wouldn't look good for the bookstore if the first project we sponsor doesn't get finished."

I was so relieved at not being fired and that Mrs. Shedd didn't seem to know I might be the one Detective Heather was talking about arresting that I told her not to worry. She had my word the blanket would be finished. I did, however, mention that the mixed-needle part might not go over too well with the group, and it was best to stick to just crochet.

"And the Will Hunter book signing? It's a lock?"

"Almost," I said in my most confident voice, leaving out the fact that we had to impress Natalie Shaw at our next event.

"Good, because I can't wait to meet him."

"Why?" I asked, surprised. I couldn't imagine she'd be interested in the memoirs of a slacker-type actor.

"I'm a big fan. I've seen all his movies. I think he's just dreamy."

Oh, no, that was all I needed. It wasn't just a matter of foot traffic. Mrs. Shedd had a crush on the guy. She went on to describe the new dress she'd bought for the event, which meant that, unlike with most of the author programs, she planned to attend. Only as an afterthought did she mention Detective Heather's comment.

"It isn't anybody we know, is it?"

"I hope not," I answered in the understatement of my life, before heading to the door.

That night I thought I would go to bed early, so I'd get a good night's sleep before the *Hook Down the Pounds* author event. I wanted to be alert and ready to tackle any disaster that might come up. That was, unless Detective Heather arrested me first.

It was a good plan—if I had been able to sleep. I couldn't find a comfortable spot in my bed. It suddenly seemed big and empty, and I got up in the dark. It may sound kooky, but I didn't want to turn on the lights. The house was faintly illuminated by the floodlights outside, and when I got to the kitchen, I opened the refrigerator.

The five bottles of Hefeweizen were still there. I reached for an amber bottle, thinking that nobody was going to drink it and it might help me sleep.

I took it to the kitchen table. With the refrigerator shut, the only light was from the backyard floodlights.

I heard Blondie's claws on the living room floor as she came across the house. I let her out and stood in the silent yard while she disappeared into the darkness. When she was finished, she bounded back inside.

With the door shut and locked, I sat down and opened the beer. I took a sip and made a face, expecting it to taste terrible. Actually it was quite good—for beer, anyway.

By the time I had a third sip, I was feeling the effects. Charlie had always said I was a cheap drunk. A few sips of anything, and I was ready to dance on a table.

The smell of the beer reminded me of Charlie, and I felt a whomp of pain hit me in the gut. Even now, sometimes when I first awoke, for just a moment I would forget. I'd think everything was as it had been, and Charlie had just gotten up early and was in the kitchen, reading the trades.

We had reached that place where we were comfortable together and knew each other's habits. Without thinking, I would scramble his eggs so lightly they were almost undercooked. And he automatically bought me a red-eye along with movie tickets.

I always thought we'd be like those older couples I saw who still held hands.

I took another drag on the bottle. It seemed so unfair that he'd died at fifty-one.

Blondie got up. I heard her lapping up water from her bowl and knew that any second she'd go off by herself. Though she looked like a terrier mix, she had the personality of a cat. I guessed it was from being alone in an enclosure at the shelter for so long. But slowly she was beginning to bond with me. I reached down to pet her, and she stayed put and leaned against my leg.

The beer was working. I felt the tension melt out of my shoulders. I wondered what Charlie would think about my being suspected of being a murderess, though I suppose that was politically incorrect. There were just murderers now.

He probably wouldn't be happy that Samuel was a street musician—excuse me, open-air entertainer. At least if he was playing inside somewhere, he wouldn't have to worry about rain or low-flying pigeons.

I drained the last of the bottle. My thoughts were running together. Worries were crashing into other worries. Thanks to my meeting with Mrs. Shedd, I was now worried about my job. If the afghan didn't get finished or she wasn't able to meet her idol, the blame was going to fall on me.

It wasn't the money. Charlie had left me with enough. It was the idea of failing. The whole episode with Ellen had beaten down my confidence. This job was my chance to climb back up. But there was nothing more I could do tonight.

I dropped the empty into the recycling bag, and Blondie and I headed across the dark house, anxious for bed.

CHAPTER 15

"DON'T WORRY. NO MATTER WHAT HAPPENS, you'll work it out," Dinah said in a reassuring voice. "You always do. Remember the *See Jack Cook* event?"

"And I thought I'd mentally gone over every disaster," I said, wringing my hands. Dinah reached over, separated them and suggested I take a deep breath.

"I thought it was cute that his name was Cook and that's what he liked to do. Actually, he was pretty cute, too, as I remember," Dinah said.

"Whatever cuteness there was ended as far as I was concerned when he did the candy-making demonstration and the sugar boiled over and got on the hot plate and made a bunch of smoke." I shuddered when I thought about what had happened next.

"It wasn't so bad, really. The smoke alarm went off, and the fire department came," Dinah said. I looked at her and rolled my eyes.

"Author programs aren't supposed to end with the audience being evacuated."

"That wasn't the end, really. You had him finish his demonstration in the parking lot, and the fire department guys even hung around and helped." Dinah's sparkling eyes danced. "And those caramels he made." She kissed her fingers.

"The fire guys did like the caramels, and we did sell all of Jack's books. But tonight is different. I have more than books riding on this. I need to wow Natalie Shaw."

"Just be glad it's not another book by Fern Darling. What was her erotic romance called?" Dinah smiled as she remembered. "*Hot and Hard.*"

I blushed just thinking about it. Fern had been planning to read a section of her book, but her husband and kids showed up unexpectedly just as she was about to start, and she'd freaked and ran out the door.

"But you stepped in when she left. You got up there in front of God and everybody and read that selection she'd chosen," Dinah said. "That woman had a way with euphemisms." Dinah giggled as I squirmed, thinking of all those eyes on me as I'd read Fern's prose. "Let's see, there was *joystick*, *love handle*, *pleasure lever* and my personal fave, *passion baton*," Dinah said. "But by far her best line was something about Amber's rising moans as she rode Connor's hot rod."

I nodded, willing the redness to leave my face. "And we sold out her book, too. Even without her there to sign." I let out a sigh. "And even Mr. Stink Bomb's book did okay. A bunch of people came in the next day and wanted copies of his soap book. I think you made me feel better," I said, glancing around the bookstore.

"That's what best friends are for," Dinah said, hugging me. "Besides, Debbee Stewart isn't cooking anything, and her book isn't one long sex scene. You had her come in and do her demonstration, and it went fine. You got in some balls of string and hooks to sell. What could go wrong?"

"Right," I said, brightening. What could go wrong?

In a show of support, the crochet group had said they would come to the event. Adele had stuck around when she finished her stint in the children's department, and now joined Dinah and me. She was into neutrals at the moment. Her skirt, vest and shirt were all shades of beige and brown, but what they lacked in color they made up for in texture. The vest was some phony fur thing, the shirt was crinkly stuff and the skirt was ruffly.

"You look worried, dear," CeeCee said, joining our little group. "Not a good face to show the world. I say, if you act as if everything is okay, it will be." She sniffed the air. "Oh, my, what are they baking in the café?"

"Rustic apple pie cookies," I said. It had been a deliberate plan. The smell of apples and of spices like cinnamon was supposed to make people feel good. I was pulling out all the stops on this one.

I had called Natalie to remind her, and she had said she would try to come. I couldn't push too hard, but the word *try* made me nervous. Everything could go smooth as glass, but if she wasn't there to see it, it wouldn't help me in the Will Hunter department. She'd told me at least three times how busy she was. There were so many changes to make and clients' needs to take care of. And Ellen's computer had been brought back to life and into the office.

I sparked at that and asked whether it had shown whom Ellen had the lunch appointment with.

"Sorry, there was nothing about her lunch date that day, or about much else. Not that I was surprised," Natalie said. "Ellen was a worst-case scenario kind of person, and she didn't trust anything that wouldn't work in a power failure or that needed batteries."

Sheila walked past the bargain section and joined us, clutching her fabric bag of crochet supplies as though it was her blankie.

I moved everyone en masse to the event area and had them take seats. Dinah sat with the others and gave me a good-luck power fist sign. I was glad to have her moral support.

I had spent the afternoon arranging everything and was pleased with the setup. The arrangement of chairs in a fan shape around the small table afforded everyone a good line of sight. Even from the last row, the stack of copies of *Hook Down the Pounds: The Magic Way to Lose Weight with Crochet* was visible, particularly the upright one on top. There was still plenty of room on the table for Debbee to do her demonstration. Nearby there was an end cap with more books, a pyramid of balls of string and a coffee mug holding a bunch of medium-size crochet hooks. I wanted it to look like a full house to Natalie, so to make sure there weren't a lot of empty seats, I had put out only twenty. Four of them were already filled with the crochet women.

People began filtering in, and the seats were filling up quickly. Many had stopped in the café first and gotten drinks and cookies. I checked the clock and felt my stomach clench. I had been so busy worrying about whether or not Natalie was going to show, I hadn't noticed that Debbee hadn't arrived. If the program didn't start soon, the crowd would get bored and leave.

Adele looked over at me and gave a disparaging shake of her head. "Pink, the natives are getting restless. You better do something."

I felt a momentary panic, but then an answer showed up. It was really quite obvious. I waved the Tarzana Hookers to the table. Adele rushed up and, before the others had even made it to the front, was already telling the crowd about the crochet group and the charity project. I was glad to let Adele take over. CeeCee seemed a little less pleased, though when someone asked for her autograph, she brightened up right away.

Someone mentioned the newspaper column and asked about the blanket, and when Sheila showed off another of her impressionist scarf creations, the audience responded with *wow*s. Things got a little thorny when Adele started talking about yarn and spent way too much time describing the differences between worsted and sports weight. Now more concerned about Debbee's arrival than about Natalie's, I had my eyes glued to the door.

Finally Debbee arrived with several friends. By now all the seats were filled, and people were gathering at the back and around the sides. I regretted not bringing in more chairs from the storage shed. I should have realized the words *magic* and *lose weight* would draw a big crowd. It was a mixed bag of women, some teenage girls and a few men. I checked the crowd again. Still no Natalie.

I introduced Debbee, and she took over. She was warm and friendly and—though nobody seemed to notice—a little on the round side for having written a magic-diet book. I glanced out at the crowd, which had grown even bigger. She talked about how the book could change your life, help you lose weight and even break bad habits. She was going to demonstrate one of her strategies.

"I call this the EFOMO maneuver, short for Emergency Food Moment maneuver. You know how it is. You are tense or upset, and the desire to eat something crunchy and salty is almost hypnotic. Instead of ripping open a bag of chips, reach for these." Debbee took out a green crochet hook and a ball of string. She cut off a long length of the string and explained that the two items took up no more space than a couple of pencils, and could be carried everywhere.

"The EFOMO maneuver will work in a restaurant, too. When you're looking at the menu and have an overwhelming desire for the all-fried plate or the giant hot fudge sundae, take out your kit," she said, making a slipknot and beginning a foundation chain, "and you'll be able to get past that moment and back to your good sense.

"Personally, I like to make something if I'm crocheting, even with string." When she'd made fifteen chain stitches, she turned her work and began doing single crochet. She kept going, doing row upon row, and then she held up a little square.

"So I make little coasters and get past the chip moment." She went on to explain that the book had charts showing how many calories you could save by crocheting for different amounts of time. For example, if you crocheted for five minutes instead of eating an iced cupcake, you just saved four hundred calories from hitting your hips. And if you crocheted five hundred calories' worth a day, in a week you'd have knocked off enough calories to lose a pound."

There was a sudden gush of excited voices as the audience started talking. I had the sense that this event was going really well, and that Debbee was going to sell a lot of books. I felt even better when I glanced toward the door and saw Natalie coming in.

She wasn't alone. Will Hunter trailed in after her. His dark brown hair had that just-woke-up look. He was wearing lambskin moccasin slippers, baggy khakis and a T-shirt under a flannel shirt. In other words, his typical outfit. Surprisingly, nobody noticed him. They were too intent on listening to Debbee say that she'd be happy to sign books and mention there was a limited supply of hooks and string available for people who wanted to get started on the plan right away.

All at once the chairs emptied, and everyone funneled toward the display. At first they walked; then they began to run.

"I think you've got a problem," Dinah said, coming up next to me. There were clearly more people than supplies. The pushing and shoving had already begun. I saw at least one person snatch a ball of string from someone else's hands. Balls of string had fallen onto the floor and were rolling off, with people running after them. The customers who had managed to get a hook and string were crowding around the table as Debbee did another demonstration.

Others were walking away, crocheting little chains and not looking where they were going. It was chaos, pure and simple.

The people who were still empty-handed were milling around, looking angry.

"What are you going to do, Pink?" Adele said, surveying the hostile group.

I knew how the woman with the erotic book had felt. I just wanted to run away. Natalie was standing outside the throng, and her lips were pursed in a judgmental pose. So much for things going well.

The hookless crowd had surrounded CeeCee, but when they saw Will Hunter, they abandoned her. Between asking for autographs, they asked for his help. They seemed to think that since he was a movie star, he had some extra clout, and they started complaining to him about the lack of hooks and string. Being the movie hero that he was, he came over and told me about the problem, like I didn't know.

"Hey, dude, you've got to do something. This mob is turning nasty," he said with his usual laconic delivery. No question, he was right. Reading Fern's passage out loud, with all its love nubs and shuddering, volconic eruption orgasms, was nothing compared to this. All eyes seemed to be on me. I started to feel panicky, but then an obvious solution appeared. It turned out everyone in the crochet group had brought along their tools. A few minutes later, I had a handful of hooks, and Adele cut lengths of her yarn. Will Hunter helped pass them and even kept a set for himself.

The pushing and shoving stopped, and the tone of the crowd turned excited as they all began making chains of stitches. Dinah gave me a thumbs-up.

"This is cool," Will said, showing me the coaster he'd made out of some of Adele's pink yarn. Natalie was standing next to him. She didn't have a hook or string, but she looked as though she could use one. There was a tired tension around her eyes.

By the time the group dispersed, all the books had sold, everyone had a hook and some string or yarn, along with the hope of losing a thousand pounds, and the café was cleaned out of rustic apple pie cookies.

As Natalie and Will headed toward the door, she stopped to say good-bye. "That was interesting," she said cryptically. "I'll have to let you know." Will gave me a little salute as they left. I noticed he took the hook and yarn with him.

THOUGH THE BOOKSTORE NEEDED MAJOR STRAIGHTening the next morning, money wise the event had been a big success. In addition to selling out Debbee's books, we'd moved a lot of crochet books and calorie counters. As I collected stray bits of string and abandoned coffee cups, I kept listening for the phone. Natalie had said she'd let me know, but she hadn't said when.

Since the whole Will Hunter venture was more important to me than to Natalie, I knew I might never hear from her. When there was no word from her by lunchtime, I cut to the chase and called. It seemed like a good sign when she took my call.

"I was going to get back to you later this afternoon," she said. Who knew whether that was publicist baloney or whether she'd really intended to. All I wanted now was the answer either way. Before I could get to my point, she began on hers.

"I like the way you handle things. I really meant it about having some work for you. There is just too much for me to do," she began. "It would be on a consultant basis, and Lawrence can't know about it. He keeps fussing with that blond detective for not arresting you." She asked me to come in the next day to discuss it. "I'm booked solid, so it'll have to be late," she said, suggesting I come to her office around nine-thirty p.m. "By the way, you were right: Ellen did have an appointment book. I was going through some things in her closet, and I saw the bag she used for a brief-case. And there it was."

"Did you look at her schedule? Who did Ellen have down for lunch?" It was hard to hide my impatience.

"It's not so much what was there—more what wasn't," Natalie said, hesitating. "You can look at it tomorrow and decide for yourself." There was some noise in the background, and Natalie seemed distracted. "Oh, I didn't real-ize you were here," she said to someone. She suddenly seemed anxious to get off the phone, and I had to rush to get in the real reason for my call—her answer about the book signing.

She sounded hurried. "I may be sorry for this, but okay. I like the idea of doing something different from what Ellen would have done."

I pumped my arm with a *yes* gesture as we agreed on a date.

When I got off the phone, at first all I could think of was that I had scored Will Hunter. But as I was congratulating myself, somewhere in the back of my mind it registered that if Natalie had been in Ellen's closet, she must have been in Lawrence's bedroom first.

CHAPTER 16

As I walked across the bookstore, I was mentally reeling off everything I had to do now that Will Hunter was a go. The crochet group was already in full swing, and I couldn't wait to tell Dinah the good news. And I was thankful I didn't have to tell Mrs. Shedd any bad news.

Just then, two women stepped in front of me and blocked my path. "We want to join the Tarzana Hookers," a woman with rust-colored hair said. She introduced herself as Stacy Hart and her friend, who had a brown ponytail, as Meg Hauser. "We were here last night," Stacy continued. "What a wonderful program. Who knew crochet had so much to offer?"

"We saw the column in the paper, too," Meg said in a conspiratorial voice as we approached the event area. She looked at the table and seemed awestruck, as if she suddenly found herself in the presence of Queen Elizabeth. "Wow, is CeeCee Collins in your group?" I almost thought she was going to curtsy when CeeCee looked up and smiled at the new arrivals.

"I just loved your weight-loss commercial. You were so inspiring," Meg gushed, though as her gaze wandered down CeeCee's body, it was obvious that she noticed some of the inspiring weight loss hadn't lasted.

"I grew up watching *The CeeCee Collins Show*," Stacy said. "Imagine, being able to crochet with a genuine legend."

CeeCee fluttered her eyelids and patted Stacy's hand. Somehow she pulled off being humble and the star in the same gesture.

I explained that Meg and Stacy wanted to join us.

"That's just wonderful," CeeCee said. They were still giving her awed looks, and CeeCee gestured toward a couple of chairs and introduced Dinah, Sheila and Adele.

"Where's the afghan we read about in the paper? It was just terrible about Elaine Sheridan," Meg said as they sat down.

"Ellen," I corrected.

"Whatever," Meg said, looking up and down the table. "Where are the squares that she made?"

Stacy nodded. "We want to make squares for it, too. We want to be part of history."

Adele got up and came beside the newbies. "Then you know how to crochet?"

"Sure. We learned last night," the redhead said as they both held up their hooks and string. Each had just a trail of chain stitches.

Adele touched the trail hanging off Meg's hook. "That's not quite crochet. These are just the foundation."

"Oh," Meg said, sounding deflated.

"But they're nice and loose," Sheila said from down the table. Dinah caught my gaze, and we both rolled our eyes. Even at our most clueless, we'd been better than that.

"Dear, I'm afraid the author's plan was more about keeping your hands out of a bag of chips than making anything."

"She said you could make a little coaster." Meg looked

at her trail of stitches and wrinkled her nose. "We got there kind of late. Maybe I missed part of what she said."

CeeCee's expression changed to impatience. "We're working under deadline and could certainly use some help. But you'd both have to learn how to crochet properly." Meg and Stacy both nodded in agreement, and CeeCee gestured toward Adele and said she'd teach them.

Adele didn't look that happy at being bossed around by CeeCee, but took the new members down to the end of the table anyway. She turned out to be a surprisingly patient teacher. Once she was satisfied that they understood single crochet, she left them to practice and rejoined the rest of us.

Finally I got a chance to tell Dinah the good news. She jumped up and hugged me.

CeeCee was laying out paper squares on the floor, in a life-size mock-up of the afghan. She placed the completed squares on top of the paper ones. She looked up at us and gave me a dirty look.

"Can't you save all that until after the group?" she said in an irritated tone. Sheila handed her four squares made out of blue heathery yarn. They seemed fuzzier than the others and had stitches that were much looser.

CeeCee shook her head in disgust. "I would think that by now you would know you have to use the same kind of yarn as the rest of us, and you can't use that giant hook."

Sheila's expression tightened before our eyes. Her shoulders hunched together, and instinctively she began to rub the back of her neck.

I couldn't believe how harsh CeeCee had been. Apparently Adele noticed, too. She picked up Sheila's work and patted her on the shoulder.

"The colors are a little bland for me, but you could make a great scarf out of these. All you have to do is make some more of them and join them together," Adele said. Sheila relaxed a little and thanked her for the suggestion.

"Where are the squares you did?" Adele asked CeeCee.

CeeCee suddenly looked disconcerted. "I've just been too busy the last few days with the face cream infomercial to think about anything else."

Adele shook her head in disapproval and showed off a stack she'd completed. "But you had time to make those paper squares?"

CeeCee's voice had now turned shrill. "I was just trying to keep things organized. It's the kind of thing Ellen would have done." The paper squares started to scatter, and CeeCee struggled to put them back the way they'd been. "They're all marked either done or not done, and I was going to hand out the not-done ones."

"I have some to count in the finished ones." I held out the three granny squares I had completed, and CeeCee took them with no comment. I was disappointed when she barely looked at them. I was really proud of my work. True, I'd had to unravel and start over again a number of times, and the three had taken much longer to make than I wanted to admit, but I thought the orange and light blue with the black border looked really nice.

Dinah gave her two she'd made. CeeCee seemed just as uninterested and dropped them in a pile on the floor. Adele leaned over and picked up one of mine. "Pink, you made this?" It was obvious by her tone that she thought my piece was good, but she sounded too surprised for it to come off as a compliment.

CeeCee finished laying our completed squares over the paper ones. But there were still way too many blanks. The newbies had stopped practicing and were hanging over the mock-up.

"Is that the murder blanket?" Stacy asked, gazing at it with a strange fascination.

CeeCee stood up and put her hands on her hips. "Dear, we like to think of it as Ellen's legacy, or the tribute afghan. Nobody is calling it a murder blanket. 'Murder blanket' sounds so negative," CeeCee said before asking to see their practice work.

"Have they figured out yet who did it?" Meg asked in a low voice. Then she directed her attention at me. "Weren't you the one who found her?"

"I bet it was her husband. That's who it always is," Stacy offered.

"We're not here to play detective," CeeCee snapped. She reached for the practice swatches Stacy and Meg had made, actually pulling them out of their hands. "Let's see what you've done."

I watched in amazement as CeeCee measured the swatches and counted stitches and rows, and was able to tell our new members how many of each they needed to do to end up with squares that would match the size of the rest of ours. She started to explain about making black borders and then threw up her hands.

"Just do what you can and we'll add the borders," she said impatiently. CeeCee glared at the rest of us. "Don't just sit there. Get those hooks going."

"She's sure in a mood," Dinah said, leaning close to me.

"I heard that," CeeCee said. "You'd be in a mood, too, if your name was attached to something and it looked like it was going to be a disaster."

I had a feeling she was talking about more than the afghan, and I asked how the infomercial was going. Her glare said it all, and I dropped it. For the rest of the time, we all crocheted in silence.

By the end, with the exception of the newbies, we had each completed another square. CeeCee didn't seem any happier as we handed them to her. She had collected all the blank paper squares, and she started handing them to Adele, Sheila, Dinah and me, telling us those were what we were responsible for. As an afterthought she took two from Dinah and me, and handed them to the newbies.

Adele's face looked stormy, and she complained about being lumped in with the rest of us when she was not only a top-of-the-line crocheter but at the very least cohead of the group. CeeCee ignored her comment and started to lecture all of us.

"We are running out of time. You need to take your crochet things with you everywhere, so you can work whenever you have a spare moment—"

"That's just what Debbee Stewart told us to do," Meg said, interrupting and holding up her hook and trail of chain stitches. She turned to the rest of us. "You're carrying, too, aren't you?"

It turned out that, with the exception of CeeCee, we had all taken Debbee's advice, and we all showed off our "Debbee's kits," as we'd come to call them.

"It isn't just about staying out of the chip bag," Sheila said. "I used mine at the gym. You wouldn't believe how fanatical those women are about getting their spaces in the classes. I took too long to scan some woman's card, and somebody else took her spot and she raised holy hell until I went in and got the first woman to move. It really made me tense, but I took out my hook and string and by the second row of single crochets, I felt the tension melt away. I want to get my boyfriend to carry one. He's been under a lot of stress lately."

Meg was taking what she had just learned and making a row of single crochets on the foundation chain and said she was going to make a coaster.

CeeCee looked more and more exasperated as the talking and string-crocheting continued, and then she just lost it.

"Didn't any of you hear me?" she shouted. "We need squares. Squares, ladies. Lots and lots of them. Made out of yarn, not string." She snatched Meg's two rows of work and unraveled them until they were just string again. "Stop making string coasters."

We were all staring at her. I had never seen CeeCee come so unglued. Sheila patted her arm and handed her a hook and some string.

"I think you need this more than I do."

CHAPTER 17

DINAH AND I DECIDED WE NEEDED A GIRLS' night out. Another Mr. Online had turned into Mr. Dud, and I wanted to get my mind off the fact that Detective Heather was still lurking around, trying to build a case against me. After CeeCee's meltdown during the group meeting, we figured she needed a night out, too, and we invited her to join us. But by then she seemed to have gotten over whatever was bothering her, and said she was busy.

When Dinah arrived at my house, we both laughed. We'd changed into nicer clothes, but courtesy of our identical choice of black slacks, black turtlenecks and black jackets, we looked like the ninja Bobbsey Twins.

The Encino restaurant we chose for dinner was located in an upscale shopping center with two levels of stores around a large pond with a series of waterfalls. Once seated in the dark booth we threw our diets to the wind and had fettuccine Alfredo, garlic bread and Caesar salad. We ended by sharing a piece of cheesecake.

We had planned on a movie, too, but when we came out of the restaurant, we realized it had already started.

"We might as well walk a little of dinner off." I pointed toward the walkway.

All during dinner, I'd managed not to talk about Ellen's murder, but as soon as we started walking, I couldn't help myself and brought up how we really hadn't gotten anywhere in our attempt to investigate.

"Sorry I haven't been much help," Dinah said. "I don't have much experience beyond reading mysteries and watching *Tina & Terry Bolton, PIs*, that fast-talking mother/daughter team of sleuths on television."

"They would have tied up this case by now for sure," I said, thinking of the TV team. Half the time the pair caught the guilty party by talking his or her ear off, and the culprit confessed just to get them to be quiet. Unfortunately in real life it wasn't that easy.

The stores were still open, and I noticed a sign for a yarn shop. Through the window we could see several women sitting around a table in the center, knitting.

"What do you think?" Dinah said as we stood looking inside. We'd never been in a real yarn store. So far all of our supplies had come from the Super Craft Mart, where the "always-friendly staff" knew nothing about yarn or hooks except where they were kept in the store.

All the yarn for the auction project had been purchased by Ellen and, since the bookstore was sponsoring it, paid for by Mrs. Shedd.

"Let's do it," I said, opening the door. Inside, the walls were lined with cubbies full of yarn. The knitters looked up as we passed their table, and then they went back to their work.

"Adele would have a fit," I said with a laugh. I watched their needles clack as they went back and forth on rows of knits and purls. It seemed boring compared to the excitement of going in a circle and then having spaces and yarn going around edges like I'd done in the granny square.

An older woman in a gorgeous heather blue sweater asked if she could help us.

I was going to say we were just looking, but before I knew it, I'd told her who we were.

"So you're part of the Tarzana Hookers," she said, nodding with recognition. "I saw the article in the paper. Too bad about your leader." The knitters looked up at us again. Was there just a note of superiority in their expressions?

"Crocheters are welcome here," she said, gesturing toward the cubbies full of yarn.

Dinah and I hesitated. "We've only shopped at the Super Craft Mart," I explained. Everyone in the place laughed.

"Comparing that place to here, it's like apples and oranges," the woman in the sweater said, leading us toward the back. The selection was amazing, and so different from the craft superstore. We wanted everything, but finally narrowed it down to some merino wool. We both left with lovely little shopping bags holding yarn to make a long scarf with a ruffly edge.

I couldn't wait to go home and start crocheting. The owner had tucked in printed instructions which said the pattern was rated "beginner."

On the way back to my place, we passed the Sheridan house. The lights were on, and there was a car in the driveway.

"Lawrence has company," I said. I couldn't tell what kind of car it was, but it appeared to be some type of small economy model. His Bentley was always parked in the garage. I pulled over to the curb and told Dinah how Natalie mentioned being in Ellen's closet. "I wonder if it's her."

The street was empty and quiet. The main foot traffic around here was pretty much restricted to the dog walkers in the morning, along with the joggers and the maids walking up from the bus stop. At night there was nobody beyond an occasional out-of-sync dog walker like me.

"I want to find out," I said, cutting the lights.

Even in the dark, I could see Dinah's stunned expression. "You mean like creep around and look in the windows?"

I nodded.

"I hate to bring it up, but isn't that trespassing?" she said.

"Only if we get caught, and we won't." I shrugged confidently, though I wasn't quite sure where the confidence was coming from. Dinah was usually the daring one.

"Okay, then, if you're in, so am I," Dinah said, ever up for an adventure. "I still can't believe he's already got another woman. Ellen's barely cold. So, if we catch him with Natalie, what are we going to do with the information?"

This time I groaned. "I haven't figured that part out yet."

I moved the greenmobile farther up the street so there would be no chance Lawrence or his guest could look out the window and see it. We closed the doors with hardly a click and headed across the street.

We stopped outside the fence and looked in. All the curtains were open, but the rooms appeared empty. I knew from being inside that we were facing the dining room, kitchen and two bedrooms, one of which was used as Ellen's crochet room and the other as the home office.

"We've got to get in the backyard. They're probably in the living room or den," I said, crouching low and slipping around the side of the house.

"Or the master bedroom," Dinah whispered, following me.

"I hope not. I don't think I'm ready for Lawrence in boxer shorts or less," I said as we reached the gate.

It had a lock.

"Let's try the other side," I whispered.

We stayed low and tried the gate by the garage, but it was locked, too.

"Well, I guess that's it," Dinah said. We crept past the bushes and went back toward the street. My back said a big thank-you when I stood up. I gave it a few rubs as I looked back at the house.

"Didn't this sort of thing used to be easier?" I said.

Dinah laughed. "You've done stuff like this before?" Dinah started toward the car, but I stayed put.

"I don't want to give up. I want to see who is with Lawrence."

"I don't think there's a choice," Dinah said, putting up her hands in capitulation.

Not making a move to leave, I surveyed the area. Then I smiled. I had a fabulous idea. "We can get in through there," I said, pointing at the property next door. When Dinah hesitated, I indicated the FOR SALE sign out front and explained that the house was empty. Dinah smiled, and she gave me a thumbs-up.

The gate to the yard was ajar, so there was no problem walking onto the property. The backyard was easily accessible, too. Everything had been left open to make it easy for prospective buyers to look around.

The backyard was big and dark. The border with the Sheridans' was thick with ivy and tall bushes, which were probably filled with spiders and other creepy things.

"There's a chain-link fence behind all the foliage, and there's probably a gate somewhere," I told Dinah. "When these houses were first built, this was out in the sticks, and nobody was all bent out of shape about security. All the fences had gates so the kids in the area could cut through yards. My house has the same kind of fence behind the bushes and ivy, and there's a gate somewhere on each side."

I pushed behind the row of greenery until I touched metal. Dinah kept close behind me as I began to feel my way along the fence. Something scampered through the bushes, brushing past us. Dinah started to squeal, but caught herself and muffled it. "What was that?"

"I don't think we want to know," I said, moving along the chain-link barrier.

"Is it really that important to find out who's visiting Lawrence?"

"What happened to your sense of adventure?"

"It ended when something crawled inside my ear," she said in a frantic whisper. She squirmed around, and I heard her brush something off as she made an *ew* sound.

"Found it," I said, feeling the post and then metal top of the gate. It was old and probably rusted, but with some jiggling, it finally opened. We slipped through and hit another wall of greenery on the Sheridan side. I remembered admiring it the day I found Ellen. The whole perimeter of the yard was filled with trees and artfully trimmed bushes. Beautiful to look at, but difficult to get through. We had to feel our way until we found some kind of opening in the hedge. Dinah was holding on to my belt loop by now and brushing things away from her face.

We managed to squeeze through, but not without getting souvenir leaves and twigs stuck in our hair and clothes. Dinah met up with more crawly things and did her best not to shriek.

The crouching had gotten painful, and we began to crawl around the side of the yard. It saved our backs, but our knees paid the price. The Sheridans apparently weren't big on window coverings, and just like in the front, all the windows on the back of the house were exposed.

With a certain degree of relief, I noticed that while the lights were on in the master bedroom, it appeared empty. No chance of seeing Lawrence in his undies. Yay.

The living room seemed to be where the action was. I made out the top of Lawrence's head, but couldn't see into the room well enough to make out whom he was with. We'd have to get closer.

I sent up a silent prayer for our convenient clothing choices. Not only did the ninja black make us hard to see as we crawled along the edge of the yard toward the house, but all the grass and mud stains would hardly show. We turned when we reached the perimeter of the house, and crawled through the flower bed past all the windows until we reached the living room.

A little voice in my head went off, asking me if I had lost my mind. Was I really crawling through the Sheridans' backyard? Thank heavens Barry didn't know.

We were right below the living room. Just a little peek, and I'd have my answer. I swallowed a few times and gathered up my courage. Slowly I began to inch up. Finally I took the plunge and lifted my head eye-level with the window. I dropped down abruptly.

"Who is it?" Dinah demanded.

"It can't be. You look," I said. Dinah did the same sort of move I had done.

She dropped down and was about to say something when two things happened that changed everything. From inside, the black poodle began to bark, and from outside, the sprinklers went on.

I heard the sound of someone unlocking one of the French doors.

I grabbed Dinah's hand, and we made a run for it across the yard through the cold spray. The dog ran out and stopped at the sprinklers, but kept up the barking. I caught a glimpse of Lawrence peering out into the darkness. "Stop," he yelled.

Like we were really going to do that. I pushed Dinah into the bushes and we found our way to the gate. Somewhere Dinah lost a shoe, and I really had to go to the bathroom, but we made it out into the other yard. With amazing energy and grace, we ran to my car, started the motor and pulled away.

By the time we got the two blocks to my house, we

heard the unmistakable *thwack* of a police helicopter as it began circling the area, flashing down its bright beam.

Only when we were inside and we had collapsed on the couch did Dinah and I look at each other.

"What was Sheila doing with Lawrence Sheridan?" I said.

"Do you think she's Miss Water Glass?" Dinah said, referring to my discovery during my snooping when the crochet group had met at the Sheridans' to get the squares. "Wow, she's really full of surprises. First she starts making those gorgeous scarves, and now we find her hanging out with Lawrence. Go figure."

As soon as the helicopter gave up, a soggy Dinah hobbled out on one shoe and went home. I changed into dry clothes but was too wired to do anything. Finally, glad that CeeCee couldn't see what I was working on, I pulled out the yarn store shopping bag and began making the chain-stitch foundation for my scarf. The phone rang, making me jump. It was Barry on his cell, telling me that he and Jeffrey were at my back door, which for once was locked.

I let them in, trying to act as if everything was normal.

"We were on our way home when I saw the helicopter," Barry explained. "I wanted to make sure you were all right. The 911 call said something about an intruder in the Sheridan backyard." He gave me a funny look.

"Really?" I said innocently. "I've just been here crocheting." I held up the beginning of the ruffly scarf. But then Barry leaned toward me and pulled a twig and a leaf out of my hair.

CHAPTER 18

AFTER THE LEAF REMOVAL MANEUVER, BARRY and Jeffrey hung around for a while. Being the good detective he was, Barry got me to spill everything about our backyard adventure. I tried to tell him about Lawrence and Sheila, but he waved it off.

"Are you out of your mind?" His tone was serious. "Just think, if Sheridan had seen it was you."

"But I am just trying to find out who really killed Ellen Sheridan," I protested.

"You have something more immediate to worry about." He'd cornered Detective Heather's partner and found out she was close to making an arrest. "Molly, honey, I hate to tell you this, and I hate even more that there doesn't seem to be anything I can do about it—but the someone she's about to arrest is you."

"Me!" I shrieked, feeling my legs go weak. Barry noticed and started to put his arm around my waist for support, but he glanced toward Jeffrey and held my arm instead.

"Molly, you should line up an attorney." He was all business, and the exhilaration of escaping the yard was replaced by a feeling of doom.

"Maybe this is when I should take off for Brazil," I said.

"This isn't a joke. I mean it about the attorney." He made a move toward me again, but looked over at Jeffrey playing with the dog and stopped himself. Blondie had appeared when they came in and immediately bonded with Jeffrey. It was the happiest I'd seen Jeffrey, and the most excited I'd seen Blondie.

I told him Peter already had somebody in mind. Barry seemed relieved, but not when he heard I didn't even have the lawyer's number.

"This is really serious. You should talk to him and make arrangements."

I gave him my best you-don't-really-mean-that look, and he just gave me his serious-detective blank face back.

Barry reluctantly looked at his watch and said something about having to get Jeffrey home. It was obvious neither one of them wanted to go, but Barry was caught up in doing his superconscientious dad act. Because of his son's presence, Barry gave me a restrained hug and whispered that he'd try to come back later. Blondie followed them to the door, and Jeffrey gave her a final pat before they walked out.

I looked back at my crocheting and realized I'd totally lost my place in the foundation chain for the scarf. I tried counting all the chain stitches, but my mind kept wandering. I'd been worried before, but it was somehow vague and I was able to brush it off. It was just too ridiculous to think anyone could believe I killed somebody. I was the person who wrapped up spiders in paper towels and took them outside rather than squashing them. But having Barry tell me to find an attorney meant it was serious, real.

Even if I did get arrested, I'd get off, right? Maybe there were a few facts that made me look guilty, like I was found hanging over the body. And yes, I did seem to be doing better since Ellen died. I felt a shiver of doom. It probably didn't help either that Lawrence seemed convinced I did it, and he had probably been complaining to some bigwig that I was free on the street while his wife was dead. Didn't anyone see that he might be making all that noise to get the spotlight off of himself? That thought brought me back to the earlier adventure and seeing Sheila with Lawrence.

She hadn't been *with him*, with him. They weren't touching or anything, but there was a definite friendliness in their eye contact. I racked my brain trying to remember what Sheila had said about her boyfriend. He'd done some kind of intervention to get her on drugs for her nerves, which sounded like the kind of thing Lawrence might try. He wasn't your meditation sort of guy. Ah, but she'd said they'd broken up when she wouldn't go for it. Then I remembered something she said at the crochet group about her boyfriend being stressed, which had to mean they were back together. Lawrence and Sheila? They weren't a couple I would put together if I were playing matchmaker, but, then, who knew what attracted people to each other?

I finally undid the whole chain and tried to start at the beginning, determined to keep track of my ten-stitch groups. The phone rang, and it was Barry. He apologized for not being able to make it back. Work called. He didn't give any details, but I knew it was a body or bodies with blood and who knew what other gore. I would be freaked if that was facing me. Not Barry. There was a hint of excitement in his voice. I wondered whether an outsider would think we were an odd couple.

I was feeling hopeless with my foundation chain. Maybe someday I'd be able to think about other things while crocheting, but not yet. I still needed to give it my full attention, and that just wasn't going to happen now. As I put the yarn back into the shopping bag, I remembered my meeting with Natalie and felt a ray of hope. Maybe Ellen's appoint-

ment book would get me off the hook. That was, if I didn't
get arrested first.

My eyes were swimming with sleepiness by now. I went
to bed and hoped for happy dreams.

I spent the next day looking out for Detective Heather
and her handcuffs. Every time someone came in the bookstore, I was afraid it was her, but she never showed. Adele
and I spent our break together working on squares for the
blanket. I didn't tell Adele, but I wanted to do as much as I
could in case I got arrested. Though I was still in a certain
degree of denial.

I refused to think of what a shambles it would make of
my life. It had been an uphill battle since Charlie's death,
and I was just beginning to see the light. Would I get fired?
Would the crochet group shun me? Would Adele get my
job? At least Jeffrey would take care of Blondie for me.

I worked late at the bookstore, putting everything in order just in case, even though Barry had said he thought I
would get bonded out quickly. I was relieved to still be a
free person when I left the bookstore and headed over to
Natalie's office.

Natalie had told me to come to her office so late, it
seemed as though she was practically living there. It had to
be a daunting task to run the public-relations firm and try to
convince all of Ellen's clients to stay, on top of doing all
the hand-holding chores such as showing up at CeeCee's
commercial shoot.

The front parking lot was almost empty, and I supposed
the one in the back was, too. It was well after office hours,
and the retail stores and restaurants were all closed. It felt a
little eerie to go into the empty office building. The elevator stood open and waiting.

I had my fingers crossed that something in that date
book would point to somebody else, though I still hadn't
figured how I would get that information to Detective
Heather.

The corridor was silent as I turned down the hall. All the other offices were closed and their inhabitants long gone.

At the end, I saw the door with the new sign: PSS PR. No matter how modern it was, it still looked stupid to me. But Natalie was going for a whole new look. I had my hand on the door and was pulling it open when it pushed toward me from the inside. I almost choked when I looked up and found myself eye to eye with Detective Heather.

Instinctively I put my hands in my pockets.

"What are you doing here?" she demanded.

"I have an appointment to see Natalie Shaw," I said, trying to look beyond her and into the office. "Is something wrong?"

"I'm the one who gets to ask the questions," she said curtly and then told me to wait in the hall. "And don't go anywhere," she commanded before closing the door.

My automatic thought was to run, but I stopped myself. Like where was I going to go that she couldn't find me? I'd wait and deal with the consequences, even if it felt as if my heart was going to thump its way out of my chest. It seemed like eternity but was more like ten minutes when another detective opened the door. I recognized him as Detective Heather's partner, Rick Allen. I closed my eyes and held out my hands, waiting for the feeling of cold metal and the inevitable click as the handcuffs locked shut.

After a moment when I felt and heard nothing, I opened my eyes. The detective was looking at me oddly.

"You okay?" he said. I nodded, though I was feeling a little queasy from nerves. Before he could blink, I'd pulled my hands down and out of sight. "What are you doing here?" he asked in a benign tone.

"I had an appointment to see Natalie Shaw. What's going on?" I again tried to see into the office.

"It might be better if you sat down." He took me into the reception area. His suggestion of sitting down made me tense up again. I figured he wanted me to sit because I might fall down when he said whatever he had to say. Somebody had gone overboard with air freshener, and the fragrance only added to my unease. That was when I noticed there was yellow tape across the entrance to Natalie's office.

He took out a recorder and a notebook and pen. "I'd like to ask you a few questions here. It seems more efficient than going to the station. Is that okay?"

My heart rate accelerated. This was beginning to remind me of the Ellen episode. I nodded, and he asked for my personal information and took it down.

"How well did you know Natalie Shaw?"

"Something happened to her, didn't it?" I said, staring at the yellow-tape barricade.

He looked at me levelly. "Natalie Shaw is dead."

I swallowed hard, and for a moment the room started to spin. I was glad I was sitting, because my legs suddenly felt like they were made out of Gummi Worms.

"I had nothing to do with it. I wasn't even here. Why would I kill her? She agreed to the Will Hunter book signing, and she wants to give me work. Where were all of you, anyway? The parking lot was empty when I got here."

He put up his hands to stop me. "One of the cleaning crew found her in the courtyard and called 911. The first officers and the rescue ambulance went into the other parking lot." He gestured toward the back and then looked at me directly. "It appears she jumped off the balcony. There was a note on her computer."

"Suicide?" I said, choking on the word. "But she was just getting what she always wanted." I explained how she had worked for Ellen and been pretty much an invisible slave, and now she was in charge.

"In the note she confessed to killing Ellen Sheridan and said she couldn't live with herself anymore."

If my legs had felt weak before, they felt like they had

melted now. I was having trouble wrapping my mind around what he was saying. Natalie was dead? And she had killed Ellen?

He asked me again how I knew Natalie. Somehow I pulled my thoughts together and told him my whole history with Natalie, from my last day at Pink Sheridan to the present.

"How has her mood been lately?"

I explained that she had been stressed out trying to keep all the clients from leaving after Ellen died. "But she seemed like she was happy with what she was doing. Her dreams were coming true. . . ." I let my words trail off as another thought made its way into my mind. If Natalie had confessed to killing Ellen, they couldn't arrest me. There would be no middle-of-the-night raid with Detective Heather barging into my bedroom and handcuffing me. I didn't have to worry about a lawyer anymore or how to make bail. I was embarrassed by my own self-serving thoughts in the face of everything, but I also felt a tremendous sense of relief.

It was a tidy little circle. Killer confesses and then kills self. However, when you knew the actual people in that circle, it wasn't tidy anymore. It was shocking. I knew without looking in a mirror that I could give any ghost a run for their money in the paleness department. The blood that had drained from my face had pooled in my rubbery legs, and I felt light-headed.

Detective Allen appeared concerned and asked if I was all right to drive. I appreciated his thought, but I just wanted to get out of there, and I assured him I was fine.

"Of course there will be an investigation, but I doubt anything will change," he said as I hobbled out the door.

I held on to the wall as I made my way to the elevator. I realized why Detective Heather had sent her partner: Her whole plan had just collapsed, and she probably couldn't stand to be the one to tell me.

The cool night air revived me as I walked outside. The

front parking lot was no longer quiet. There were several police cruisers, and the news vans had just started arriving. How convenient for them; it was just in time for the eleven o'clock news. The loud *thwack* of several helicopters announced the arrival of their partners in the sky. As the only person exiting the building, I suddenly found myself surrounded, as though it was some kind of news conference.

The reporters already had the basic details, and were running with the idea the suicide note was also a confession. Having celebrities involved upped the ante of the story.

"I understand Will Hunter was one of Shaw's clients, and was Ellen Sheridan's client before her death. What's he going to do?" The eager young reporter from Channel 3 stuck a microphone in front of me. I tried to explain that I wasn't Will's spokesperson. They kept badgering me with questions, hoping I'd give them something good. Poor CeeCee would be upset that no one was asking about her.

One of the reporters brought up the fact that I had been at the Ellen Sheridan murder scene. In an effort to say something, without regard for how stupid it was, she asked me if I was some kind of death groupie.

I finally escaped and went to my car. As I was getting in, I noticed another car parked next to me. It had a lighted Yummie Pizza sign on top, and there was someone in the driver's seat. The door opened, and he hopped out and grabbed an insulated bag from the back. He looked at the news vans and police cars, and stayed put.

"What's going on?" he asked me. He looked about eighteen, and nervous.

I gave him the rundown, and he looked more uneasy. "Her name wasn't Natalie Shaw, was it?"

When I nodded, he looked worse. "My boss is going to be pissed. It's the second time this week I've shown up with a pizza and not been able to deliver it. It's not like it's my fault. The first one was a prank, and this time it's a dead woman."

I felt for him. Peter'd had a delivery job during high school. I paid the kid for the pizza and put it in my car. The kid seemed relieved and thanked me before he drove off.

Once I was back home, I saved Peter the trouble and called him. His response surprised me: no recriminations for showing up on the news again. He didn't even mention the death-groupie comment.

"Are you okay, Mother?" He sounded genuinely concerned about me. "You looked pretty pasty."

I assured him that I had recovered, and the pasty look was more a product of the news van's lights. That wasn't altogether true, but it was hard to admit weakness to my son. "You can cancel the attorney. I don't think I'll be needing him now."

Peter breathed a sigh of relief. "I'm glad. Brunch can be a celebration of sorts. No more worries."

I agreed before hanging up, though I didn't feel much like celebrating. Yes, I was off the hook, but Natalie was dead. Then there was a barrage of phone calls, from Dinah, the crochet group and Samuel, all expressing shock and wanting to know if I knew any secret details. Barry also called on his cell from the back door, which was locked again. He hugged me and seemed relieved.

"Now I won't have to get you a cake with a file in it," he said as we sat down in the living room. I expressed some concern about Natalie's death, but he cut me off.

"I'm just glad you aren't a suspect anymore. You don't know how close it was."

"And I probably don't want to know, either."

"Where'd the pizza come from?" he asked, opening the box on the coffee table. Without waiting for an answer, he helped himself to a piece. When he lifted the lid, the order invoice fluttered to the floor. I picked it up and read it.

"Why would Natalie call up and order a pizza to be delivered at ten p.m. if she was planning to kill herself?"

CHAPTER 19

"DEAR, I THOUGHT THAT DEATH-GROUPIE COM-
ment was a little crude," CeeCee said as I joined the group
at the event table the next day. I was glad to see that
CeeCee appeared to be back to her usual self, although I
got in at the tail end of her reprimanding everyone for not
crocheting more squares on their own time. CeeCee un-
zipped her amethyst-colored warm-up jacket and set out
skeins of different-colored yarn. "Though I suppose it must
have seemed strange to the reporters, running into you at
both scenes." She shook her head. "I can't get used to the
idea that Natalie killed Ellen. I mean, it was obvious that
she stood to gain from Ellen's death. But then to take her
own life . . . Well, at least it closes the circle."

"It leaves you in kind of a bind, doesn't it? Who's going
to handle your publicity now?"

"I hardly thought about it." CeeCee's comment was a
little too quick, and it gave the opposite impression. I was
sure she had figured it out exactly. "For now I think I'll just

handle things myself. Who knows what will become of the business?"

"Pink, what were you doing there so late, anyway?" Adele joined CeeCee at the head of the table. She seemed to be trying a toned-down look, wearing boxy jeans with layered tank tops of different shades of blue under a safari jacket. She'd pulled her hair back into a minuscule ponytail with the help of an army of hair clips. When I explained that it had been about doing some consulting work for Natalie, Adele looked pleased, then stricken as the reality that it wasn't going to happen sank in.

CeeCee interrupted and said she thought we ought to have a moment of silence for Natalie. We all agreed and spent a minute looking down. When it was done, everything was back to business as usual.

"If you had worked for Natalie, it would have been hard for you to keep your job here," Adele said, dejected. When CeeCee and I gave her a dirty look, she protested, "It's not like with Ellen. We barely knew Natalie."

With Dinah's arrival, we got down to business. Stacy and Meg had come back and begun working on single-color squares. Two other women had shown up, brought in by the book signing. They shared in the moment of silence, even though they didn't have a clue who Natalie was.

"I hope you two know something about crochet," CeeCee said. They pulled out their hooks and lengths of string and held them up proudly. Then they displayed their string coasters.

CeeCee hit her forehead with the heel of her hand. She looked at Adele. "You deal with them." Then she leaned close to me. "It's nice that we're getting more members, but they're more hindrance than help. Nobody seems to understand that we're facing a crisis."

"Which reminds me," I said. "The chairwoman from the charity called me all frantic. She was shocked about Natalie and suddenly very nervous about the afghan. She wanted some word on its progress."

CeeCee and Adele both swivelled their heads toward me. "She called you?" they said in unison. "Why didn't she call me?" Again said together by the pair.

"That was probably the work Natalie was going to give me, handling her pro bono clients. She probably gave them the number and told her to deal with me before she . . ." I couldn't say the rest. CeeCee and Adele bought the excuse and relaxed.

"We really need to change the subject to something more cheerful," CeeCee said. Appearing to have a sudden thought, she patted her face. "What do you think of this face cream? I could swear I see the years melting away every time I look in the mirror."

Adele looked and shook her head. "You look the same to me."

"We have to talk," Dinah said, sitting down next to me.

"Not here, not now," I said between my teeth.

Sheila had a pile of string coasters next to her work. It must have helped relax her, because she was busy at work on a patterned square and for once seemed to be having no trouble with too-tight stitches. Dinah and I both watched her. . I knew we were thinking the same thing. *Sheila and Lawrence?*

Adele stayed with the newest of the newbies and looked at their swatches. The two women eyed her like she was some kind of crochet goddess. Sensing that she was finally on the pedestal where she belonged, Adele drank it in. When she finished with them, they looked over at me.

"Wow, you're the death groupie," one of the newbies said. Her name was Jen, and she came in the bookstore a lot with her young kids. She was all bright eyed and enthusiastic. "You keep turning up on the news, don't you? I saw you when they found Ellen Sheridan . . ." She stopped herself.

"Maybe that's an uncomfortable topic. Since she was your founder and everything."

"Ladies, I know we are all very saddened by the death of Natalie Shaw, but we really need to be putting this energy into crocheting. We are getting closer and closer to the date of the auction." CeeCee glanced around the table.

"Who was Natalie Shaw?" the other newbie asked. Her name was Bonnie, and she had great hopes of losing enough weight with the crochet plan that she'd be able to wear a size two.

CeeCee explained who Natalie Shaw was and said she'd committed suicide out of guilt for having killed Ellen Sheridan.

"And Ellen Sheridan was?" Bonnie asked, appearing confused.

I left CeeCee to explain. I picked up my crochet hook and some yarn and tried to just concentrate on making a granny square. Dinah leaned in close.

"Lunch after?" she said. "Then we can talk." She glanced at my granny square and gave me a thumbs-up.

AN HOUR LATER DINAH AND I WERE SITTING IN the corner booth of a Thai restaurant down the street from the bookstore.

"Tell me everything. Last night on the phone you sounded shocked, overwrought and not too coherent."

"I think I earned the right to sound that way after the night I had."

"Did I hear you right? You mumbled something about Natalie not really killing herself."

"Okay, here it is. Would you order a pizza if you were going to kill yourself?"

Dinah considered it. "She ordered a pizza?"

I waved the receipt and told her how I'd ended up with it.

"What did Barry say?"

"He said to leave it alone. He'd seen the report. There was no sign of a struggle in the office or on the balcony. He was short on details of how she looked when they found her. I'm sure it wasn't good. He said sometimes a cigar is just a cigar."

"I see his point," Dinah said, "particularly since you are now off the hook. Why would you want to stir things up and put yourself back on the hook? You did show up at the crime scene. I can't believe Detective Heather isn't trying to pin it on you."

"She was at the office before I got there. It turned out all the cop cars and rescue ambulances were in the back parking lot. I know I should leave it alone like Barry says, but I just can't."

Dinah nodded. "I hear you. So where do we start?"

"By ordering lunch. No good detective works hungry," I said as the waitress came to the table. "The pad Thai is the best."

Since I had the afternoon off and Dinah didn't have a class until evening, we stopped by Yummie Pizza after lunch. An older man with *Hal* embroidered on his shirt was behind the counter. I showed him the receipt and asked what he knew about it.

"Was there a problem with the pizza? We have a money-back guarantee." He pulled out a form in triplicate. "Just fill this out and send it in, and in six to ten weeks, Corporate will send you a coupon for a free pizza."

"That's not it," I said, pushing the form back toward him. I was glad it wasn't. That was an awfully long wait on a money-back guarantee, and a coupon didn't seem as though it would count as money back. But all that was really beside the point. "I wondered what time the order came in and who exactly ordered it." As an afterthought I added, "It wasn't a standing order, was it?" That, I realized, would have taken the wind right out of my investigative sails.

Hal looked from me to Dinah and shook his head. "Who are you ladies and why are you asking all these questions?"

I made the mistake of telling the truth. "It's about a suicide that we don't think is a suicide. Like, why would someone order a pizza if they were going to . . . ?"

"Unless you're cops, which I highly doubt," he said in unfriendly tone, "I'm not answering any more of your questions. And if you think about it, you should be glad. You can order from Yummie with confidence that your privacy will be respected."

"That went well," I said when we were outside.

"I could have told you honesty was definitely not the best policy in this case. Did you see his face when you said the word 'suicide'? I thought he was going to call the cops."

We were standing around the front, trying to figure out our next move, when a car with a Yummie Pizza sign stuck on top pulled in. A teenage boy got out, holding an empty insulated carrier.

"Hey, Mrs. Lyons," he called as he crossed the sidewalk. "You waiting for a pizza?"

Dinah's face brightened. "Jason?"

He took off his baseball cap, which as I recalled had been the problem when I saw him in Dinah's office.

"You can put the cap back on. I never meant that you had to take it off in my presence. Just in class. So, you work here?"

He balanced the carrier on his hip and flipped the hat back on. "You've broken me, Mrs. Lyons. My mom wanted to know what happened. All I did was open the car door for her. I thought she was going to freak or something."

Dinah showed him the receipt and asked the same questions I had. Jason might have improved his manners, but he was still low on the curiosity scale. He never asked why; he just told us what we wanted to know.

He could tell that the pizza had been ordered at eight p.m. by Natalie, to be delivered at ten p.m., and it wasn't a standing order. Hal apparently always marked those with a "reg," so the delivery person would give them extra-good service. Jason looked at the receipt again. "I know her. I delivered to her a couple of times. She worked late a lot and gave big tips. I made some comment that she must have a really tough boss to make her work so late, but she said she was the boss and she didn't mind. Different strokes, I guess." He handed back the receipt. "If you guys want a pizza, I get a discount. We're having a special this week on stuffed pizza. Everybody loves that double crust," he said, the last part sounding like a well-practiced pitch, like the ones you hear from restaurant waiters trying to get you to order fancy appetizers with some catchy phrase.

Dinah thanked him but said we'd just had lunch. She also told him she'd finished marking his paper and that he had really made a big improvement quickly.

He did some kind of happy dance that included pointing at her and saying, "You're the man."

"I can't believe he's the same kid I saw slouching in your office," I said as we walked away.

"It's just the Lyons effect," she said with a chuckle. "I take overaged high school kids and turn them into college students."

We got in the greenmobile, and Dinah read over the receipt. "I can't believe Barry told you to drop it."

"Really what he said was to stay out of it. He said they do a psychological autopsy to make sure it really is a suicide. Now that I'm no longer a suspect, he's started telling me how much it bothered him that he hadn't been able to do anything. And he finally accepted that Detective Heather was trying to get me out of the way, but apparently she was so cool about it, even her partner didn't get that she had an agenda."

There was more. I mentioned that Barry had waved a brochure for a resort in Maui in front of my face.

His exact words had been, "Just imagine three days and

nights in paradise, alone with me. Just moonlight, and mai tais, and absolutely no murder."

"Sounds nice," Dinah said.

"I told him I couldn't think about it right now. There is so much going on at the bookstore. The crochet group is fighting a deadline." I sighed. "And the Will Hunter thing is up in the air now that Natalie is gone."

"I'm sure Mrs. Shedd will understand," Dinah said.

I shook my head. "That's not it. I need to pull off something big for the bookstore. It's not just that his appearance would bring in people; it could also open the door to other celebrity signings. We'd be *the* place in the Valley. And there's something else," I said, dropping my voice. "I need to prove that Mrs. Shedd was right about hiring me." Dinah gave my arm a sympathetic squeeze and reassured me that Mrs. Shedd probably already felt that way.

"What was Super Dad going to do with Jeffrey?" Dinah asked, bringing the subject back to Barry's proposed trip.

I shrugged it off. "It was all very somedayish. We never talked dates, and I didn't say yes."

Dinah's expression said it all. She would have locked in the trip.

I steered the car out into the traffic on Ventura Boulevard and headed east. "I was thinking we'd stop by and see what's happening to Pink Sheridan."

"Sounds like a good idea," Dinah said.

Everything seemed back to normal at the office and retail center. The front parking lot was full, and people were going in and out of the stores and restaurants as if nothing had happened in the courtyard.

Dinah followed close behind as I walked in the front door of the building. This time I didn't go upstairs, but headed for the door that led to the courtyard. The building was shaped like a U around it. Along the back there was a one-story building with a jewelry store and another that sold educational toys. Behind that was the back parking lot.

Outside in the courtyard, it looked like just another warm September day. The created creek meandered between minihills that were landscaped to death, with bushes and flowers and patches of grass. Around the edge there was a big concrete walkway.

I looked up at the wooden stairway. It led to the balconies that ran along each floor that housed offices. I noticed remnants of yellow police tape flapping in the breeze on the fourth floor.

My eyes traveled straight down. I shuddered. Orange cones sectioned off a small area of the concrete, and I realized that was where Natalie had landed. When we reached the cones, I shuddered again. The concrete appeared mottled, as if it had been cleaned but everything wouldn't come up.

"We're going to redo the sidewalk there," a man in a sport jacket and slacks said. He held out his hand and introduced himself as Derek Sanderson, the leasing agent for the center. "You ladies are the ones who called about leasing some space?" He smiled with artificial friendliness.

Dinah and I looked at each other, and I took the lead. Why not take this unexpected opportunity?

"It was just terrible what happened." I gestured up toward the PSS PR office. "What's going to happen to their space?"

Derek did the salesman thing of telling me he had something much better to show us, and he pointed to an empty suite on the second floor. "And what line of work are you ladies in?" He glanced at our clothes, which did look a bit casual for two titans of industry.

"Tutoring. We run a tutoring service," Dinah said, winking at me. She explained she was an instructor at Beasley Community College. She started a rant on how unprepared all the students were, explaining that our tutoring service was to catch them while they were still in high school. I watched Derek's eyes glaze over, and he waved his hand and nodded.

"That office will be perfect for you."

I nodded, then glanced back up toward the fourth floor. "Is that where it happened?"

Derek tried to avoid the subject. "We're having the railing redone to make it higher."

"But that's where she fell?" I said, getting dizzy thinking about what it would be like to go over the edge.

"Jumped," he corrected. "No matter what anybody says, we're not liable. But, ladies, let's not be morbid," he said in a cheerful tone. He gestured for us to follow him to the available office.

"We're really interested in that one." I pointed up toward the fourth floor. I could hear Derek groaning quietly. "Is it available?"

"You're not lookie-loo crime-scene groupies, are you?" We both shook our heads vehemently. "We've seen a lot of those." He adopted a singsongy voice. "They want to be part of history. That's what they all say."

I rolled my eyes at Dinah. We both thought that be-part-of-history business was way overused. Being invited to the presidential inaugural ball counted as being part of history. Seeing a crime scene or making some squares for a charity afghan connected to a dead woman did not.

Derek hesitated, but finally relented. I guess he decided it was better to err on the side of our being what we actually said we were, on the slight chance we were legit. I felt just the smallest smidgen of guilt at misleading him, but, then, I wasn't there like the others with their morbid curiosity. I was investigating.

He took us inside to the elevator. As we rode up, he suddenly got chatty and said that the public-relations firm was going to be relocating to some talent-management company in the city. This office wasn't immediately available like the second-floor one, but if we had our hearts set on it, he was sure arrangements could be made.

It felt strange going inside, and I was surprised to hear

voices. Derek explained that the office staff was still working there. He assured us the office would be recarpeted,
pointing to a round stain in the center of the reception area.
I bent down to look at it more closely. Derek said they'd
shampooed it several times, but the spot wouldn't come
out. I touched it, and it felt faintly greasy. Instinctively I
sniffed my fingers, but the scent of freshly brewed coffee
overpowered any residue.

Leo, the receptionist, was sipping the source of the fragrance at his desk, and I was relieved that he didn't seem to
recognize me. Mostly, he just looked stunned.

Derek Sanderson seemed anxious to have us look and
leave. But I didn't need to check *The Average Joe's Guide
to Criminal Investigation* to know I should seize the opportunity. I boldly walked into Natalie's office as if checking
out the dimensions. I glanced at the desktop, hoping to see
CeeCee's file, but it was clear. Any drawer-opening was out
of the question under the circumstances, but there might be
a way I could check out the boxes lined up against the wall.
If Ellen's appointment book was in one of them, this was
the only chance I'd get to look for it.

I made some excuse about wanting to check the window
and wall sizes, saying the office was just what we were
looking for. I even got Derek to get me a tape measure.

Dinah picked up on what I was doing and distracted him
as I supposedly measured. While supposedly taking notes
on the sizes, I kept conveniently dropping my pencil into
boxes, which gave me a perfect excuse to ruffle through
their contents.

Dinah kept talking at Derek Sanderson, lecturing him
on the trickle-down effect of our supposed tutoring center.
She was so convincing, I almost believed we were doing it.
But she could only hold his attention so long. I needed to
move fast and unobtrusively. Luckily, nobody seemed to
notice I had to be the klutziest person on earth. Most of the
open-top boxes seemed to contain papers and things like

press kits and office supplies. I was down to two boxes and beginning to lose hope. I'd gone from dropping my pencil to letting the tape measure slip. I bent down to rummage and felt my heart rate go up. Next to a file of newspaper clippings there was a medium-size leather notebook. I flipped it over, and my breath caught. Its cover said AP-POINTMENTS in gold letters. My hands were shaking as I opened it and thumbed through the pages. I was so intent on my mission, I didn't hear the real estate agent's cell phone go off. The pages stuck together as I tried to locate the page for the day Ellen died.

"Hey, what are you doing?" Sanderson yelled, staring at me as he flipped his phone shut. He stepped over, grabbed the book out of my hand and dropped it into the box.

He grasped my arm and then Dinah's and hustled us out the door. "Not lookie-loos, my foot. I should call the cops."

As we stepped out into the hall, two women in black power suits approached. He gave us a rough push toward the elevators and turned on a full-beam smile at them.

It wasn't until we were safely ensconced in Starbucks that my heart stopped pounding. "I can't believe how close I was, again. If only the pages hadn't stuck together, I might have seen the page before he ripped the book out of my hands."

Dinah tried to make me feel better, saying I had done the best I could. Then she asked me about the last time I'd talked to Natalie.

Having a rapid heart rate hadn't stopped me from getting a red-eye, and I took a sip as I thought back to the call, wanting to get what Natalie said right. In the process something else surfaced.

"Wow, I'd forgotten. Someone came in the room while we were talking. Natalie sounded surprised and something else. Maybe worried. She'd been telling me about finding Ellen's book and said something that didn't make sense." I struggled, trying to recall Natalie's exact words. "It was something about not what was there, but what wasn't."

Dinah ran a wooden stirrer through her chai latte. "What do you think she meant?"

I sighed. "I never got a chance to ask her. She had to get off the phone. I thought I would straighten it out when I saw her. But . . ." I swallowed hard.

Two men with laptops came in and sat down at the small round table next to us. I leaned closer and dropped my voice to keep our conversation private.

"Suppose whoever overheard Natalie understood what she meant, and they realized Natalie knew something about Ellen's death, and they—"

"Faked the suicide," Dinah said, almost in a whisper.

"And in one move," I said in a voice so low I could barely hear myself, "got rid of Natalie and ended the investigation of Ellen's death."

Dinah wanted to know whether I remembered anything from the call that might give away the person's identity. But I came up blank. "Natalie didn't even make any reference to whether it was a man or woman. But it certainly could have been Lawrence. We know he was working with her. He could have stopped by the office and overheard her." I thought back to Barry's saying that Ellen had known her killer and that the crime wasn't planned. "And as for killing Ellen, suppose Lawrence came home for lunch and said he wanted a divorce to go off with Miss Water Glass and they started to argue. He could have suddenly decided it would be more efficient and more cost-effective to just strangle her."

"But I thought Natalie was Miss Water Glass," Dinah said, confused.

"Maybe she wasn't. Or maybe she was, but Lawrence decided she was a problem because she could tie him to Ellen's murder. He'd already killed once, so doing it again probably wouldn't have been as hard, and this time he planned it. And the suicide note ties everything in a nice little bow, and he's off the hook."

"You sure aren't a fan of his," Dinah said.

"And you are?" I countered. "Besides, whether I like him or not has nothing to do with it. I'm just thinking about motive and opportunity."

"You've been looking at that investigating book again," Dinah said. I nodded and admitted I'd broken down and bought it.

"And there's CeeCee."

"CeeCee?" Dinah repeated. "But she's so—"

"Exactly. You wouldn't expect her to be a serial killer. But don't you remember the part she played in that movie *Whatever Happened to Aunt Peggy?* The whole point was, nobody suspected her character of being the killer. The tinkly laugh and the sweet smile made her seem sugar and spice and everything nice. And you know, I think she even killed the people by strangling them." My voice had started to rise with my excitement, and I had to force myself to slow down and soften my tone. "And as for motive— there's her secret, and I don't mean the toilet paper."

Dinah pushed away her cup. "Don't forget, there are always the wild cards, like Sheila. We did see her with Lawrence. And Will Hunter. Who knows what's really underneath that laid-back charm?"

"Don't say that," I protested. "He can't be the murderer. Then I'd have no chance of getting him back for the book signing."

CHAPTER 20

I WAS MULLING OVER THE EVENTS OF THE afternoon as I moved around my kitchen. Dinah and I had come up with many possibilities, but no proof. Again I regretted not having the few seconds more to see the entry in Ellen's book. Seeing a name would have narrowed things down.

It was strange how quickly Pink Sheridan Shaw Public Relations had gone back to business. But, then, there was really no choice if you wanted to have a business. Clients were sympathetic for about five minutes, and then if you weren't back up and operating, they were off looking for someone else. They always talk about the show having to go on, but it is even truer in show business.

Mrs. Shedd had gone off to an Arizona spa for a few days, and I hadn't enlightened her yet about losing Will Hunter. I was afraid she wouldn't take it well. Besides, I hadn't given up hope on fixing it before she returned.

I had left the bookstore around noon, but since I would

be working until closing for the next couple of days, I had decided to cook some meals in advance. I was in the kitchen when Barry came to the back door. He gave me his usual warning when he discovered it was unlocked.

A big pot of corn chowder simmered on the stove along with a saucepan of boiling water with matzo balls in it. The yeasty smell of baking bread filled the kitchen as the bread machine did its thing. I was at the counter, making up some individual salads.

Barry sniffed the air before checking what was under the pot lids. "Smells great. Interesting concept, corn chowder with matzo balls," he said with a chuckle. As usual, he couldn't stay long. He had to get Jeffrey to the dentist and then go back to work.

"Everything goes with matzo balls. What about your dinner?"

"Pizza. I'm picking it up on the way home," he said, displaying a coupon from Yummie's.

"That's the place Natalie Shaw got the pizza from," I said in an excited voice. "The one she ordered the night she supposedly killed herself." I took enough salad for two, put it into a ziplock bag and poured some of the balsamic honey-mustard dressing I'd just made into a plastic cup. I liked to think I excelled at salad. None of that bland iceberg lettuce with a few cucumber slices. I went all out. I bought herb salad mix and put in cucumber, grated carrots, blue cheese, walnuts and dried mixed berries.

Barry smiled in appreciation as I handed him the salad to go.

"You know, I remembered that she was talking to someone in her office when we were on the phone. I'm thinking . . ."

Barry put up his hand to cut me off. "They finished the psychological autopsy. It turns out she'd been treated in the past for a drug overdose, which had all the trappings of a suicide attempt. Something about getting fired from a job.

And one of the assistants in the office said Natalie had been talking about feeling guilty about ending up with the business, along with being worried that she wouldn't be able to handle it. The coroner ruled her death a suicide."

"But what about the pizza and the somebody in the office and . . . ?"

Barry quieted me the way he knew best. He kissed me with a long, slow, mind-blowing dance of tongues that definitely would have been a gateway to other things if he hadn't had to leave. When he pulled away, he waved a piece of paper in front of me.

I snatched it and read it over. It was an e-mail confirmation of the trip to Maui, including flights. In large type along the bottom, it read *nonrefundable*.

"I can't believe you did this."

He smiled, appearing pleased with himself, until he checked my expression and realized he'd misunderstood.

"But I never said yes. I don't have the time off." I handed him back the paper with a less-than-thrilled expression.

"Taken care of. I talked to your boss, and she was fine with it."

"I can't believe that you went ahead without telling me." If I'd been upset about his showing up unannounced, it was nothing compared to this.

Barry began to pick up that I wasn't overjoyed with what he'd done. "Molly, you're making a big deal out of nothing. We'll go and have a good time. So what if I didn't wait to get the official yes from you?"

"So what?" I didn't mean to, but my voice rose. "You can't just assume."

He made an annoyed face, and his eyes flared. "It's about Charlie, isn't it? You really have to let go and get on with your life."

"It isn't about Charlie this time. I can't believe you don't get it."

"And I can't believe you're making such a fuss over a

small detail. I knew you would agree, and time was running out on the deal." He shrugged and put the paper in his pocket. "It was a nothing detail."

My mouth dropped open. "A nothing detail." I might have sounded a little crazed by now. I even had some awareness of it, but no way was I backing down. Not when he wouldn't even acknowledge that he'd been wrong to assume. "It's not a nothing detail. You can't just decide for me."

"If I'd had any idea you were going to act like such a crazy woman over this, I never would have gone ahead with the plans." He still sounded way too calm. The only giveaway was the clenching of his jaw.

"Now I'm a crazy woman because I won't let you just bulldoze over me. Maybe you can take Jeffrey instead."

It was hard to believe that a few moments ago we'd been kissing, and now everything was falling apart right before my eyes.

Then he smiled. "No, I have a better idea. I just happen to know someone who would love to spend a long, romantic weekend on the beach with me." Aghast, I felt my mouth fall open as he walked out the door. I would have slammed it if I were Barry, but he was too controlled and shut it quietly. His threat of going with Detective Heather made enough of a bang.

"That went well," I said as the soup began to boil over.

Did we just break up?

When Barry didn't call later or stop over, it became apparent that we had. Being older didn't make it any easier to deal with. Maybe I hadn't wanted the committed relationship he did, but I didn't want *no* relationship, either. I played depressing music, made myself a large, gooey hot fudge sundae and spent a tough night alone. Was Barry inviting Detective Heather on our trip right now? I couldn't get the picture of them on a moonlit beach out of my mind. I thought about calling Dinah, but it was far too late.

I forced myself to get a grip. I got my hands busy crocheting squares and got my mind off Barry by thinking about the two crime scenes. At least mostly off Barry, anyway. No matter how much I tried to focus my thoughts on how odd it was that I had ended up at both scenes, he kept popping up. Was I wrong for making such an issue out of his assuming things? I forced my thoughts back on the two crime scenes, and something flitted through my mind. I had a feeling of some similarity, something about smell. I rubbed my temples. All this thinking had given me a headache.

I HAD THE NEXT DAY OFF. EVEN THE CROCHET group didn't meet. CeeCee had some appointment and insisted we couldn't meet without her. I buried myself in work around the house and rearranged Peter's old bedroom into a crochet room for myself. It wasn't as elaborate as Ellen's, but I used Peter's bookcase to store my yarn, arranged by color. I'd been buying crochet books like crazy, and I put them all on a shelf. I moved a comfortable chair in and vowed to get one of those fancy lamps that offered full-spectrum light. When it was done, I sat in the chair and made a square. But as evening approached, I began to feel glum. I missed Barry's stopovers.

Even though I went into the bookstore early the next day, I stayed until closing, trying to keep busy, which was hard. There was no book signing to handle, and there weren't even many shoppers. In the last hour, I felt more like a maid than like an events coordinator as I gathered up abandoned coffee cups and put the magazines in their rightful spots. As I was doing a final walk-through, I saw Adele sitting in the children's department. She was on one of the minichairs, which put her knees somewhere in the vicinity of her chin. She looked kind of forlorn in spite of the red outfit and black and white striped tights. She was crocheting one of her double-size squares.

"It looks nice," I said, coming up next to her. I glanced around the empty bookstore. "I think Mrs. Shedd should rethink staying open so late; there's no business."

I expected some zinger from Adele, but all she did was blink.

"Welcome to my little corner of the bookstore," she said in an unhappy voice.

"Why don't I get my crochet stuff?" She barely nodded as I left to get my things from the office.

After I turned the *open* sign to *closed* and made sure the door was locked, I joined her, almost dislocating my knee as I sat on the small chair. As lousy as I felt, Adele seemed worse. She looked as though she needed to hear something nice, so I complimented her on the piece she was working on.

"Pink, cut the pity compliments." She sighed. "I've been sitting here thinking about Natalie. We went to the same noon executive kickboxing class at Women's Work-out World. We were friends, you know."

I was having trouble wrapping my mind around Adele in a kickboxing class, but when she mentioned being friends with Natalie, it interrupted my mental picture. When Natalie had stopped by the crochet group, she hadn't talked to Adele. Maybe she had nodded some kind of acknowledgment at Adele, as if she had recognized her, but it was hardly a greeting between friends. I felt a clutch in my heart as I realized that might be as close to a friend as Adele had. On another note, it made me wonder about her relationship with her "hunk." Did he even know she considered him a boyfriend?

I felt bad about all of my previous frustration with her and vowed to act differently. I took out a J hook and began making yet another granny square. What kept it from getting boring, aside from my sheer joy at knowing how to make one, was varying the colors. This one was going to be rose, pink and cream, bordered in black.

"This is nice, just the two of us crocheting together," I said, feeling a wave of kindness toward her.

She made a grunt of agreement and nodded. "It's better than being stuck here with a bunch of kids with runny noses who hate me. I don't think I can face one more story time."

"I'm sure they don't hate you."

"I'm just not good at it."

"We all have days when we feel like that. Don't sell yourself short. Mrs. Shedd thinks the kids' department is doing very well. And that's all because of you." I began to think the whole adversarial relationship with Adele had been my fault, and I was glad that I was fixing it.

"Ha, Pink, you can't fool me. Look at you. You never have days like that. You have friends and a family. Even your crochet stuff isn't that bad."

"You really think so?" I waited to see whether she'd add a zinger, but instead she pulled out a sell sheet for *Uncle Harry's Idea Factory.*

"How am I ever going to put on a story time for this book?"

I read over the sell sheet and handed it back to her. I gave her some hints such as having the kids do some of Uncle Harry's ideas, preferably ones that weren't messy. I quickly read through the copy again. "Here you go—Charades. Have them play Charades." To my surprise Adele hugged me.

My cell rang, and since the store was closed, I answered it. It was Dinah. We'd been playing phone tag all day.

"No, no, there's nothing important to talk about," I said, looking toward Adele. We might have had a warm moment, but I wasn't ready to let on about Barry in front of her. "Tomorrow. Right. We'll go to Century City like we planned." I glanced Adele's way. She gave me her sad look and muttered something about having the afternoon off, too.

"If I went with, I could show you this fabulous yarn store," she said.

When I got off the phone, she said something about how nice it would be to have a girlfriend trip. She had a sad puppy-dog look, and the yarn store sounded promising, so I invited her to come along. She said yes right away.

I was feeling all good inside about our moment, thinking we'd at last torn down the walls between us. We would be friends from now on. I picked up my stuff and went through the bookstore, turning off the lights and shutting down the air. I met Adele at the front.

"Pink, your ideas for the kids' thing were perfect. You should be doing those events, not me. How about we switch jobs?"

Okay, so maybe things hadn't changed.

"WE HAVE TO PICK SOMEONE UP," I SAID TO Dinah as I got in her car the next morning. When I explained it was Adele, Dinah looked surprised and none too happy. "What's that about?"

"You should have seen her last night," I said before giving Dinah the rundown on Adele's and my moment. "And then she went back to her usual self. Unfortunately I'd already invited her."

"Is there something else wrong?" Dinah gave me a funny look. I swear she had some kind of best-friend radar.

We were almost at the bookstore, where we were meeting Adele. "I waited because I thought it was just a fight, but Barry and I broke up." It felt good to finally say it out loud to somebody.

"What?" she squealed as we pulled into the parking lot. Adele was waiting outside. Who could miss her, in her orange warm-up suit and the purple scarf she'd fashioned into a headband?

"Adele doesn't know, and I'm not talking about it in front of her. I'll give you details later." The last word was barely out of my mouth when Adele jumped into the backseat.

This trip into the city was supposed to be a change for all of us. There was a different feeling on the other side of the hill, as it was referred to. I don't know why it was called over *the hill* since it was really over the mountains.

Dinah got on the 101 and then took the 405 through the Santa Monica Mountains. We'd timed it so that traffic wasn't bad, which meant that it was at least moving. When Adele started giving Dinah driving tips, I knew I'd made a mistake in inviting her.

"Any word on what's going to happen to the PR firm now that Natalie's gone?" Adele asked.

I repeated what Derek the rental agent had said about Lawrence folding the PR firm into his company.

"Hmm, then they'll be needing some new people. Maybe I should apply," she said, adjusting the purple scarf headband. "I'm probably just what he's looking for."

I just nodded and let her think whatever made her happy.

Every chance she could, Dinah slipped me a look of concern and squeezed my hand. I knew she was sympathetic but also dying to hear all the details.

We stopped at the Century City mall and checked out the stores, with Adele giving a running commentary on how much she preferred indoor shopping centers.

"That was fun," Dinah said with a touch of sarcasm, as we got back into the car. "Okay, Adele, where's the yarn store?"

"I'll just direct you," Adele said, insisting that she needed to sit in the front seat.

Her directions took us to Third Street near La Cienega, where old, oddball stores were being replaced by new trendy businesses.

Adele told Dinah to park around the corner. The street

that ran parallel was all residential, with mostly two-story stucco duplexes and apartment buildings.

Adele led us back to the commercial street, where there was a lot more foot traffic than in the Valley, and fewer people wearing shorts. I would have passed the actual store without seeing it, if Adele hadn't stopped our progress and taken us inside.

"Remember, his place stays a secret," Adele said before we went in. It was called Frank's International Button, Fabric and Yarn Mart, and was the complete opposite of the store Dinah and I had visited. We had to walk in sideways because there was so much of everything heaped on the counter of the tiny shop. The yarn was displayed in the back corner. *Displayed* was a nice way of saying it. Actually, sample skeins were tacked to a piece of cardboard.

Adele knew Frank and kept making conversation with him to make sure the other sideways shoppers knew she was a regular.

Dinah found some black yarn with gold threads running through it. I picked a green-blue cotton yarn that was the color of the greenmobile, and Adele went for some fuzzy stuff that seemed to be pink mixed with a lot of other colors.

Shaking her head with disbelief, Dinah looked down at the shopping bag Frank had just handed her. "I can't believe I bought more yarn. I haven't even finished the scarf I started."

Adele chuckled. "Welcome to the club." Loving to be the one in the know, she explained how once you started crocheting, you picked up the yarn habit. "You see something beautiful, and you have to have it. Particularly here. Did I mention that when whatever stock he has is gone, that's it?"

Dinah pulled me aside while Adele was going through a long good-bye with her yarn store friend. "Give me details. What happened with Barry?"

I started to explain, but Adele interrupted.

"Ladies," Adele said, breezing out of the store and dragging us along with her. "Let's stop at the pastry shop down the street. I can personally vouch for the apple dumplings, but everyone says their cakes are fabulous, too."

I looked at Dinah, and she took it from there, explaining that we'd been planning to stop at Farmers Market. It was a quaint bunch of outdoor stalls nearby that had been an L.A. landmark forever. Adele cut her off.

"Trust me on this—you'll be happier with my choice." Without waiting for us to answer, Adele merely walked down the street. For just a second it occurred to me that Dinah had driven, which meant we had the car keys and hence the power, and we could flex it. It annoyed me that I'd invited Adele because she'd seemed so upset, and now she'd managed to take over Dinah's and my day. But not wanting to be stubborn for stubborn's sake, I realized the pastry place sounded really good, and I followed Adele.

It turned out to be one of those places with bistro tables, wrought-iron chairs and a huge display of mouthwatering cakes and pastries.

Adele went with her apple dumping, Dinah chose the triple chocolate cake and I picked the berry shortcake. We found a table by the window. Adele definitely knew her desserts; the combo of whipped cream, yellow cake and slightly tart berries was amazing.

Adele was checking some text messages on her phone between bites of her apple dumpling. Dinah was totally focusing on her dessert, pointing out that it had chocolate cake, fudge icing and bits of chocolate bars in both. I listened while looking out the window. All the chocoholic talk was somewhat lost on me. I was one of the few people who liked chocolate only occasionally. My weakness was whipped-cream cake, and this one was worth every calorie.

There seemed to be a constant flow of people going to a place across the street. I squinted to read the sign, and recognized the name as one of the new celebrity hangouts. It looked like an ordinary storefront restaurant, but every few seconds another car pulled up and the valet jumped in while the owners got out.

I watched the flow for a few minutes, but then I almost choked on my cake. CeeCee got out of her Jaguar and walked over to the person getting out of the car behind her. There was no mistaking Lawrence Sheridan. They stood facing each other, talking. Then CeeCee's facial expression crumbled into distress. Lawrence was doing a lot of head shaking, which looked to me like he was telling her something she didn't want to hear. I nudged Dinah, who looked up from her chocoholic stupor. We both watched as the still-arguing pair went inside.

"What's with you two?" Adele said, looking up from her text messages.

Neither of us said a word.

IT WAS ONLY LATER, WHEN WE'D DROPPED ADELE off, that I brought up CeeCee and Lawrence.

"I'm betting it was something about business. Maybe he found out CeeCee's secret," I said. "Mabye that's what CeeCee's been so upset about."

Dinah shook her head. "Maybe, but I'm more interested in you and Barry. What happened? How could you have broken up?"

When I told her about his booking the trip without an official yes from me, I expected a true-blue girlfriend response, something along the lines of, "Of course you did the right thing. He was ridiculous to just assume you'd go." Or even just a "yeah, right." Instead she regarded me with a puzzled expression, and not a good kind of puzzled.

"Have you ever heard the one about throwing out the baby with the bathwater? So maybe he made a little mistake. It sounds like his intent was good. I'm out there in the dating trenches, and believe me, it's not a pretty sight. Sometimes you have to let things slide.".

"You're missing the point. He wouldn't even acknowledge that he did anything wrong. He acted like I was crazy for being upset. The man went ahead with a vacation without even getting my okay. And then he wanted me just to go along with his plan. He talked to Mrs. Shedd without consulting me."

"Some people would consider that a romantic gesture. I keep meeting men who can't commit to a cup of coffee on Tuesday, and you find the one guy who wants a real relationship, even marriage. . . ."

I explained again. I had married young and had kids right away. I had loved all of it, but now that I was alone and starting over, I wanted to concentrate on my life and on my job for a while. I wanted the freedom to make my own plans. "I wanted Barry, too, but on my terms." It was hard to keep the sadness out of my voice. Dinah hugged me in understanding.

"Maybe Barry didn't realize he hit such a sensitive spot."

"It doesn't matter. It's over. I can't undo what's done."

"Do you really think he'll go with Detective Heather?"

I just gave Dinah a dirty look.

I might have sounded as though I had it all together, but when Dinah left, I crumbled. What if she was right? Maybe I had overreacted. I started to berate myself for making a mess of things. Even the Will Hunter appearance had gone south.

I had tried calling Lawrence Sheridan's office and, no surprise, hadn't gotten a call back. I would have called Will Hunter directly, but his number was beyond unlisted. Mrs. Shedd still didn't know anything was amiss. I was going to have to tell her soon, and I didn't look forward to it. Even though it wasn't my fault, I felt as if I had failed.

For a brief moment my thoughts went back to Barry, and I wondered what he was doing that very second. Did he miss me? I glanced at the lamp with the switch that wouldn't work. Barry would have fixed it in no time.

WHEN THE CROCHET GROUP NEXT MET, WE HAD lost our momentum because of the time off. All of CeeCee's paper squares had been ignored, and none of us had been doing much square making on our own. All the newbies had forgotten how to crochet, and CeeCee seemed preoccupied. Her mind was clearly elsewhere: She didn't even blink when Adele stepped in and started ordering everyone around. CeeCee just kept putting a black border around one of the newbies' single-color squares.

Adele told Sheila, Dinah and me to get our hooks going, and then she gave a group refresher lesson to the newbies. She even handed out some sheets with descriptions of the basic stitches for them to keep as a reference. I had moved up from granny squares of two colors plus a black border to squares with four colors plus black.

Adele ran the whole meeting. Only at the end, when Adele was calculating what we had versus what we needed, did CeeCee come to and join the group. It was as if she'd awakened from a trance or something.

With a start, CeeCee began ruffling through the box of squares. When she'd finished, she looked up.

"Am I the only one who realizes we are at the end of our time? That auction is going to go on whether this afghan is completed or not. If we aren't able to turn it in, I'll look bad as your leader for not keeping on top of you, and you, the Tarzana Hookers, will look bad for not living up to your promise. But that isn't the real shame. Just think of all those dogs and cats that won't be spayed or neutered because their owners can't afford it, and Hearts and Barks won't have the money from the afghan to help them. Or the seniors who won't get Hearts and Barks's assistance and won't be able to keep their pets. Or the poor little strays that won't find homes because there won't be money for the Hearts and Barks foster program.

"We've all had personal crises and other interferences with our crocheting, but, ladies, we are down to the wire and it is now-or-never time. Which is it going to be?"

Everything CeeCee said was true, and surprisingly well said after her trance state.

We all held up our hooks and waved them in a sign of unity. Inspired by her impassioned speech, we all recommitted ourselves to making the needed squares. It was agreed that we'd all work independently and meet again the night before the auction to assemble our donation.

I just hoped nothing would get in our way.

CHAPTER 21

WITH EVERYTHING ON MY MIND, I HAD FORGOT-
ten about Peter's invitation to brunch until he called to give
me the time and the suggestion that I might want to wear
something nice instead of the khaki pants and shirts I wore
all the time.

"Do you have a dress or something? It is the Belle Vue
Hotel," he reminded me.

I rolled my eyes and assured him I would wear something appropriate. Actually, the idea of a dress sounded
nice for a change, and I found a long, sheer Indian one in
my closet. It was black with tiny yellow flowers, and always seemed in style. I matched it with a pair of sandals
and a smaller purse than the satchel I usually carried. I did
a whole number with my makeup, too, along with a com-
petent blow-dry job on my hair.

Sometimes Peter's attention to appearances had its ben-
efits. The Belle Vue was tucked into a canyon, and once
you drove through the gate, it was like leaving everyday reality behind. The hotel was known to be frequented by

celebrities, visiting royalty and people with healthy expense accounts.

A valet whisked the greenmobile away, giving the old Mercedes just the slightest of disdainful looks.

I crossed the grounds, marveling how anything real could look so perfect. The lawn was a solid green carpet without a blemish on it. Carnations, impatiens and roses, all in either white or a shade of pink coral, filled the area along the walkway. They were so painstakingly maintained, there wasn't a wilted blossom or a dead head among them.

I crossed over a small arched bridge, glancing down at the stream that passed under it, joining the ponds on either side. Graceful swans glided over the water.

The peachy pink main building was small and inviting, with a lobby that looked more like a living room. When I reached the restaurant, the host announced that everyone was already seated, and led me across the patio to an umbrella-covered table surrounded by pink coral rose bushes. I was surprised at the number of people there.

I gathered that the woman next to Peter must be his date. I wondered if that meant he was serious about her, as I rarely met his women these days. I had the unfortunate habit of getting attached to my sons' girlfriends, and it got sticky when they broke up. Their solution had been to keep me out of the loop. Samuel had a woman with him as well. She was the one I'd seen manning the CD table the night I'd seen him play. But it was the person seated next to the empty chair meant for me who most caught my attention.

He stood as I approached the table, and pulled out my chair.

"Mason Fields," he said, introducing himself, as he touched my arm. "And you must be Molly." I smiled tentatively, wondering what was going on.

I slid into my chair as Peter took over the job of host. He introduced the woman next to him as Sunny and mentioned

that she was in development at Universal. She looked like a
perfect match for Peter. Not a hair out of place; very poised
and aggressive. Her clothes were elegantly casual, just like
Peter's.

Samuel had his golden hair pulled back in a ponytail
and was nicely dressed in a T-shirt with an offbeat open
vest over black jeans. His date's name was Morgan, and
something in the way she moved made me think she was a
dancer, probably ballet.

Mason, Peter explained, was the lawyer he'd told me
about. And also the lawyer I no longer needed now that I was
not about to be arrested. So why was he here? Unless . . .
had Peter decided to play matchmaker? That felt way too
weird. All along I had thought he had a problem with me dating, but I realized maybe it was just a problem with whom I
was dating.

I glanced over at Mason again, and he caught my gaze.
He was certainly easy on the eyes. His dark brown hair was
shot with silver, and a lock of it fell across his forehead and
somehow gave the impression that he was sincere and
hardworking.

Though Peter didn't go through Mason's credits, I realized I knew who he was. He was the lawyer known for
keeping his celebrity clients out of jail. He was always
popping up on the news, giving a statement as he came out
of the courthouse. Recently he'd represented a well-known
actress accused of killing her husband.

The details came back to me. Everyone had thought she
was guilty, but apparently, thanks to Mason, the jury had
some doubts, and she got off. There had been a civil trial
after it. She had lost that one and was found responsible for
her spouse's drowning in the pool. Though she had to pay a
hefty amount, she stayed out of jail and went on with her
life. She'd probably earned the amount she'd had to pay
doing her next movie. Afterward the case had been the fod-
der of Jay Leno's monologues for weeks.

It was a comfort knowing that Peter had set me up with an attorney who obviously would have kept me out of the big house. Except, since Mason had the reputation for getting guilty people off, everyone would have believed I really did kill Ellen. It was all beside the point now anyway. I glanced around the beautiful patio, with the graceful trees offering shade and all the people enjoying the ambiance, and I breathed a sigh of relief, knowing Detective Heather wasn't going to pop out of the bushes, dangling handcuffs.

Mason started talking to Peter and Sunny about a TV show idea they were all working on, which explained how Peter had gotten Mason to show up. I realized that as far as Mason was concerned, this was a story meeting, even if it was Sunday. Leave it to Peter to work from all different angles. Mason was all smiles when he turned back to me.

"Peter said you've had a very stressful couple of weeks." Something about Mason's manner put me at ease, and I poured out my adventure of being a murder suspect, including my roller-coaster ride of trying to get Will Hunter for the bookstore.

"And now I'm back to square one," I said with dismay. "All things considered, it shouldn't be that important, but the owner is really counting on his showing up." I mentioned all the arrangements I'd made and the crowd it would bring in, and how I was hoping it would open the door to more celebrity book signings, since they all seemed to be coming out with books these days.

Mason listened attentively, nodding at the right moments and smiling enough to appear to be amused by the lighter parts of the story. When I finished, he touched my arm.

"If it's any consolation, I would have gotten you off," he said. Of course he didn't mention the stigma that would have gone with it. "And I can help you with Will Hunter. I'll have my people track him down."

"Mother, why don't you just get in touch with Lawrence

Sheridan? I heard he's moved the PR business to his office and is overseeing it now," Peter said.

I mentioned my unsuccessful attempts to get a call back from Lawrence. But Peter persisted.

"We saw him and his girlfriend at a charity event the other evening. He came up to me and said he owed you an apology for accusing you . . ."

"Girlfriend?" I said, interrupting. "Who is she?"

"I don't know if she's his girlfriend. I just called her that. Maybe they were just there together."

"She was definitely his girlfriend," Sunny interjected. "I remember thinking she was pretty obviously staking her claim, the way she kept putting her hand on his neck."

But when I started asking for details about things like her name or what she looked like, both of them came up vague. "She was a lot younger," was the best I got.

"I think that's pretty shocking that he was out with another woman right after his wife died," I said to the table.

Mason again put his hand on my arm, a gesture that I began to realize was natural to him. "Don't be so quick to judge him. Everybody deals with grief differently. I know Lawrence, and he's the kind of guy who just gets on with things. I'm sure he's keeping himself going by taking care of Ellen's clients. And the hand on his neck could have just been a sign of reassurance."

I supposed he had a point. Mason was good. He had succeeded in getting me to believe that Lawrence was secretly grieving and just being comforted by some younger, unidentified woman.

"I'll still take care of putting you together with Will Hunter, and if you really want to know who Lawrence was with, I can get hold of a seating chart. I'm on the board of directors for the charity," Mason said as brunch arrived. With the arrival of the food, the conversation lightened up. Everybody was oohing and aahing about theirs, except for Morgan, who'd ordered some plain steamed-vegetable plate that she was barely eating. The combo of her ultrathin body and her manner with the food shouted *anorexia* to me, but I reminded myself that it was none of my business.

"This reminds me of how much I wish I got to spend more time with my kids," Mason said, gazing around the table. He explained to me that he was divorced with a grown son and daughter, both of whom had moved out of state.

The nice family moment survived the main course, but everything changed with the arrival of dessert. We had all ordered something gooey and delicious, except for Morgan, who had opted for only a double espresso.

As we worked on our desserts, I made the mistake of asking Samuel how his gig was going. Since he had told me about it so proudly, I thought it would seem unmotherly not to inquire. Of course, I made no mention that I'd seen him or that I even knew any of the details.

Samuel muttered something about everything going okay. Morgan, juiced from little food and lots of espresso, spoke up. "I don't know why you don't just tell them. It's nothing to be ashamed of."

On the word *ashamed*, Peter's head shot up. It was one of his biggest worries—being embarrassed by his family.

"Okay, I was going to tell you eventually," Samuel started. Then he blurted out that he was playing in the courtyard at the Valley Promenade.

"But that's outside," Peter began, his face lapsing into upset. "That's where the people play and push their homemade CDs and have guitar cases open for handouts."

"They're not handouts," Samuel said, growing angry. As usual, his brother had hit a sensitive spot. "They're tips on top of a salary. And if you hadn't been so high and mighty, you might have helped me get something better. . . ."

Peter started to speak, but Samuel stopped him. "And don't even think of saying that 'if I wanted to play a musician' thing."

All this was being said in tense whispers so as not to alert the whole place that a family squabble was in session. But if it kept up, the loudness level was likely to explode. Mason leaned in front of the two of them and held up his hands in a time-out gesture.

To my surprise, both of my sons stopped and turned their attention to him. Getting in the middle had never worked for me. No wonder Mason always won cases. Not only was he brave enough to jump into the middle of a family argument when the family wasn't even his, but he handled himself with such charismatic power that he settled the whole thing so everybody was happy.

First he defended what Samuel was doing. "I personally know that the Promenade is very selective about who they hire as outdoor entertainers," he said to Peter. "If your brother got a gig there, he has to be good."

Then he turned to Samuel. "Don't be too hard on your brother for not trying to bring you into William Morris. It's not the right place for you right now." He went on to say in the most face-saving of ways that Samuel would be lost in the shuffle there, but that Mason knew the place for him. "I know somebody who books small clubs. He's a genius at developing talent, too." Mason offered to set up something between them. Then he turned to me and winked with a smile. Peace again reigned at the table as Peter and Samuel began talking to each other about sports.

"Have you ever thought of being a judge?" I said, pleased and amazed at how everything had turned out.

"I'll take that as a compliment," he said, waving the waiter over for refills on our coffee.

By the time we left the patio, everyone was talking in a new, friendly way. The only moment of contention had been when the check came. Since it was Peter's party, he had gone to pick it up, but Mason beat him to the small leatherette folder.

Though Peter protested, there wasn't a chance Mason

was going to acquiesce. Mason knew how to win whatever he was after.

"This was the best afternoon I've had in a while," he said. "It was nice being part of a family."

There was a flurry of hugs and good-bye kisses to Peter and Samuel and their dates before they headed to the valet stand. Mason asked for my valet ticket, but hung back on the walkway.

"I just realized I *did* see you on the news when Ellen Sheridan died," he said.

"I hope you're not going to tell me I looked pasty," I said.

He chuckled and said I certainly looked better in person. I thanked him again for jumping into the lion's den.

"I meant what I said. This was the best afternoon I've had in a while." Our eyes met for a moment, and there was a sizzle in his. I didn't know quite what to do, so I started to babble about something. He chuckled again and pressed his card on me.

"I'll be in touch about Will Hunter, but in case you are a suspect in another murder, or need someone to bring you an aspirin in the middle of the night . . ." He touched my arm again; then we walked the last few steps to the valet stand and he handed over our tickets.

They brought his car first—a shiny black Mercedes S-class. He gestured for them to pull it aside, and waited until the greenmobile arrived.

He walked me to the car. "I always thought that design of Mercedes was the best." As I turned to acknowledge his comment, I noticed a black Crown Victoria pull up to the valet stand. Barry got out, dressed in his work suit and with his on-duty persona. Although he appeared to be talking to the valet, I knew he'd seen me.

Mason waited while I slid into the driver's seat, then leaned in and gave me a kiss on the cheek and a squeeze on my shoulder, and again mentioned being in touch. I didn't have to look to know that Barry was taking all this in.

When I finally drove away, I glanced in the rearview mirror. Barry had turned away from the valet and was watching my car. He was wearing sunglasses, but there was just the slightest twitch in his mouth that gave away his emotions. He didn't look happy.

It was only when I drove outside the gates that I realized it appeared for all intents and purposes as if I had just been at a hotel with another man.

CHAPTER 22

TRUE TO HIS WORD, MASON CALLED ME AT THE bookstore with Will Hunter's number. He was still working on Lawrence's escort's name. He also asked me out. I felt a little funny about it, but, then, Barry and I really seemed over. I bought a little time to think about it, saying I needed a rain check, because I was in over my head with my crochet group. I mentioned the Tarzana Hookers and our Hearts and Barks auction donation.

"What a small world," Mason said. "I'm on the Hearts and Barks board of directors." I made a comment that he seemed to be on every board of directors, and he chuckled in response. "I suppose it does seem that way. It's my attempt to counteract being a lawyer."

This time I chuckled. I liked that he had a sense of humor about himself. He asked some more about the afghan and seemed to remember seeing it listed in a catalog he'd received for the silent auction.

"I wasn't planning to go to the fair, but you've changed

my mind. Maybe we can meet up there. If you've caught up with your knitting."

I gasped. "Crocheting. They aren't the same, you know."

"You're cute," he said with a smile in his voice, before hanging up.

Who would have thought I'd end up so popular this time around? But it was too much to sort out now, so I threw all thoughts of my social life onto the back burner.

I wasted no time getting in touch with Will Hunter. He was his usual laconic self and didn't even question how I'd gotten his number.

"I am stunned and saddened by what happened to Natalie," he said when I asked how he was doing under the circumstances. I wasn't sure he even knew who I was, until I brought up the book signing and his tone lightened. "Oh, yeah, the bookstore lady. Love your place. I still have my hook and string."

I went right for the order and asked if he would still be making his appearance on the agreed-upon date.

"It's all been kind of strange. My agent wanted me to go with another publicist, but I'm sticking with Ellen's husband for the moment. He seems like a know-the-ropes kind of dude. I'll tell him I'm going to do it, and you just cross wires with him for a confirmation."

I couldn't very well say that even though Lawrence claimed he owed me an apology, he wasn't returning my calls. I told Will about the pressure to finish the auction donation and used it as an excuse to get the confirmation from him.

Instead of giving me the unequivocal yes I wanted, he picked up on the fair and started asking a lot of questions about it. I explained that it raised money for all kinds of animal services, and I mentioned we were down to the wire to finish the afghan. "We're assembling it the night before, at the bookstore."

"I don't want to give you any more worries, so I'll just say yes for sure."

I gave myself a high five of sorts. It was more like a high hook, since I'd been attempting to crochet during both phone calls. I discovered I still needed to give my full attention to what I was making and had to unravel both times.

I had taken my promise to CeeCee seriously and been working on squares in every spare moment. When I got stuck cashiering at the bookstore, I crocheted between customers. Dinah came over, and we made squares and had Chinese takeout.

I was so focused on making parts for the afghan, I stopped thinking about Ellen and Natalie and who had really killed whom. There would be time enough for that when the auction was over.

Some of my grannies still ended up missing a corner and had to be unraveled, but most of them looked really good, if I said so myself. Most of all I loved watching a ball of yarn turn into something concrete.

The plan was, we'd all meet at the bookstore the night before the fair and work all night if need be to get the afghan assembled. But as it got closer and closer to the appointed night, one by one, as they came to Shedd & Royal to deliver their squares, the newbies begged off. The story was always pretty much the same: They had young kids and couldn't get out of mommy duty. In desperation, I had tried to get Meredith to help, but I kept getting her message machine and no call back.

THE BOX OF SQUARES LOOKED FULL AS I CARRIED it to the event area. I was setting things up for the long night ahead. I'd already brought in cardboard carriers of coffee and trays of cookies to keep us going. I set the box down on the long table and began to take the contents out, counting squares as I went. It was looking promising until

I caught my breath. Some of the newbies' work had gotten pushed to the bottom. In all our rushing, no one had added the black borders to seven of their single-stitch squares. Not only that, but when I put them next to the rest of our work, they didn't match the quality. These must have been the first ones they made.

Adele joined me and looked over my shoulder. "We can't use those," she said, taking them out of the mix. We discussed what to do, and decided to wait until CeeCee got there, hoping she would bring more squares with her.

Sheila and Dinah came in together. They helped themselves to cookies and coffee while we waited for CeeCee. She arrived late and without even an apology. When I explained the problem, she didn't seem to hear it the first time, and I repeated it.

I expected some kind of hysteria, but she just muttered something about how it would be all right. She'd whip up the needed squares now. She absently put down her things, took out a hook and several balls of yarn and began crocheting.

Adele nudged me and pointed. I couldn't believe my eyes. CeeCee, the queen of crochet, had missed a corner on the granny and didn't even seem aware it had only three. Adele put her hand out to stop CeeCee's hook. CeeCee gasped when she realized what she'd done, and then avoided everyone's gaze, obviously embarrassed. She threw the piece aside, not even bothering to unravel, and just started a new one instead.

Whatever had been bothering CeeCee had apparently gotten worse.

"Pink, we're not going to make it," Adele said, shaking her head.

"Don't even say that. We can't fail," I said, my voice rising in power. I looked at my watch. It was just ten. "We have all night. C'mon, ladies, if we all make one square and some of us make two, we'll have enough. Then all we have to do is assemble it."

"Pink, we're not putting it together with a sewing machine. It's a lot of work." Adele had found an assortment of yarn and laid it on the table. I had just set out skeins and skeins of black, thinking it was all we would need. Sheila and Dinah put down their coffee cups and picked up their hooks. CeeCee's new piece seemed to have all its corners, but there was a certain speed missing in the delivery of the stitches.

"Do you want to talk about it, CeeCee?" I asked, watching as she dropped the half-finished square and began another without seeming to be aware she hadn't finished the first.

There was a delay in her response. She looked at me, but her eyes were darting, as if her mind was elsewhere. "No. Everything is just hunky-dory," she said with an edge in her voice that clearly meant things weren't, but she wasn't going to give details.

"Adele, you do know how to assemble the afghan?" I said.

"Of course, Pink," she said, and began to explain that we would put it together in strips and then crochet the strips together.

She found CeeCee's map and began laying out the squares to see exactly where we were. A noise cut into my awareness. It took a few moments for me to realize it was a knock at the bookstore's door. Once everyone had arrived and the bookstore officially closed, I'd locked it.

I wasn't prepared for who was at the door. I opened it just as he was about to knock again.

"Will?" I said as he stepped inside. He looked around. I had turned off a lot of the lights, so it was kind of dim in the entrance. He handed me an advance copy of his book, *Walk a Mile in My Shoes*.

"Dude, I signed it to you, too," he said. "With publicists dropping like ants, I realized I better stay on top of my sh—stuff."

"Okay," I said. "Is that it? You wanted to give me the book and tell me that?"

"No, dude, that is definitely not all of it." His brow was furrowed, and his head bobbed up and down as if he was frustrated. "I heard your SOS, and I'm here to help." He pulled out a crochet hook and headed for the back.

Now I remembered I had made some comment about being worried we were cutting things too close and that we were meeting at the bookstore the night before the fair. I had never expected him to show up.

"Yeah, I've taken up the hook." He leaned in close and dropped his voice. "I'm trying to quit smoking, and that coaster idea works great."

Adele almost swallowed her tongue when she heard he was here to help.

"So, how'd you learn how to crochet anyway?" she asked in a doubtful voice.

He disappeared and returned holding the same kids' kit I'd bought. "I figured if the directions were simple enough for little guys, they'd work for me." In order to prove himself, he pulled out a wad of string and made a coaster right in front of us.

"We need squares. Like this," Adele said, holding up the ruby and white one Meredith had made.

"I can't do anything that fancy, but . . ." Will pointed to the array of classic granny squares, which outnumbered the elegant motif of Meredith's. "I can make one of those." He grabbed a ball of yarn from in front of CeeCee and whipped up the first two rounds of a granny square, and it had all four corners.

"He's in as far as I'm concerned," Dinah said. Sheila echoed her sentiment. CeeCee came out of her thoughts only long enough to notice that he'd arrived.

"It's fine with me. We need all the help we can get," CeeCee said vaguely, and went back to her work.

Adele smoothed out her leopard-print pants and black

tunic. She touched the black scarf she had tied around her head and, seeming to find herself in order, voted him in too.

She then began prattling about how she'd seen everything he was in, including the commercial he'd done as a kid for chocolate-chip cookies. He shrugged off the fawning and glanced around the table. "Doing something real like this beats out playing a part any day."

I kept watching CeeCee. It was so unlike her to not get in the middle of some entertainment business conversation. She wasn't pushing us to work faster, either. Something was wrong, and it had to be big to make her act so strangely.

Dinah wasn't starstruck, and made easy banter with Will. She even asked about the slippers.

"Someone finally asked," he laughed. "Everybody looks, but you're the first person to give me the question. I'm a firm believer that if your feet feel comfy, your world totally rocks. My feet just get hugged by all that lamb's wool." He moaned with pleasure and then offered to let Dinah try them. She declined.

CeeCee looked up for a moment and gazed around at all of us, then shook her head absently and went back to her work, which now looked like slow motion. Even with Will's help, and he actually was helping, I was worried.

By midnight we had all the squares we needed, but the job of putting them together was daunting. CeeCee came to again, and started to talk about the map and big needles. Then she just looked at Adele and said, "You handle it."

Adele gave us each some squares and showed us how to use single crochet to join them into a strip. She skipped CeeCee, who had put her head down on the table and gone to sleep.

Sheila had been staying very quiet. Along with being generally nervous, she seemed shy as well. But by the way she paid close attention to the conversation and kept opening her mouth and then saying nothing, it was obvious she wanted to join in.

Finally she took a deep breath, and the words just came out as she looked at Will. "In my other life, I work at Tarzana Women's Workout World."

Will nodded in recognition. The little bit of encouragement got her to keep going.

"Both Ellen and Natalie are—I mean, were—members." Sheila's expression darkened as she appeared to remember something. "You know, I don't think Ellen ever realized me, the receptionist, was the same person as me, the crochet group member. But, then, she never seemed to pay attention to anyone, just went through her routine, weights, treadmill and out." She seemed to have gone off on a tangent about how so many of the gym members were stuck in a rut. "I could always tell who was in a class even if I just saw the back of their heads."

Apparently the class area had a glass wall and was in clear view of the reception desk. I was only half listening until she got to the part about the day Ellen died.

"And, like always, Natalie was in her regular spot for the lunchtime kickboxing class." Adele glanced Will's way and mentioned that she was a regular in that class, too, and offered to show off some of her kicks.

I asked Sheila whether she knew the exact time all this had taken place. She knew down to the minute when Natalie had arrived and left. It turned out Sheila was a little more fanatical than I'd realized.

Dinah turned toward me and nodded with comprehension. Sheila had just given Natalie a perfect alibi. She had been at the gym from before until well after Ellen's approximate time of death. Unless Natalie had known how to dematerialize, there was no way she could have killed Ellen, which meant the suicide and note were both fakes. And I'd thought her pizza order was compelling.

What had Natalie said to me about Ellen's appointment book?

By now my mind was getting fuzzy and my vision a little

blurred from stitching together the squares. But even in my muddled mind, I knew there wasn't much I could do with Natalie's alibi. With Barry out of my life, I couldn't tell him. Detective Heather? No way.

I glanced around the table. Everyone had fallen into a stupor. The coffee was long gone, and the cookies, too. We were almost there. We just needed to join all the strips, and we'd be finished. CeeCee was still asleep, hugging an unfinished granny.

Even Adele looked glassy-eyed.

Will stood up and stretched. "You need to get your blood flowing." Somehow he got everybody, including CeeCee, to stand, and he led the group through a tai chi routine, which magically revived us all—except for CeeCee, who went back to sleep.

In a burst of energy, we connected all the strips.

The sun was up, and life along Ventura Boulevard was starting to stir, when we finally finished. Who knew Will Hunter would end up saving the day?

I looked at the finished afghan lying on the table. I was amazed that we had done it. Before CeeCee had become unfunctional, she had laid out a plan for the afghan that balanced the intricate patterned pieces Ellen and the others had crocheted in the beginning with the granny squares and plain Janes we'd made later as time became short. Adele's oversize squares, with their floppy flowers and bright colors, made up the center and added some texture. I was surprised to see how, when placed in to the finished product, her work looked quite beautiful. Ellen's and Meredith's similarly patterned squares were arranged to add accents. Sheila's color choices made her work stand out. She used mostly complementing shades of blue and green. CeeCee had spruced up most of the newbies' work with shell stitches in the black borders. Dinah's and my grannies blended in with the others, which seemed like a good sign. The final touch was the four solid double-crochet blocks

CeeCee had made for the corners. She had tacked a crocheted red heart to two corners, and on the other two she had tacked a white dog and a white cat.

As far as I was concerned, the whole thing was flat-out beautiful, and I was proud to think I had a part in making it. It was partly lack of sleep and partly emotion, but my eyes got misty.

The morning crew arrived at the bookstore and began going through the opening procedures as we packed up the afghan. Everybody had a reason why he or she couldn't take the finished product to the fair, most of which probably had to do with wanting to grab some sleep and a shower. I was left holding the blanket.

Bob, the barista, handed me a coffee as I headed out to make the delivery.

As I turned to go, CeeCee came out of her trance long enough to make a remark about the health cookies Bob had just made. "It's not what's in them," she said, putting one down with disdain after taking a bite. "It's what's not."

Why did that ring a bell?

CHAPTER 23

S‌ince it was early S‌aturday morning, traffic on the 101 was manageable. If I hadn't felt so out of
sorts from being up all night, and if I hadn't been been so
focused on getting the afghan delivered, I might have appreciated the silvery mist hanging over the San Gabriel
Mountains as they loomed over the Valley. But I wasn't
noticing anything but the car in front of me, and wondering
how much longer until I got to the World Studio back lot in
Burbank, where the fair was being held. Even the feeling of
unease that had started when I realized Natalie had an alibi
was pushed to the back of my mind.

As usual, nothing went smoothly, and I had to go
through a bunch of wrangling to get in since the fair wasn't
officially open and I wasn't on any list. The security guard
finally got hold of someone from the auction committee,
who got me in.

I parked and walked into what seemed like the center of a
sweet little town—except it was a set that had been used on
countless TV shows and movies. The signs and decorations

on the storefronts changed according to what was being filmed. Judging from the current state of the storefronts, I guessed they were doing the talkative mother-and-daughter sleuths in their small Connecticut town.

There was lots of activity as booths and pet corrals were set up in the center of "town." There were going to be animals available for adoption, booths selling pet products, information booths for animal organizations, and a lot of food.

I found the large white tent that was to be used for the auction. Inside, a bunch of people were arranging the items on long tables. I snagged one of the volunteers and held up the afghan.

"Oh, thank heavens," the dark-haired woman said. She was wearing her glasses on a chain around her neck and had a puffy black hairstyle. I recognized her from several old TV series. She was always the boisterous sidekick.

"Oh, it's so fabulous. A lot of dogs are going to get spayed or neutered because of your contribution." She looked around for the rest of my posse, and I explained that we'd worked all night and they'd be there soon.

With the blanket delivered, I breathed a sigh of relief and wandered through all the setups, wondering if anyone had coffee. I noticed that some of the storefronts were actually being used for the fair. There were signs for tarot card readings, astrology charts, chiropractic adjustments and massages. The smell of coffee got my attention, and I followed it. I got a "black eye" this time. It was definitely a two-shot-of-espresso day. I didn't even want to think what I looked like, still in yesterday's clothes. I was glad I'd worn the khakis that promised not to wrinkle.

There were several benches in the grassy center area, and I settled on one. Even with the espresso-and-coffee mixture, my eyes got heavy, and though I didn't mean to, I fell asleep.

"Molly, are you all right? Speak to me," a voice said,

cutting into my sleep. When I opened my eyes, Sheila's face was inches from mine, and she was shaking my shoulders. "Sorry, but when I saw you slumped over, I thought you were . . ." she said with a nervous laugh.

"Dead?" I said, finishing her thought.

"After Ellen and then Natalie . . . You know how they say things travel in threes," she said with a trace of warning in her voice. As I looked around, I realized I must have been asleep for quite a while, as the fair was now in full swing. I don't know if it was from sleeping sitting up in public and wearing yesterday's clothes or because of Sheila's comment, but the feeling of unease had moved up from the back of my mind.

My eyes felt kind of gritty, and slumping had left me with a nice kink in my neck. There was still some coffee in the cup, and I drank it cold, then began rubbing the back of my neck.

"Meredith is doing massages." Sheila pointed to a row of storefronts. "You ought to sign up. I'm first on the list." Sheila sat down with me. She seemed very tense again, and I wondered what was up. Looking as if she was on autopilot, she took out her hook and wad of string and started crocheting a coaster.

A massage by Meredith sounded like just what I needed, but before I could act on the thought, I looked toward the shaded area where the dogs for adoption were in enclosures. Barry and Jeffrey were leaning over the metal fencing, petting a black and gray mutt. It felt like a rock had dropped in my stomach. Without realizing it, I reached into my pocket, took out my hook and string, and joined Sheila in nervous crocheting. I wasn't looking at what I was doing, and I made a long tail of chain stitches and then turned the work and started going back over the chain with single crochets.

"There's CeeCee," Sheila said. I pulled my eyes away from Barry just as a man handed the dog's leash to Jeffrey.

When I saw CeeCee, I did a double take. She was freshly attired and seemed to have joined the living again, but what really got my attention was who she was talking to— Lawrence Sheridan. He had Felix with him, and his head was leaning toward CeeCee's as if they were in some deep, friendly conversation. Something had definitely changed between them.

I got up and stretched.

"Hey, Pink, did you deliver the blanket?" Adele asked as she walked over. The lavender pedal pushers and aqua top, finished off with a silver baseball cap, were apparently her casual mode.

"Of course," I said, starting to rub my neck again. "I'm signing up for one of those massages."

Adele followed me—well, she actually tried to pass me, but her platform sandals slowed her down and I got to the storefront massage parlor first. The windows had been papered over to give privacy, and there was a clipboard with a sign-up sheet on a chair by the door.

I signed my name and handed the board to Adele just as she clomped up. Unfortunately my allotted time wasn't for a while, and I decided to walk around.

There was a nice turnout, and lots of people had brought their pets with them. But I didn't think it would have been Blondie's cup of tea.

I ran into more familiar faces. Meg and Stacy, two of the newbies, had come with their kids. They were on the way to the auction tent to show them the "murder" blanket. Farther on, I passed Will Hunter. He'd brought his dog, a mutt with one blue eye and one black one, and multicolored fur. He'd already seen the blanket and was proud to say he'd played a part in it.

"Molly," a male voice called. I turned and squinted into the sun, trying to find its owner.

"Mason?" I said, surprised.

"I hoped I'd run into you. Here's that name." He handed

me a business card. "I saw the afghan, and it looks great," he said, touching my arm in his signature gesture. I caught sight of his watch and realized it was time for my massage. After saying I'd see him at the auction, I rushed off, slipping the business card into my pocket. I assumed it was the booking agent for Samuel.

When I reached the massage storefront, a sign was hanging on the door, saying MASSAGE IN SESSION. Apparently Meredith was running late. I hung around the door, waiting.

When it finally opened, a smiling man walked out. "You're in for a treat," he said, before disappearing into the crowd.

When Meredith saw that I was next, she hugged me and brought me inside. I walked across the smooth tile floor, hoping the massage would take away this feeling of something not being right, but if anything, the lingering fragrance in the air made me feel even more uneasy, and I started rubbing my temples.

I tried to push it all away, making small talk with Meredith.

"I promise this will be better than what I did in the bookstore," she said as she helped me into her special chair. She explained that she'd begin with me leaning forward while she worked on my back; then she'd recline the seat. It all sounded good to me. She undid my shirt, pulled it off my shoulders and laid some flat, warm stones on my shoulders and neck. They felt soothing, and I closed my eyes, hoping I would relax.

I felt Meredith take the stones off, and I heard her squeeze something onto her hands. Suddenly I smelled a stronger version of the disquieting fragrance. My stomach felt queasy, and I opened my eyes and sat up.

I blinked and looked around, hoping my stomach would settle. The makeshift massage parlor was empty except for a shelving unit with some supplies left from the last shoot.

I'd put my purse on it next to Meredith's things. I tried taking some deep breaths. I noticed my purse had fallen over, pulling Meredith's scarf away from her bag. Something about it got my attention. It was messenger style and crocheted out of granny squares. I couldn't take my eyes off of it, and she followed my gaze.

"Beautiful, isn't it?" she said. "It was a gift from Ellen."

I nodded in agreement. It was beautiful, and perfect except for the hanging yarn around the button closure.

"It's better if you close your eyes," she said, gently pushing my shoulders and easing me against the special chair.

Even with my eyes closed, I couldn't get my mind off the bag. There was something about the beige yarn in the middle of the squares that bothered me.

Meredith worked on my arms and shoulders, and moved on to the pressure points in my back. It was supposed to relax me, but if anything I was feeling more tense. The yarn was the color of coffee with lots of milk, and it was fuzzy. A halo, that's what CeeCee had called it. I swallowed hard as I realized what bag it was. It was the one Ellen had made for her daughter, with the yarn from her cat. No way would Ellen have given that to Meredith. I remembered the ball of yarn and hook next to Ellen when I'd found her. Ellen must have been finishing it when . . .

Meredith's hands were back on my shoulders. Her hands felt powerful as they squeezed and kneaded. Then she began working on my neck, and the smell of the massage oil was so strong, I felt like I couldn't breathe. I had to get out of there.

I sat upright. "I've changed my mind about the massage," I said, trying to keep my voice calm.

Meredith didn't release her hands, and for the first time I realized just how strong she was. I couldn't get up. "Nonsense, Molly, nobody leaves in the middle of a massage."

"I really have to go," I protested. Using my arms for

leverage I gathered my strength, thrust against her grip, and stood up abruptly. I was relieved when her hands fell away.

With my shirt still pulled down from my shoulders, I quickly took a step toward the door, but then I felt something cold and metallic against the base of my neck.

"I don't think you want to leave just yet," Meredith said in a menacing tone. She pushed me back into the chair and came around to the front. A small blue steel handgun was now pointed at my face. She explained that it was a gift from her boyfriend and small enough to keep in her pocket. He was concerned for her safety, with so many people showing up dead. I swallowed hard when she said his name. "Lawrence."

I looked toward the door. It was maybe fifteen feet away. Outside, the fair was in full swing. If I could just get to the door.

"You think you know something, don't you? You have been trouble since day one. I thought once you were off the hook, you'd back off."

I'd always thought Meredith was pretty, but seeing how hard her blue eyes were, I changed my mind. Her mouth was set in a grim, straight line.

"It was all Ellen's fault, you know," she said. "I just wanted her to shut up. She was going on and on about Lawrence and his women, and how he always promised he was going to get a divorce and marry them. Like I'd believe I was like the others. She kept saying it over and over. . . ."

This wasn't good, I thought, getting a sinking feeling. Meredith was spilling her guts, confessing. I considered making a run for it. She'd have to be crazy to shoot me here. She would never get away with it. But the more she talked, the clearer it became that she was crazy and I had no doubt if I moved, she'd shoot.

"It was Ellen's way of telling me she knew about Lawrence and me. Then she started saying how terrible it was when someone you'd helped betrayed you. She'd set me up massaging Lawrence. It was supposed to help relieve all his stress." Meredith got a sly smile and continued. "I found a better way to relieve his stress. And Lawrence meant it when he told me he wanted to marry me. Best proof, we're together now." She grimaced in annoyance. "I just wish he'd stop talking about her."

Was I supposed to say something here? Did Meredith want me to tell her to hang in there, that Lawrence was sure to come around and make all her dreams come true?

"Ellen just kept going on and on. Crocheting and talking as I was giving her a massage. I just wanted her to shut up, and I did this thing called the sleep maneuver. They actually demonstrated it in massage school and said never to hold a client that way.

"I reached around her neck with the crook of my arm. She thought it was part of the massage, like I was steadying her while I did her back. Then I squeezed. In a few seconds she passed out, and the yacking stopped. I wanted to let go, but I knew she'd just start up again. And then she stopped breathing."

Meredith rambled on about setting it up to look like a burglary, but since she had no experience, she'd bungled it. Now I understood why the smell of the massage oil bothered me. It must have been lingering on Ellen when I'd found her. And it had been in the air when I'd gone to Pink Sheridan that night. For a moment I thought I was going to throw up at the strong scent of lavender and eucalyptus, but the wave of nausea passed.

Now that Meredith had started, she was letting it all go. There was a certain look of relief on her face as she started talking about Natalie. Not telling anyone must have been hard.

"I came in from setting up my massage chair, and Natalie was talking to you on the phone. She didn't realize I heard her tell you about finding Ellen's appointment book.

Everybody had bought my story that I left Ellen's early because Ellen said she had an important lunch meeting. Even that blond detective." Meredith glared at me hard. "It was all working out very nicely when the detective thought you were Ellen's lunch date, but once I knew about Ellen's appointment book, I realized it was only a matter of time before Natalie figured out Ellen had no lunch meeting. I couldn't afford to be caught in a lie. Natalie was getting too cozy with Lawrence, anyway. I had to protect my interests. And setting it up so it looked like she killed Ellen and then herself over the guilt made the date book irrelevant."

I finally understood Natalie's cryptic comment about not what was there, but what wasn't. Not that it was any help to me now.

Meredith smiled again at her own cleverness as she described how she'd begun the massage in the outer office. "I had to leave off the massage oil—the residue on her skin would have been a giveaway. She was easy to fool. When she wasn't looking, I dumped a little on the carpet, then showed her the spot, claiming I'd spilled the whole bottle. When I excused myself to use the restroom, I wrote the suicide note on Natalie's computer. I was wearing gloves, of carse. Then I suggested we finish on the balcony. Natalie fell for all the nonsense about ions and the special properties of a fresh-air massage. Everybody in the building was gone. Even the cleaning crew wasn't there. I did the same move on her. Once she passed out, I just pushed her over the edge." Meredith's expression changed to concern. "They really should consider a higher railing."

I looked longingly toward the door. Meredith followed my gaze and gave me a shake of her head.

"Sorry, but it looks like you'll be missing the auction." She took a step closer, and I could smell the metal of the gun. "I don't like killing people. And I'm sure you'll be my last. I'll just say you had some kind of seizure while I was giving you a massage." She rambled on about how she'd say she tried CPR, but it didn't work. I was feeling light-headed now. Time was definitely running out.

I felt my throat catch when she pulled a dispenser of duct tape off the shelving unit and positioned it with the gun under her arm. With her free hand, she pulled out a length and tore it against the cutting edge. She slapped it across my mouth, and I felt an instant sense of panic, as if I couldn't breathe. I sucked air hard through my nose and fought the dizzying feeling. She pulled off a longer piece of the metallic tape and went behind me. I felt it stick to one ankle and then go around the other before they were pulled together. With my feet bound together behind the chair, any thought of escaping on foot went out the window.

Meredith came back in front of me. She pulled off another long piece, and I knew it was meant for my hands. Once she secured them, I would be totally helpless. I looked around for something, anything that could help me. There was nothing near me except for a small table with the bottle of massage oil.

She stepped toward my right arm, but the tape caught a bit of air and blew against itself, sticking together. As she shook her hand to free it, I made my move. She was looking down at the tape, which now had flipped up, the end sticking to her hand.

I grabbed the bottle and squeezed hard. The stream of strong-scented oil hit the floor and made an ever-enlarging puddle on the smooth tile. Meredith picked up on the movement and turned toward me.

"What are you doing?" she said, making a lunge to get the bottle. Big mistake. The oil made the slick floor impossible. Meredith lost her footing and fell with a large *plop*. The gun flew out of her hand and went off to points unknown. She tried to get up, but her hands and feet slid away and she did a belly flop.

I tore the tape off my mouth, not something I'd like to

repeat. I could taste blood on my lip. I took a deep breath and tried to call for help, but my voice wouldn't work. Desperately, I leaned down to get the tape off my legs. It was not an easy proposition. I couldn't tear it or find the end to pull it, and I had no scissors to cut it.

Meredith had made it to her hands and knees and was trying to crawl out of the puddle, but her legs kept slipping from under her. Eventually she was going to figure out a way to get up, so I had to work fast. I rolled the tape into a band and pulled my legs against it, eventually getting it slack enough that I pulled out one foot at a time.

Being careful to avoid the oil, I jumped off the chair. I needed to restrain Meredith, but she was so oily, the tape wouldn't stick to her. Then I remembered the nervous crocheting I'd done, and pulled it out of my pocket. It had been just aimless work, and instead of making a coaster, I had just made a long foundation chain with several rows of single crochet. I took it and wrapped it around Meredith's feet. She was wiggling on the ground now, trying to get across the room to find the gun.

Suddenly the door flew open, and Adele marched in. "Pink, what's taking so long? It's my turn." Then she looked down and saw Meredith writhing in the oil on the floor with her feet tied together.

"She killed Ellen and Natalie, and she was trying to kill me." I called out a number and told Adele to use her cell. For once, Adele didn't ask any questions.

A few moments later Barry sprinted in, gun drawn. I held up my hand to stop him before he hit the oil. He gave me an odd look, and I realized my shirt was still pulled down around my shoulders and unbuttoned in the front.

After that it seemed as though half the fair was crowded outside. Barry kept Meredith handcuffed until some uniforms arrived, along with Detective Heather, who, it turned out, was also at the fair. It seemed strange to see her in shorts. She was talking to Meredith and wanted a statement from Adele and me. Someone had found a roll of paper towels and covered the oily area with layer upon layer of them. Adele was making the most of her moment and was telling everyone she had saved me.

I was sitting on the massage chair, giddy from it all and at the same time about to cry. I can only imagine how I looked. I had at least pulled my shirt on and closed it.

I saw CeeCee, Sheila and some of the other crocheters just outside. CeeCee was talking to the various newspeople and camera crews that were there to cover the fair. Mason Fields stuck his head in the door. He took one look at me and disappeared. He reappeared a few minutes later and used his attorney powers to get inside. He had some wet paper towels for my mouth, and a frozen lemonade. Both were greatly appreciated. Barry glanced over, and I saw his expression darken. He left Detective Heather and came over.

"Do you need a rescue ambulance?" He had positioned himself in front of Mason. My lip was still oozing, and I was feeling a little shaky, but I told him I was okay. He stayed a little too long. He just kept looking at me and breathing. His jaw clenched a few times and then he went back to business. Mason watched him go, and when Barry looked back, they exchanged glances.

"Do you know him?" Mason asked me.

I just nodded.

Dinah arrived after that. I saw her look through the door. Her eyes widened when she saw me, and she blew me a kiss.

As Meredith was about to be led out, I went over to Detective Heather and pointed toward the messenger bag. "You might want to take that as evidence." I told her Ellen had made it for her daughter, and the only way Meredith could have gotten it was if she had killed Ellen. "The beige yarn in the middle and on the catch match the yarn Ellen was holding when she died. She must have been just finishing the bag."

"You can't prove that's Dakota's bag," she screamed. I started to answer, but Adele stepped in first and explained to Meredith and everyone else within earshot that the center of the bag Ellen had made used yarn spun from her daughter's Siamese cat's fur. Adele gave Meredith a haughty stare. "I don't suppose you know about DNA. Well, just like people's hair, cats and dogs and other animals, too, have DNA in their fur. All we have to do is to take a sample from the bag and a sample from the yarn Ellen was holding and compare the DNA."

Even in my state, I had to laugh at Adele's use of "we."

I followed the crowd outside as Meredith was led to the parking lot. No matter how I looked, she looked worse. Her white cotton pants and top were like oil rags. Her ponytail was clumped together and resembled a rat's tail. Remnants of my crocheted restraint were still stuck to her leg, and the fragrance of lavender and eucalyptus trailed after her. I hoped they'd offer her a shower in jail.

She passed Lawrence, who for once didn't look collected. He moaned with such pain, it made the hair on my neck stand up. His eyes were wet, and his emotions bared. Felix was in his arms and was trying to lick his face to comfort him.

"You killed my Ellen?" he said in a ragged voice. "You killed my Ellen," he repeated. Meredith told him she did it for him. Lawrence reacted as if the words were a punch to the gut. She yelled for him to get her an attorney, and he just shook his head.

"You're on your own," he muttered.

Meredith called to Mason just before the cops turned toward the parking lot and the cluster of cruisers. She asked for his card. He shook his head, too.

I wanted to think it was on principle, rather than because she was the one person he didn't believe he could get off.

I was still standing there, recovering from it all, when Jeffrey rushed up to me with a fuzzy little dog in tow. "Are you okay? Like, are you hurt or anything?" I thanked him and told him I was fine. Then he leaned closer. "You have to get back with my dad. He's going nuts. I can't take his moping around, and he's paying way too much attention to me. He even tried to cook." Jeffrey did a mock throw-up move.

With Meredith and the police gone, the crowd dispersed, and Dinah caught up with me. We watched as things began to return to normal. A few minutes later, there was an announcement that the live auction was about to begin.

Only as an afterthought did I find Mason's card in my pocket. On the back was the promised name, but it wasn't the agent for Samuel as I had thought. It was Lawrence's date from the charity event. It was no surprise that the name was Meredith Brancussi.

CHAPTER 24

IT TOOK A FEW WEEKS AFTER THE FAIR FOR THE crochet group to meet. We had all been in shock about Meredith and amazed that she had hidden such a dark side under such a seemingly pleasant demeanor. CeeCee remembered that Meredith had said once that she wanted to have the kind of life Ellen had. But CeeCee never guessed how serious she was.

And Meredith probably never guessed how far from that life she would end up. She was charged with two completed murders and one attempted, and was awaiting trial, forced to depend on the services of a public defender.

Lawrence formally apologized for behaving as though I'd killed Ellen. In a gesture of conciliation, he'd not only agreed to let Will Hunter's book signing go forward, but he'd also promised a second event with another of his celebrity author clients.

"It's good to be together again," CeeCee said when we'd gathered around the long table in the event area. She looked like her old self, maybe even better. "I have an announcement to make." The whole group turned toward her, and she beamed. "You are looking at the host of the new reality show *Making Amends*."

Meg and Stacy clapped excitedly and gushed about being part of a group with a TV personality.

Dinah and I looked at each other. They were hearing the happy ending. We knew the whole story, and why CeeCee had been acting so strangely.

I'd made another pound cake and taken it to CeeCee's, and she'd confided in us. It turned out CeeCee's late husband, the world-famous dentist, had been an idiot with money. When he died, she'd found out he'd blown it all. She'd taken the diet infomercial as a way to make some much-needed cash, but her runaway sweet tooth had made it impossible to lose the weight she'd promised strictly using the diet herbs.

Ellen had helped her get prescription diet pills. However, when CeeCee tried leaving the PR firm in a cost-cutting move, Ellen used copies she'd made of the prescriptions to stop CeeCee. When Natalie took over, she'd found the file and gone down a similar road.

CeeCee couldn't afford to let the information come out, as she'd instantly lose the face cream infomercial and any chance for future spokesperson work. However, when the PR business landed in Lawrence's lap and he saw the file, he pressed CeeCee to come forward and admit what she'd done. Who knew he'd be the one with ethics?

She didn't agree at first, but the night we put together the afghan, he'd worn her down. The news conference was set for several days hence.

Sound bites of it appeared on the eleven o'clock news, the entertainment news programs and all the morning shows. The next day all the shows forwarded the flood of e-mails they'd gotten. The public had spoken, and they loved CeeCee for admitting what she'd done.

Lawrence, manager, TV producer, and now publicist as

well, took all the e-mails and sold the XBS channel on doing a reality show hosted by CeeCee that followed people making amends for past mistakes.

"Of course, even with the show, I'll still be part of the crochet group. I have a bunch of ideas for our next charity project," CeeCee said. "I'll have to depend on Adele's help, though."

Adele didn't react. She sat with her face resting on her hands, staring into space, no doubt reliving her moment of glory. The newspeople had snagged her at the fair, and she'd told them how she had caught Meredith and saved me, and pointed out the DNA evidence in the cat fur yarn. She had been all over the news, even on CNN. At last she had what she thought was her due. One of the kids even asked for her autograph at story time.

"I'll be glad to help." Sheila smiled at CeeCee. She had been all nerves when she'd heard about Meredith's other side. On a positive note, she had turned that frantic energy into the beautiful shawl she'd laid out on the table. It was done with three strands of mohair in royal blue, sea foam green and lavender yarn on the huge hook. We all gushed praise.

"The yarn was Ellen's. I asked Lawrence if he would sell some of hers to me. But when I went over there and we talked, he insisted on giving it to me," Sheila said, modeling her creation. "Funny thing, though, he had to call the cops because there was a Peeping Tom creeping around his yard."

Dinah and I rolled our eyes at each other. We'd never tell.

Another newbie had joined, who surprised us all. Will Hunter sat with his slippered feet resting on a chair, working on a cream-colored afghan. He was doing his best to ignore the adoring glances of Stacy and Meg.

He'd ended up being the auctioneer at the Hearts and Barks auction. Lawrence was originally slated for the job, but under the circumstances he hadn't been in any shape to handle it.

Just as expected, our afghan had drawn a big price. There had been a lot of action, and then one bid that so far outdid everyone else's, the bidding stopped and that buyer won the auction.

Our beautiful creation was now proudly hanging on the wall in Mason Fields's den. He'd told me I was welcome to visit it anytime.

For now I was holding off on that.

Peter and Samuel had come over together the night of the fair. They brought flowers and hugs, and there was no fussing. At least for the moment, we were all on the same team.

Barry had come over after they left. He had been all business in public, but alone he just held me and kept asking me if I was okay. In between there were a few questions about what was I doing with Mason Fields. It was obvious Barry didn't like him. Not only because of anything I might be doing with him, but because cops weren't fond of lawyers, particularly high-profile ones who made mincemeat out of their cases and got guilty people off.

I took the fifth.

I asked whether Barry and Detective Heather were getting ready for their trip. He clenched his jaw a few times and narrowed his eyes.

"It's been postponed," he said, attempting to sound casual. It was nonrefundable but, it turned out, changeable. He looked at me hopefully. "I thought we might be able to start over. Would you like to go to Maui?" he asked. When I didn't answer, he said I could get back to him. If the answer was yes, we would discuss dates. Before he left, he fixed my light switch.

I was going to call him after the crochet group meeting. Though I still wasn't sure what I was going to say.

Dinah nudged me. "How is it that you end up with two guys you don't know what to do with, and I am still ending up with online duds?"

It was a good question, and I didn't have the foggiest. Probably something about things showing up when you weren't looking for them.

CeeCee handed out some sheets with patterns for prayer shawls, baby blankets and quick afghans as potentials for our next project, and asked for our input.

Just then, Trish and Nicole, the Encino twins, rushed up to the table, holding tote bags of yarn and waving plastic holders with an assortment of hooks. "We want to join. We heard crochet is the next big thing."

CeeCee's Granny Square Washcloth

Materials:	Two 2.5-oz. skeins of 100% cotton, worsted, 4-ply yarn (such as Lily Sugar n' Cream) in two different colors. (There will be enough to make several.)
	J-10 (6.00mm) hook
	Large needle for finishing
Stitches:	Chain = Ch
	Double Crochet = DC
	Slip Stitch = Sl St
Gauge:	Doesn't matter for this project

HEART OF THE SQUARE

Attach color 1 to hook with a slipknot. Ch 4, join to first Ch with Sl St to form a ring. Ch 3 to raise the yarn (counts as DC), 2 DC in the ring, Ch 2, 3 DC in the ring, Ch 2, 3 DC in the ring, Ch 2, 3 DC in the ring, Ch 2. Join to top of Ch 3 with a Sl St, fasten off by cutting approx. 4-inch tail and pulling back through stitch. Pull tight.

There should be 4 groups of 3 DC separated by 4 corners made by Ch 2s.

ROUND 1
Attach color 2 to hook with a slipknot. Attach color 2 to a corner with Sl St, Ch 3 to raise the yarn (counts as DC), 2 DC in space, Ch 2, 3 DC in space, Ch 1; * 3 DC in space, Ch 2, 3 DC in space, Ch 1; repeat from * 2 times. Join to top of Ch 3 with Sl St, fasten off.

ROUND 2
Attach color 1 to hook with slipknot. Attach color 1 to a corner with Sl St, Ch 3 to raise yarn (counts as DC), 2 DC in space, Ch 2, 3 DC in space, Ch 1, 3 DC in space, Ch 1; * 3 DC in space, Ch 2, 3 DC in space, Ch 1, 3 DC in space, Ch 1; repeat from * 3 times. Join to top of Ch 2 with Sl St, fasten off.

ROUND 3
Attach color 2 to hook with slipknot. Attach color 2 to a corner with Sl St, Ch 3 to raise yarn (counts as DC), 2 DC in space, Ch 2, 3 DC in space, Ch 1, 3 DC in space, Ch 1, 3 DC in space, Ch 1; * 3 DC in space, Ch 2, 3 DC in space, Ch 1, 3 DC in space, Ch 1, 3 DC in space, Ch 1; repeat from * 2 times. Join to top of Ch 3 with Sl St, fasten off.

ROUND 4
Attach color 1 to hook with slipknot. Attach color 1 to a corner with Sl St, Ch 3 to raise yarn (counts as DC), 2 DC in space, Ch 2, 3 DC in space, Ch 1, 3 DC in space, Ch 1, 3 DC in space, Ch 1, 3 DC in space, Ch 1; * 3 DC in space, Ch 2, 3 DC in space, Ch 1, 3 DC in space, Ch 1, 3 DC in space, Ch 1, 3 DC in space, Ch 1; repeat from * 2 times. Join to top of Ch 3 with Sl St, fasten off.

ROUND 5

Attach color 2 to hook with slipknot. Attach color 2 to a corner with Sl St, Ch 3 to raise yarn (counts as DC), 2 DC in space, Ch 2, 3 DC in space, Ch 1, 3 DC in space, Ch 1, 3 DC in space, Ch 1, 3 DC in space, Ch 1, 3 DC in space, Ch 1; * 3 DC in space, Ch 2, 3 DC in space, Ch 1, 3 DC in space, Ch 1, 3 DC in space, Ch 1, 3 DC in space, Ch 1, 3 DC in space, Ch 1; repeat from * 2 times. Join to top of Ch 3 with Sl St, fasten off.

Finish by working yarn tails into body of washcloth using large needle.

Helen's Pound Cake

1 lb butter, room temperature, cut into pieces
1 lb confectioners' sugar, sifted
8 eggs
4 cups cake flour, sifted
1 teaspoon baking powder (sift with cake flour)
1½ teaspoons vanilla paste or vanilla extract

Cream butter until fluffy. Add sifted confectioners' sugar gradually, scraping bowl occasionally. Mix two eggs at a time and add to batter; beat between additions. Add the sifted cake flour and baking powder gradually, beating between additions. Add vanilla and mix in.

Pour into a 10-inch greased tube pan and bake at 350 degrees for approx. 60–70 minutes. When a toothpick comes out clean, it's done.

Let cool in pan for 5–10 minutes. Then cool on rack. When completely cool, frost.

Buttercream Frosting

6 tablespoons butter at room temperature
2 cups confectioners' sugar
1 teaspoon heavy cream
1 teaspoon vanilla paste or vanilla extract

Beat butter until fluffy. Add confectioners' sugar gradually, beating between additions. Add heavy cream and vanilla and beat until smooth.

Spread over cake. •

Optional: Lay strawberry halves around the top.